DANNY'S WAR

PJ FIALA

Booktrope Editions
Seattle, WA 2015

Cover Design by Chelsea Barnes
Edited by Wendy Garfinkle

This is a work of fiction. Names, characters, places, brands, media, and incidents are either the product of the author's imagination or are used fictitiously. Any resemblance to similarly named places or to persons living or deceased is unintentional.

PRINT ISBN 978-1-5137-0461-6
EPUB ISBN 978-1-5137-0511-8
Library of Congress Control Number: 2015915904

ACKNOWLEDGMENTS

I would like to thank everyone who has read my book and loved it. Without you all, my books wouldn't exist. Thank you.

Thank you to my amazing husband, Gene. Babe, you are my life and you've made me the woman I am today. Thank you for being you and helping me become me. Thank you for not minding that the house isn't always clean and dinner isn't always made. Aw, who am I kidding? Never. Dinner is never made, by me anyway.

Thank you to my children. You guys are amazing and I thank you from the bottom of my heart for the people you've become. You should all be very proud of yourselves. Know that I am proud of you.

Thank you to my friends for always being there for me. I love you guys.

Thank you to my beta readers—Mitzi, Maureen, Danni, and Terri. Your suggestions and support have made this story memorable. Your willingness to read and critique are invaluable to me.

Thank you to my Booktrope family. Your hard work and dedication to authors is fantastic.

Thank you to all the veterans in this world. My grandfather, father, brother, two of my sons, and one of my daughters-in-law are veterans. Needless to say, I'm proud. Proud to be an American and proud of the service my amazing family has given. Thank you all for your sacrifices. I love you.

To my husband, Gene,
who has been a constant support in my life.
Always encouraging me and loving me all the way.
Thanks, babe. You've made this thing called life an amazing adventure.

To my children,
who have helped shape me into who I am today.
Thanks guys, you mean the world to me.

And, of course, thank you to all the men and women
who serve in the various branches of the military.
Thank you for your sacrifices and your devotion.
The tag line in my email is:
We are the land of the free, because of the brave.
I believe this whole-heartedly.
Words cannot convey the gratitude I feel for all you do.
Thank you.

OTHER TITLES BY PJ FIALA

Second Chances Series
Designing Samantha's Love
Securing Kiera's Love
Engineering Jessie's Love

Rolling Thunder Series
Dog Days of Summer, Book 1
Rydin' the Storm Out, Book 2
Gunnin' for You, Book 4

CHAPTER 1

DANNY TRIED TO BREATHE through the pain of his heart slamming into his chest. Trying to clear the fog in his head, he listened to the sounds around him, trying to remember where he was. His skin wore a fine sheen of sweat as he swallowed rapidly to moisten his throat. His leg hurt and the ringing in his ears made him nauseous.

Nothing but the fucking ringing in his ears. *Breathe, just breathe.* A sharp slap on the face had his eyes flying open, looking into Lex's face. Lex was yelling at him, but Danny couldn't hear a word. His mouth was moving, the chords were standing out in his neck, his eyes were wild…something was wrong. Terribly wrong. Danny's eyes darted behind Lex to see Coop and Dirks looking down at him. They wore blood and dirt and they looked scared shitless. Danny closed his eyes. *Think, dammit, think. What the fuck happened?*

As his heartbeat began to slow and the ringing subsided, a whirring sound caught his attention. His eyelids were heavy as though something weighed them down and he struggled to open them. Then he remembered, he was deaf and Lex couldn't talk. Fuck! Did someone drug him? Danny's heart rate picked up as he fought against the fog in his brain. Trying to sit up, he felt strong hands push at his shoulders.

"Easy, Sergeant, take it easy, we've got you now. It'll be fine."

Danny looked up into dark brown eyes peering through a full face helmet. The man looked to be about his age, maybe a little older.

"It's going to be okay, Sergeant, we're flying you to base in Kandahar and from there, you'll be flown to Germany. Try and relax, we'll be there in a few minutes."

Danny looked to the man's left and saw a pole holding several bags of liquids and tubes running down to his arm. Behind the pole, he saw the sky and felt the pitch and sway of the helicopter. He tried sitting up again, but the man gently held him in place. "You'll need to lie down, Sergeant, we're almost there."

Finding his voice, Danny said. "My leg hurts. What happened? Where are my men?" He licked his lips and looked into those brown eyes, close to the color of his own. Pleading silently for information.

"Your unit hit an IED. One casualty, two injuries. You were hit in the leg, the rest of your men are back at camp. The other injury is flying right behind us."

IED, that's right. Pot or water was the usual question before going out on a mission. Pot was a primary crop in Afghanistan and the insurgents usually didn't blow up their own crops. So they were most often safe if they walked through the pot. Water meant slopping through trenches where IEDs were seldom placed. But today, they had to fucking walk into a camp and check out the residents living there. Fuckers lured them in by pretending to be in need of assistance. He remembered watching Reed and Janus walk up ahead. They'd been laughing at a joke one of them had told when the explosion blasted the camp.

Danny flew through the air and landed in a heap, the wind knocked out of him, his heart racing, ears ringing. Fuck.

"Am I gonna lose it?" He waited with his breath held while the medic's eyes turned pitiful.

"Sorry, Sergeant, you already did."

Danny closed his eyes. *Don't cry. You can do this. Don't cry.*

*   *   *

A slight beeping sound invaded his sleep. What the fuck was that irritating noise? Slowly opening his eyes, Danny was assaulted with the smell of alcohol, not the drink, but the other kind. Across from him were a row of beds, each one holding a patient covered with bandages in various places, and lines running from IV bags into their arms. Moaning could be heard coming from some of the men. The low murmur of female voices was reaching his ears and growing louder. Danny turned his head in the direction of the voices and saw two nurses walk into the room, each carrying medical supplies.

The cute little blonde looked over at him and smiled, "Good morning, Sergeant. How are you feeling today?"

How the fuck do you answer that? Better to go with the usual, "Fine, ma'am. Thank you."

The redhead with her smiled and walked over to a cabinet. She unlocked it with the key she was wearing on a band around her wrist and began laying her supplies in their proper places. The blonde set her supplies on top of the cabinet for the redhead to put away and made her way over to Danny. She was tiny, maybe five feet tall. Short blonde hair and cute little dimples. It made him feel inferior. No woman would ever want him now, he was damaged goods.

Danny watched as she pulled a thermometer from her scrubs' pocket, slid the disposable end on it, and then pushed a couple buttons on the electronic unit attached to the thermometer. She looked up at him and smiled. "Need to take your temperature, Sergeant."

Danny opened his mouth to allow her to slide the thermometer under his tongue. As soon as he closed his mouth, she grabbed his wrist and looked at her watch, taking his pulse. He watched her look up when another woman walked into the room. Her little dimples creased her cheeks and her full lips formed into a smile. "Good morning, Doctor Rae."

"Good morning, Risa, how are you today?"

"Very well. The sergeant here has managed his fever and his pulse is normal. He's looking good today."

"Wonderful." Dr. Rae walked over to the side of Danny's bed. "We were worried about you, Sergeant, you've been out for a couple of days."

Danny's eyes registered surprise and Dr. Rae smiled. "Not uncommon after the trauma you've been through. I think you're finally on the mend. We'll remove the bandages in a little while and take a look at your injury. I won't lie; you're going to be in quite a bit of pain for some time now. You'll need extensive therapy and in the end be fitted for a prosthetic, but there's time for that." Dr. Rae picked up Danny's chart and reviewed it. She checked the IVs and looked him square in the eye for what seemed like minutes. Danny became uncomfortable with the doctor's close scrutiny and fidgeted with his blanket. Dr. Rae smiled softly and set the chart down as she said, "Your color looks good. Your eyes are clear. I'm impressed."

Danny had no response so he nodded slightly. As Dr. Rae walked away, Danny closed his eyes and sank back into the pillow. The pain was getting worse. He would need pain medication soon or he'd sound like the moaners across the room. Fuck.

* * *

Winter turned to spring and spring turned to summer, and now fall crept in.

"Okay, so I've changed your linens, cleaned the house, and stocked the refrigerator. I have a casserole in the oven and more in the freezer, all you have to do is heat them up." Janice Schaefer fussed with the pillows behind Danny on the sofa and then stood to her full height of five foot six. She wiped her hands on her hips and took a deep breath before slowly letting it out.

"Honey, please come home and stay with me for a while longer. I worry so much about you. I promise I won't be in your space all the time."

Danny's lips formed a straight line across his pale face. His eyes held the pain and suffering of every soldier who'd dealt with losing a limb and dealing with the months of pain and rehab. He was tired. Tired of everything, worry, pain, guilt, and the feeling that his life was changed in a way he couldn't begin to comprehend. When he left for the Army, he'd been dating Kathryn Keeting. A week after he got home, she broke up with him. She didn't blame it on his leg, said she'd changed and the distance of the past year and a half had made her rethink their relationship. Danny knew that was bullshit. He saw the look on her face when she first walked into the house and saw him sitting in his chair. He tried to not blame her, but he'd been reduced to nothing with their break-up on top of everything else.

"Mom, please. Don't." Sucking in a deep breath at the worry on his mom's face, he shook his head. "I'm sorry and I don't want you to worry, but I'll be fine. I just need this for myself. I need to move on with my life and I can't do it at your house. You've been great, but...I need this."

Janice wiped her face with her hands, trying to wipe away the worry. "I know you do, honey. I'm sorry I worry so much, it's just..." At a loss for how to finish the sentence, she dropped her hand and shrugged.

Danny gripped his crutches and, using them for leverage, stood on his one leg. Janice walked the two steps toward him and he hugged her while leaning on his crutches. "I don't mean to make you worry. You and Paul can come over every day if you like. I'm not depressed. I just want to start my life on my own. I don't want to put it off any longer. It's been nine months of therapy, doctors, and rehab. I need to move forward."

"Okay, well I'm coming over tomorrow morning to plant flowers in your garden so when you sit on the front porch you can see them. You have a beautiful home and the gardens have been calling for something pretty. Call me early if you think of anything you need. I love you."

"Love you too, Ma."

Listening to the front door open and close, Danny took a deep breath and looked around the living room. Now what?

CHAPTER 2

"GOD, I'M SO DAMN STUPID. I'm sick of being stupid." Tammy flopped on the sofa next to Molly, exasperated.

"You're not stupid, you trusted the asshole and he... well, he took full advantage. That doesn't mean you're stupid." Molly took a sip of her tea and watched Tammy pull her long, sandy-brown hair into a ponytail.

"Well, good thing I wasn't all that emotionally invested in him. Jerk. But, what am I going to do now? Gawd, this is embarrassing. My life is over."

Molly smiled and patted her friend on the knee. "You deserve so much better. You'll find someone great, don't you worry. You're amazing. As for the other thing, well, you have nothing to be ashamed of. You're beautiful. Actually, I think I've heard the word, *hot*, several times."

"That doesn't help, Mol. Gah, this is disgusting." Tammy pulled at her newly-created ponytail.

Molly stood to leave. "Gotta go, Tam, taking pictures today for a kid's birthday party. We can go out later if you'd like."

"I can make us supper here if you don't mind. It'll give me something to do when I get home from Stateside. Pizza?" Tammy stood and shoved her hands in the pockets of her worn jeans. "I don't want to go out in public for a while."

Molly threw her purse over her shoulder and smiled. "Sure. I'll be here around six. Why are you going to work on a Saturday?"

"I want to work on my mural. We're looking for financial benefactors and I want finish as much as I can."

Tammy walked her friend to the door and locked it behind her. She watched out the window as Molly got into her car.

Walking back to the kitchen to clean up the breakfast dishes and put away the leftovers, she made her plan for the day. She decided to go to the grocery store on her way home from the veteran's home. She loved working there. Her grandfather used to live there, and when she was little, her parents would take her there to visit. She grew up wanting to work there with the veterans, to be a part of making their lives better. She didn't consider it "going out in the public" in the sense that she wanted to avoid being seen. Most of the veterans were older, so she doubted they would know of her indiscretion.

*   *   *

"Hey there, Gerry, how are you today?"

"Well, Tammy, it's great to see you. You working on the mural today?" Gerry's kind, blue eyes sparkled as he smiled up at her from his wheelchair.

Tammy wrinkled her face and let out a heavy sigh. "Yeah, I think today will mostly be touch-ups here and there."

"I'll stop by in a bit. I'm setting up a mean card game for later on. You want in?"

Tammy smiled. "Not this time, I'm afraid you gentlemen would have all my money in no time. Besides, Molly's coming over for supper tonight. Which reminds me, she's photographing that big veteran's ride Rolling Thunder is putting together. Have you heard of it?"

"Veteran's Ride? I've heard about that ride. You know, we should get a bus and go see the bikers take off."

"Actually, that's a great idea, Gerry. Rolling Thunder Motorcycles has this ride every year. From what I'm told, the proceeds they collect go to help local veterans with their various needs."

Gerry's smile spread across his face. "That's perfect for us. I'm going to talk to Diane in activities and see if she can organize that. Maybe we can help in some way. See ya around, Tammy."

Gerry turned in his wheelchair, and, after a quick wave goodbye, rolled himself down the hall. Even in his sixties with no family, he was always in good spirits and trying to organize activities for the other veterans. Tammy watched him roll away, amazed at his zest for life. He'd been through so much. He lost his wife and only son in a car accident fifteen years ago and still maintained a happy disposition. She could learn something from him.

*   *   *

Tammy stood back, admiring her work. It looked good, very good. All she managed to do today was a bit of touch-up. Her creative juices just weren't flowing. She laid her brush on the table and picked up the rag lying alongside her paints. As she was wiping the paint from her fingers, she heard the door open and quietly close. She turned to see Sally, the director of the veteran's home, and her boss, walking toward her, her posture unusually stiff and her face molded into a frown.

"It looks beautiful, Tammy. You're very talented."

Tammy's lips turned up at the corners as she looked back at the mural of veterans in various wars up to present day. She'd been working on this mural for the past few months.

"Almost finished. I still need to add Operation Enduring Freedom to it."

So far, there weren't any veterans here from this war. That's why she waited to paint it last. She'd spoken to many of the veterans here before embarking on her mural painting journey. She wanted to paint the scenes accurately and many of the veterans were very helpful in sharing their experiences and more than willing to help her convey their story properly. She learned so much from these men. Their strength and endurance was astounding.

"There's time." Sally took a deep breath. "Tammy, is everything okay with you?"

Tammy's shoulders sagged as she turned to face Sally. Blowing stray strands of hair out of her face, Tammy flopped in a chair at the table.

"What did you hear?" Sad brown eyes turned to Sally as she took the seat next to Tammy. For a forty-nine-year-old woman, she was very attractive. She'd paid little attention to her hair and looks the past few years since her husband had died. She consistently dressed in business suits and flats, while her hair was blonde and bobbed, with a sprinkling of gray showing through. Tammy wondered why she didn't color it. *Her* mom wouldn't be caught dead with gray hair—not yet, anyway.

"I saw the video."

Tammy's hands flew to her face to hide as she wailed, "No. Oh, my God, no."

CHAPTER 3

"DANNY, I COULD USE your help. You're so good at figuring this stuff out. Can you come over and help me?"

Hesitating, Danny asked his brother, "Ahh, when do you want to work on it?"

"Today. Grace is working and I want to surprise her. I don't have any patients today, so anytime you can get here would be great."

Danny looked around his house; he didn't have anything going on.

"You haven't left your house in three weeks, Danny. You have to leave it sometime. Please don't make yourself a recluse. Let us help you. We love you and worry so much about you." Softening his voice, Paul said, "Please…I want things to be the way they used to be."

Biting down his anger, Danny said. "Things will never be the way they used to be again, Paul. I lost my fucking leg. Women think I'm disgusting. People stare at me when I leave the house like there's something wrong with me. I have fucking nightmares all the time. Things…" Taking another deep breath, Danny softly added, "Things *are* different. We can't change that."

Paul looked down at the floor and his scuffed shoes. Frustration bubbled to the surface. He had two and his brother only one. Fucking war. Fucking terrorists.

"Danny." Shit. "Danny, you're still you. Your body is different, but you're still my brother and I still love you. I love you more, not because you lost a leg, but because you sacrificed for all of us to protect what we have here. That's a debt we can never repay, bro. But, you're still the same caring, loving man you were and, you're going to be an uncle and we need you, man." Catching the sob trying to escape from his throat, Paul continued. "You're still you."

Danny swiped at the tears falling down his cheeks. He lost his leg almost a year ago and it was the first time he'd cried. He looked down at his scarred tennis shoe and watched one of his tears hit the toe and slide to the side. Shit.

"I'll be over in half an hour. Do you need me to bring any tools?"

Letting out the breath he was holding, Paul said, "I think I have everything we need. Thanks, bro."

Danny touched the *end call* button on his phone and slid it into his shirt pocket. He walked to the stairs going up to the second floor and his bedroom and made the laborious trek upstairs. He would need his prosthetic leg today.

*   *   *

"How the hell do you read these damn directions? This is crazy. It's a crib for fuck's sake. There must be a thousand pieces to put together. How big do you think this baby is going to be anyway?"

Paul burst out laughing. "Now you know why I needed you here. It's mind-boggling."

They worked in unison for some time, pulling pieces out of the pile and organizing them in a way that would be easy to find. Paul held the directions and read them step-by-step as Danny put the pieces together one by one. Three and a half hours later, they stood back and admired the beautiful mocha colored crib and attached dresser. It stood straight and tall and the brothers were proud of their accomplishment. Paul was proud of Danny. He slid his arm around Danny's shoulders and squeezed.

"Thank you so much, bro. Look what we did! It's beautiful. Thanks."

"I'm home," Grace called from the front room. "What are you two doing?"

Paul looked at Danny and smiled. "She's gonna squeal, get ready."

Turning his head toward the door he called back, "We're in the baby's room. Come on back and see what we did."

Paul and Danny stood together as they were, an arm around the other's shoulder, continuing to admire their handiwork when Grace rounded the corner and stopped dead in her tracks. They both looked at her, waiting for her reaction. She stared at the crib and attached dresser, frozen in place. Danny's heart began to race the longer it took Grace to speak. He fidgeted a bit and ran his hand across his jaw…waiting.

Grace finally looked at them and they saw a lone tear slide down her cheek.

Softly, while walking toward the crib, Grace said, "Thank you so much. It's…" She took a deep breath and swallowed. "It's beautiful."

She gently ran her hand along the cool, smooth wooden crib and lovingly caressed the rails. She leaned in and patted the mattress when a sob escaped. Danny stood straighter and stiffened his spine. He never knew what to do when a woman cried. He looked over at Paul, the worry etched on Danny's face.

Paul snickered. "I thought she'd squeal. Damn hormones make it impossible to predict a thing."

Grace turned toward them, wiping her cheeks and smiled. She threw herself at Paul, pushing him against the wall, wrapping her arms around his neck and loudly kissing him. "Thank you. I was worried the baby was going to be sleeping on the floor. You weren't too keen on putting this together."

Paul laughed. "I couldn't get my head around all the damn pieces. Danny did ninety-nine percent of the work. I just read the directions."

Grace pulled her arms away from Paul and looked at Danny, a smile spread across her face. Danny's face still held the tension from moments before, his brown eyes watching Grace's beautiful blue ones. She stepped forward and hugged him tightly. Danny slowly drew his arms around her thick middle and hugged her back. Tears filled his eyes. The strength of her embrace, the smell of her perfume, the softness of her curves. He missed being hugged.

Grace heard him sniffle and stood back and looked at him. "You okay?"

Danny's watery gaze held hers for long moments. Unable to say a word, he swallowed and nodded.

"What's wrong, Danny?" Grace softly inquired.

Danny shook his head. Grace held his face in her hands directing his gaze to hers. Softly but firmly she said, "What's wrong. Danny?"

"It's just…" Flicking his gaze to Paul and back to Grace, he said, "That's the first hug I've had from a woman—who isn't my mom—in months. Sorry. It felt good."

CHAPTER 4

"DON'T BE SO NERVOUS, Tammy. No one from The Wheel comes here. Now loosen up and let's have some fun."

"Sorry, Molly. I don't mean to be a drag, I'm just so darn paranoid that everyone here saw that damn video and thinks I'm trash. This past year has been horrible."

"I know it has, Tam, and I've been with you all the way. Those bitches at the restaurant last week were just jealous. Not one of them has the body you have—they just wish they did."

"You're good for my ego, Molly, I'll give you that."

Molly laughed and pulled Tammy out on the dance floor. They danced to Taylor Swift's "Shake it Off." Tammy's lime-green sheath dress hugged her body like a glove. Black heels and a cuff bracelet caught the lights as she swung her arms to the music. They both wore beautiful smiles as they wrapped themselves in the music, forgetting everything disappointing and hurtful in their lives. Molly's short dark hair was beginning to curl at the nape as she started heating up from all the dancing. The little dots of moisture began appearing across Tammy's nose indicated she was warm as well. At the end of the third song, Tammy lifted her long, wavy, sandy-brown hair off her neck and fanned her face with her hand.

"I need a drink. I think I'm melting." Tammy laughed.

"I know what you mean. Let's go cool down."

Both girls walked to their table alongside the dance floor and ordered a drink from the passing waitress. Tammy looked up and noticed a table of very nice specimens of the opposite sex staring at them. She felt her blush all the way to her toes. Watching the waitress weave in and out of patrons, Tammy noticed another table of men watching them. The waitress set their drinks in front of them, and Tammy immediately pulled her credit card from her clutch and handed it to her.

"I'll be right back with your receipt," the waitress said.

Tammy looked at Molly and said as softly as she could and still be heard over the music, "There are two tables of guys staring at us. I'm starting to feel a bit freaked out. Is it me? Do you think they know about the video? Ugh. I hate feeling paranoid."

Molly took a deep breath, slowly let it out and looked across the room at the first table of guys. They were indeed looking in Tammy and Molly's direction. It looked like about five of them standing around drinking and talking. The tall, dark-haired guy nudged his shorter, blond companion, who started laughing and shaking his head no.

"Well, they're definitely looking at us. But, I think it's more that they can't work up the courage to come over and ask us to dance. The short one just turned a few shades of red when they tall one said something to him. Probably that."

Tammy looked over at them then. Her gaze met the tall blond standing at the back of the table. He smiled and winked. Tammy smiled back and blushed.

Pushing the sleeves of her gray sweater dress up her arms to help her cool down, Molly said, "See? They just think you're sexy."

Tammy glanced over at the other table of guys and noticed them trying to be sly, but still watching them. "They think you're sexy, Molly. The guy at that table…" she said with a jerk of her head, her curls swaying, "is definitely watching you."

A smiled spread across Molly's face. "Well, tonight's about us. Finish your drink and let's hit the dance floor, girl."

Molly tossed back the last of her drink. Tammy smirked and did the same. Taking to the dance floor once more they shimmied and shook to several more songs. Their friends, Cara, and Suzy, met them during the fourth song. The girls danced and laughed. As they walked back to their table, Tammy noticed the tall, dark-haired guy sauntering towards them. The girls were smiling as he rested his elbows on the table. He looked across the table directly at Tammy, his blue eyes shining and the hint of a dimple in his right cheek.

"We couldn't keep our eyes off you ladies. Great dancing out there."

Molly smiled and looked at Tammy. Tammy looked into those blue eyes and smiled. "We noticed you all watching. So, what's the story?"

"No story. Would love a dance with you myself. Would you dance with me?"

Taking a sip of her drink, Tammy watched for sincerity in his eyes. When he didn't look away, she nodded. "Absolutely. But, I'd like to know your name first."

Laughing, he held out his right hand, "Name's Joel. What's yours?"

Tammy placed her right hand in his and said, "I'm Tammy. Nice to meet you." Nodding toward Molly, she said, "This is my best friend, Molly." Looking at her friends, she introduced them. "This is Cara and this is Suzy."

"Nice to meet you, ladies." Hearing the music slow down, he turned on a mischievous smile and said to Tammy, "Shall we?"

He walked around the table and took Tammy's hand, leading her out to the dance floor. Turning toward her, he wrapped his arm around her and pulled her close. As they swayed to the music, he bent his head down close to her ear. "My friends and I have a bet going. I think you look just like a girl in a video I recently saw. Want to make another one?"

Tammy froze. She pulled away and stared directly into the bastard's eyes. "Fuck you!" She turned and stomped off the dance floor, Joel yelling after her.

"I just offered, you stupid bitch. It's not like it's your first time."

Molly stood taller when she saw Tammy's posture and the look on her face. Tammy reached the table and grabbed her purse off the back of the chair. "I'm out of here. Fucker wanted to know if I wanted to make another video. I can't do this anymore."

Molly grabbed her purse and quickly said to Cara and Suzy, "I'll go home with Tammy."

CHAPTER 5

"HEY, REMEMBER ME telling you Joci hired me to take pictures at the house of the veteran who received the funds collected at the Veteran's Ride? I need to take pictures before the build so we can show before and after shots. Come with me, Tammy, and then we can go out and grab a bite to eat afterwards. We can call Cara and Suzie and ask them to meet us," Molly spoke into her phone.

"Okay. I'll be over in about half an hour. I want to change my clothes before I come to your place."

"Sounds great. Hurry, I don't want to miss the sun setting."

Tammy pressed the "end call" button on her phone as she walked to her bedroom to change.

The past few months had been a trial. Tammy was finally starting to feel like her old self again. The last couple of times she and Molly went out, she didn't feel like people were staring and pointing anymore. Of course, they were frequenting different bars, so nobody knew them. Last weekend they went to The Barn where Molly got wasted and Ryder, Molly's new boyfriend, took her home. Tammy, Cara, and Suzie left shortly after that without incident.

Molly and Tammy walked the perimeter of Danny Schaefer's house. The sun was low in the sky and the lighting was phenomenal. Molly captured the setting sun and the light peeking through the trees in Danny's yard. There was a gorgeous flower garden. The summer flowers had long since died, but these fall flowers, mums in burgundy and deep orange, and several varieties of kale, were so pretty. Molly stopped taking pictures of the house long enough to snap a few pictures of the flowers with the sun laying low in the background. Oh, some of these were definite screensaver shots.

Molly was lying on her belly to get close-ups of the flowers. Tammy smiled as she watched Molly in her element.

*   *   *

Danny was looking through the photo album his mom put together for him. Bittersweet. That's the only word to describe it. He was standing tall and proud as his mom buttoned the cord onto his shoulder on graduation day. Boot camp had been a bitch. It was hot in Georgia, and he'd spent three and a half months outside doing pushups, sit-ups, running, marching, shooting, and anything else his drill sergeants could think up. He'd loved every minute of it and had made good friends, too. Lex, short for Lexington, the city he came from, and Coop, short for Cooper, were the best. As he flipped the pages and watched the smile on his mom's face looking up to him, he smiled. Those were the days. On that day especially, he was proud. So damn proud. He did it. He finished boot camp. He excelled at everything they threw at him. It was the first time in his life he felt like he belonged. In school, he wasn't sports-minded or academic. He got along with everyone, but he never felt like he "fit in." He was a total motor-head. If it had a motor and burned gas, he was all over it.

Turning the page again, he came to a picture of himself standing with Kathryn. He'd just come home from boot camp and she was waiting for him. She was so damn beautiful to look at, but she was a cold fish. She didn't like sex and he usually had to do a fair amount of begging or get her drunk to get laid. But, despite that, he loved her, or thought he did. Thinking about it now, the only thing that hurt was being rejected. Danny swallowed the lump in his throat. He teetered between anger and hurt when he thought of Kathryn. Actually, since they'd broken up, he hadn't thought of her all that much until he saw a picture. Interesting.

Hearing a door slam, Danny swiveled in his chair and saw two women climb out of a car. A cute little short-haired girl was carrying a camera. The other one, damn, she was sexy as hell. Sweet little body, sandy-brown hair pulled up in a ponytail, and jeans that showed off her fine legs. She was wearing a bright red t-shirt and shit if she didn't have perfect tits. His cock sputtered to life as he watched them walk up to his house. The gal with the camera started taking pictures while the little hottie stood by her, watching. And Danny watched *her*.

Short hair said something and sexy laughed. Fuck, talk about getting sucker punched. She had a perfect smile, luscious lips. Danny groaned as he reached down and rubbed his rapidly thickening cock a few times. "Easy, boy. We're all alone now, no chick's gonna want us. Settle down."

Giving himself a moment to curb his arousal, Danny set his photo album on the table and grabbed the crutches leaning against the wall by his chair. Taking a deep breath and glancing down to make sure his cock was behaving, he pulled himself up and made his way to the front door.

Opening the door and stepping out onto the porch that surrounded most of his house he asked, "Can I help you?"

*   *   *

Molly and Tammy spun around to see the handsome man looking at them from the front entrance supported by crutches, one leg missing below the knee. Molly stood and hung the camera around her neck. She glanced at Tammy as she brushed leaves and grass from her blouse and with a slight jerk of her head they slowly approached him.

"Hi, I'm Molly, not sure if you remember me from the Veteran's Ride. This is my friend, Tammy. I'm the photographer hired to take pictures of the build tomorrow. I wanted to snap some before pictures and thought I'd do it today in case I didn't get here before the crowd converges on your property and messes things up. I'm sorry if we bothered you."

Tammy watched his beautiful, but wary chocolate-brown eyes. He looked from Molly to Tammy. He stared at Tammy much longer than necessary, causing her to fidget and slide a wayward strand of hair behind her ear.

"You think they're going to trample on my flowers?"

With a shaky voice, Molly said, "No. Sorry, I wandered through your flowers, but I don't think I've damaged anything. They're so beautiful with the sun setting...I couldn't help myself." Lowering her voice, Molly said. "Sorry. I shouldn't have."

Danny's shoulders relaxed a little. He let out a slow breath. "May I see?"

Tammy smiled at Danny. She'd been nervous when he walked out. It occurred to her then that it probably wasn't a good idea to trespass on a soldier's property, especially an injured one. For all she knew, he had guns in his house. She didn't think ahead sometimes.

Danny swung his gaze over to Tammy and then back to Molly. Molly pulled her camera up and turned it on. She hit a few buttons and brought up the pictures she'd taken. She smiled at Danny and turned the camera around so he could see them.

"You can scroll through the pictures by pushing this button," she indicated by showing him on the camera where to push.

Danny leaned into his crutches and scrolled through the pictures. He smiled a few times and looked up at the girls.

"You have a good eye for this. I guess I haven't taken the time to enjoy those flowers at all. My mom planted them to make my house feel 'cheery' or something," he said as he made air quotes with his fingers. Handing the camera back to Molly, he said, "Thank you for pointing out the beauty here."

Danny grew quiet. Both women were looking at him and wondering what to do next. He cleared his throat.

"Name's Danny. Would you like to come in and take before pictures of the inside?"

Molly raised her eyebrows in excitement and smiled. She looked back at Tammy, who was grinning at Danny.

"We don't want to put you out, but it would be nice to get some before pictures of the house on the inside. Thank you," Molly said.

Danny turned and walked into the house leaving them to follow. Molly looked over at Tammy and shrugged. They walked in behind him and closed the door. He pointed to a wall on the west side of the house.

"They're going to knock that wall out and put the addition there."

Molly walked over and started taking pictures of the wall and the room in general. It would look different in a few days.

"I *do* remember you. I thought you looked familiar, but I couldn't place where I'd seen you," Danny said.

Tammy watched Danny as he started to relax. The house was clean and he was…well, he was lean and ripped…and hot. His hair was short, military style, and sandy-brown in color. He wore a day's worth of growth on his jaw, giving him a rugged and sexy look. His t-shirt stretched across his chest and gave her a hint of the fine mass of muscle that lay just beneath. Tammy's fingers twitched as she thought about running her fingers along his chest. *I wonder if he has sandy-brown hair on his chest.*

As if he could feel her gaze, Danny turned his head and looked at Tammy. They stared for a few beats. Tammy blushed and looked down. Danny chuckled.

"How does this happen, Danny? Will you have to go and stay somewhere else for a while or can you stay here?" Molly asked.

"I can stay here," Danny said as he turned back toward Molly. "They'll frame the addition up first. They'll put the windows in and insulate and then they'll knock the wall out to allow the access. I have the plans on the table in the dining room. Do you want to see them?"

Both women nodded and Danny turned to walk into the dining room. Tammy followed last, noticing the bunching of muscle in his thighs as he moved. His powerful arms flexed with each move of his crutches. The sinew of muscle across his back tightened and relaxed as he moved. Gawd, he was simply…perfect.

As they looked at the plans, he pointed out where they were standing and where the additional bedroom and bathroom would be. Molly immediately started snapping pictures of the plans. Some up close, some from farther away.

Tammy stepped in and stood next to Danny. She loved the look of his thick fingers as he pointed to various points on the plans. The smell of his cologne swirled around her, making her weak in the knees. He smelled fabulous. Strong, clean, masculine. Spicy; Gawd, it was her kryptonite.

Molly walked around and snapped pictures of the living room. The constant click of her camera was all that was heard for a while. Tammy wanted to ask questions but was suddenly shy.

"Does she always click non-stop like that?" Danny said in a lowered voice to Tammy.

Tammy's eyes caught his, but she was tongue-tied. She could feel her heart pounding in her chest and was afraid he could hear it. Licking her lips, she said, "Yeah. It's her thing. You'll get used to her. She does have a good eye and she just loves this stuff."

Molly heard them talking about her and blushed a little. "I'll make sure you get the digitals. You can do what you like with them, but it'll be cool to see the before and after. Sometimes after a while, you forget what things looked like before. I've painted and worked on my house, not to this degree, but, months and years later when I come across the pictures, I'm still amazed at what it used to look like. That's what hooked me on photography in the first place. It's a beautiful way to memorialize the past."

Danny nodded. "Yeah, I was just looking at pictures of myself graduating from boot camp. Back when I had two legs. It's bittersweet."

Tammy, not being able to take her eyes off his, said, "Sometimes it can be. Some changes are so much bigger than others, but it's how we approach them daily that shapes our lives. We can't always control it. By the way, thank you for your service. It's appreciated more than you'll ever know." She smiled.

Danny nodded.

"Hey, we're going to head out and grab a bite to eat. Would you like to join us?" Molly asked.

* * *

Danny looked into Tammy's eyes. She had beautiful brown eyes and long, sandy-brown hair. She was petite, with a sweet little ass and breasts that his hands itched to mold themselves around. He had to grip his crutches with all his might to keep from reaching up and touching her face. Her lips, Jesus, perfect pink lips that made his dick hard. Glad to know it still worked. He didn't think any woman would want to have anything to do with him, having only one leg. Tammy seemed interested. She looked into his eyes and didn't look away.

He swallowed. "Naw. Thanks, but I think this'll be a very full weekend. I have a few things to do around here before tomorrow. I appreciate the offer."

"If you change your mind, we're going to Nicki's in De Pere. Please feel free to stop in. I'll buy you a beer." Tammy flashed her brightest smile. Danny swallowed again and cocked his head at her. She was flirting with him. She probably just wanted to pity-fuck him.

Danny watched Tammy and Molly walk down the driveway and climb into Molly's car. Tammy's ponytail swished as she walked. He couldn't help but stare at her tight little ass as it swished back and forth in time with her ponytail. Once she was in the car, he let out a low whistle. He turned from the window and made his way into the kitchen.

Pulling a casserole out of the refrigerator, he smirked. "That girl just flirted with me. What the hell do you know?"

* * *

"So? What did you think?" Tammy was looking at Molly with a huge grin on her face.

"Think about what?" Molly asked as she reached back and pulled the seat belt over her shoulder and latched it into place.

"Danny. What did you think about Danny?" Tammy pulled the visor down and looked at her face in the mirror. Gently swiping under her eye and correcting her makeup, she glanced over at Molly.

"Oh my gosh! Are you interested in Danny?" Molly slid the key into the ignition as she watched Tammy's face brighten.

"You are! You so have to come back with me tomorrow and help me with my equipment. You can make some drawings and you'll get to see Danny again."

"Okay. Yes, I want to do that. Do you think he was interested in me? Does he have a girlfriend? His house didn't look like a female lived there. It was neat and clean, but not in a feminine way. Do you think he's nice? What do you know about him?"

"Whoa, hold on with the questions, girl. One at a time." Molly laughed as she pulled away from the curb and started toward the restaurant.

"Well, does he have a girlfriend?"

"I don't know. He didn't have anyone with him at the Veteran's Ride." Molly tapped the turn signal as she slowed the car.

"Do you think he might be interested in me?" Tammy smirked at Molly.

"I don't know, Tammy. But I caught him staring at you a couple of times. Who isn't interested in you? Men always think you're hot."

"Not always. Only since that damn video. But, what do you…" Gasping, Tammy said, "Oh no, if he finds out about that friggin' video, he won't be interested in me anyway. Not for anything more than sex." Tammy's head hit the headrest in frustration.

"You don't know that," Molly countered.

Tammy's gaze slid sideways to leer at Molly. "You know what I've been through with that fucking video. My life is over. Well, my love life is over."

Molly put her car in park and twisted in her seat to look at her best friend. "Your life, your love life is not over. Just be up-front with him. Scott lied to you. He videoed you without your permission. He was probably uploading it to YouTube before you were even finished. He's a dick. If you avoid relationships because of that video, you let him win."

CHAPTER 6

"THIS IS TOO FRIGGIN' early. AND, you shouldn't have let me drink so much last night. My aspirin still hasn't taken effect."

Molly laughed as she started pulling her camera equipment out of her trunk. "It'll kick in. I think Joci has coffee on supply here, let's go get some before we start snapping pictures."

"So, you still have a hot date tonight?" Tammy smirked.

"Well, I'm going out with Ryder, who is smoking hot, so I guess that qualifies as a hot date."

Tammy shook her head. "I don't know Mol, he didn't call you all week. That's not right."

"He's shy. He opened up to me more last Sunday. And he told me he'd be busy this week. Don't be judgy."

They walked up the street toward Danny's house. There was so much activity already. As they approached the yard, they could see the siding had been removed on the side the builders were working on. There were tables and stations set up everywhere for measuring, sawing, cutting, etc. The girls spotted Joci standing by a table with food and big coffee pots on it. Molly waved and walked over to Joci.

"Hi, Joci, how are you feeling?" Molly leaned forward as they hugged.

"I'm feeling great. Jeremiah won't let me do anything, so I'm manning the beverage and food table. What would you like, coffee or hot chocolate?" Joci said.

"Coffee, please," they said in unison.

"I can get it, Joci," Tammy said. As she was pouring their coffees Molly pulled her camera out.

"We came by yesterday and I got before pictures. Take a look."

Tammy stopped paying attention. Without even realizing it, she was looking for Danny. There were so many people here, but she was sure he'd be walking around or helping out in some way.

There he was; he was walking toward them and he was fine, mighty fine. His broad shoulders filled out his long sleeve t-shirt and his jeans fit him perfectly, showing off his strong thighs. Yum.

"Good morning. How are you two doing this morning?" Danny said looking at Molly quickly, then losing himself in Tammy's big brown eyes. What was it about this woman that drew him so?

"Morning. Glad we came yesterday. With all of this stuff lying around, I wouldn't have been able to get any good before pictures." Molly said.

Danny nodded and looked around.

"Yeah. I guess it's true that it needs to get worse before it gets better."

They all nodded. Molly looked over and saw Ryder looking their way. She waved at him but he just scowled and looked away. Molly furrowed her brows and looked at Tammy. Tammy shrugged.

"He seemed a little pissed when I told him you were here taking pictures yesterday."

Molly looked at Danny with her brows still furrowed. "He's mad? Because I took pictures?"

Molly looked at Joci, who slowly shook her head. "I'm not aware of anyone being upset this morning. But you can bet I'll find out."

Molly shook her head. "Well, I didn't do anything wrong, so, whatever. I'm going to snap a few pictures of the progress then we'll come and help you here for a little while. Is that okay?"

"Sounds good. Don't worry hon, I'm sure it's nothing," Joci said.

"How was dinner last night?" Danny asked, turning toward Tammy.

Tammy tucked a hair behind her ear and without even thinking about it flashed him her brightest smile. "Good. Did you get everything done that you needed to do?"

There it was again; she could smell him. Her heart was racing and her hands were shaking. He'd shaved this morning and damn he looked good. She liked the rugged look he sported last night, but clean shaven Danny was handsome too.

"Yeah, I guess, anything else that needs to get done will have to wait." He swallowed, "You look beautiful today."

Beautiful, he thought she was beautiful? When he smiled at her butterflies lurched in her stomach and flew straight to her core. She could feel her panties dampen and her heart beat out a staccato that threatened to knock her over.

Realizing she hadn't said anything, she licked her lips and said, "Thank you. You look handsome yourself."

* * *

Handsome? She thought he was handsome? Dammit, there went his cock again. Getting lost in those dark eyes of hers made him forget everything. She literally took his breath away. He smirked and thought he heard her sigh.

Before he lost his nerve he blurted out, "Do you want to have dinner next week?"

Her eyes grew large as he waited for what? Ten minutes? No, more like seconds, but he hadn't asked anyone out since he lost his leg. This was big for him. He kicked himself all night last night for not joining her and Molly. He lay awake all night mad that he'd been enjoying a pity party and she gave him every indication she was interested and he didn't follow through. Time to get over himself.

"Yes."

Just one simple word and he felt like the weight of the world was lifted off his shoulders. "Yeah? Really?"

"Yeah. Really." Tammy laughed and his cock grew so hard he could've used it to hammer nails into his house. Then, just when he was trying to think of what to say next she giggled.

"Hello. I haven't met you. My name's Janice, I'm Danny's mom." Janice held out her hand to Tammy. She smiled when she saw Tammy blush.

"Hi. I'm Tammy." Tammy shook Janice's hand. She glanced up at Danny and lost her breath when she saw the look on his face. He looked...happy.

* * *

At first I was pissed that we were interrupted. I asked Tammy out and she accepted. Damn. Then my mom walked over. My mom. Talk about a boner kill. But I looked at the smile on Tammy's face as she shook my mom's hand, and God, Bam! Sucker punched.

"Nice to meet you, Tammy. Thank you for coming today and helping out. It's a beautiful day."

"It is. I'm actually here to help Molly with pictures, but I may just grab a hammer and help out."

"Well, there's plenty to do. I have a few things to do in the flower garden. It was nice meeting you, Tammy."

Janice smiled at Tammy and with a smirk at Danny she walked toward the flower garden.

CHAPTER 7

MOLLY TOOK PICTURES of Danny as Joci asked him questions. They stood on his front porch with a video camera because Joci wanted to add the interview to the end of the DVD she was producing for the Rolling Thunder Veterans Ride. Tammy helped with the video camera while Molly snapped pictures and Joci asked Danny questions.

"Tell me about your time in the service, Danny. Where did you do your Basic Training?"

"I did my Basic at Fort Benning. After Basic I went to Fort Stewart until I was deployed."

"When did you buy this house?"

"I bought it about 2 years before I went into the Army. I didn't go in straight out of high school; I waited. My dad was sick and I didn't want to leave. After he passed away, my mom told me she'd be fine if I still wanted to go. I did, of course, but was concerned about leaving her. Then, I had this house. Mom and my brother, Paul, took care of it for me while I was gone."

Danny's eyes kept flicking to Tammy's. He was both nervous about giving away so much of himself, and excited that she was watching him, her perfectly plump lips curved up in a sweet smile.

"Tell me about your family. You mentioned that your father passed away and you have a brother, Paul. Any other siblings?"

"No, it's just the two of us. Paul, he's so smart. He's a veterinarian in town now. He's married to Grace and they have a baby on the way. Mom still lives in town, close to here, actually."

"I want to talk to you about your injuries. When did you know you lost your leg?"

Danny took a deep breath, flicked his gaze to Tammy and swallowed. "I knew almost right away. I couldn't hear my buddies because of the ringing in my ears and didn't know if any of them were hurt." Fidgeting in his chair, he ran a hand across the back of his neck. "I passed out initially but in the helicopter, on the way to base, they told me it was gone. I lost a buddy, Reed, and another buddy, Janus, lost both of his legs and one hand."

Tammy found herself mesmerized by his voice, his eyes and his story. He didn't feel sorry for himself and he actually seemed humbled and overwhelmed with the support he was receiving from Rolling Thunder and the community as a whole. The amount of people who'd donated food, materials, tools and their time to help out was astounding. Danny teared up several times talking about everything. Tammy's heart melted.

After they finished the interview, Joci and Molly walked over to the food table. Danny and Tammy were left on the porch. Danny was trying to calm himself down before speaking to Tammy. Reliving that was rough. His heart raced and he was sweating. He hated talking about that day. That mission. And, he didn't want to look weak; not in front of Tammy. Weird. Why was she different?

Finally able to move, he stood. "Should we get a bite to eat?" he asked Tammy. She nodded and they walked silently over to the food table. Danny pulled himself and Tammy between Joci and Molly.

He leaned down and hugged Molly. "Thank you, Molly, for taking the pictures. I'm going to keep an album of them." He leaned close to her ear and said, "I hope everything will be ok with Ryder. I'm sorry I said anything."

Molly looked up at him and smiled. "You're welcome for the pictures. I'll make you a digital photo album. Don't worry about Ryder; I'm sure it's just a misunderstanding. And, if it's okay, I'd like to mention that Tammy couldn't stop talking about you last night. She's smitten."

Molly stepped back a few steps to take pictures of the women gathered around the food table. She took a few pictures of Danny as Tammy stood next to him. They looked good together. Tammy was a little sandy-haired, brown-eyed woman. Danny had sandy hair, eyes the color of dark chocolate and stood about a foot above her. He looked down at her just as Tammy looked up at him and smiled. Ahh, what a great picture. Molly snapped a few more of them talking.

"There she goes, snapping away again." Danny chuckled.

"You'll get used to it. I'd like to help today. What can I do?"

Danny looked over the yard full of people and the men helping out. He looked back at Tammy and smiled. "I was just going to go and relieve Gus from the chop saw. You want to help me with that?"

Tammy nodded as she looked into his eyes. She had to stifle the giggle that threatened to escape. Danny took her small hand in his much larger one and they walked over to the chop saw station. He looked down at their joined hands and glanced over at those gorgeous brown eyes to see her looking at their hands as well. He gave her hand a squeeze and looked straight ahead.

His heart beat furiously and his head was getting way ahead of him...them. He wasn't whole. He still struggled, every day with issues. Physical and, emotional. The PTSD took over sometimes and even though he never missed a session with his therapist, he still had so much to overcome. Then, of course, physically, he wasn't whole. Sure, days like today he looked normal, but eventually if things progressed, she would see him without his clothes. He had scars and while their bright pink tones were fading to deeper brown hues, they were still very prominent on his body. Tammy was perfect, she should have someone perfect.

"Hey, you're quiet. What's up?" Tammy smiled up at Danny and his breath caught.

"Aah, nothing, just...thinking." He smirked and looked at the saw station up ahead of them.

"Hey, Danny, how's it going today?" Gus bellowed. He was a stout, good-natured man currently wearing a red plaid flannel shirt tucked into jeans held up with suspenders.

"Good, Gus, how are you? Thanks so much for coming today and helping out, I'm speechless. And appreciative."

"Danny, I've known you since you were born. I couldn't live with myself if I didn't come to help out one of our finest soldiers."

Danny's cheeks turned bright red at the praise and he ducked his head in embarrassment.

Laughing so hard his rotund belly shook and holding his hand out, Gus said, "Name's Gus, little lady. Nice to meet you."

"Nice to meet you too, my name's Tammy. We came to relieve you so you could grab a bite to eat while the food's hot. What's the routine here?" Tammy smiled her brightest smile and Gus let out a low whistle.

Looking at Danny he said, "You better be careful, Danny, this little one will wrap you around her finger so fast your head will spin."

Tammy shrugged as her cheeks burned. Gus continued laughing. "Well, the guys will bring you boards marked up where you cut them. All you need to do is cut them and give 'em back. It goes quicker if one person mans the saw rather than everyone lining up to use it and that way, we also eliminate accidents." Lowering his voice he said, "Not everyone here should be using a saw, if you know what I mean." Laughing at his own joke, he patted Danny on the back and headed toward the food table with a quick, "Holler if you need help."

Tammy watched Gus waddle to the food table as Danny reached into a bag lying on the ground and pulled out two pairs of safety goggles.

"Put these on. Have you ever used one of these before?"

"Of course I have. My dad taught Molly and I how to use his when we helped him and his friends fix the fence at Molly's house."

Danny raised his eyebrows and smiled. "Okay. Well, sexy and uses power tools..."

"Hey, I have a few boards to cut." And that was the end of conversation as one by one men lined up to have their boards cut. Tammy and Danny took turns cutting the boards, each taking a moment to speak to the person bringing the board to ensure they understood what was needed. The afternoon passed quickly and six o'clock whizzed up to greet them.

"Hey, Tammy, I have to get going." Molly said as she strode towards them.

"Okay." Tammy took off her safety glasses and set them in the bag. Dusting her hands off on her jeans, she looked back at Danny, "I'll see you tomorrow, okay?"

Danny slid his safety glasses up on top of his head as he wiped his hands down his thighs. Not knowing what to do with his hands and itching to touch Tammy's face, he slid his fingers into his front pockets and smiled. "Yeah, see you tomorrow. Thanks for all your help today. You too, Molly, thanks."

Molly nodded, "Happy to do it and I'm stoked for you to see the pictures."

Sensing a little tension, Molly turned to Tammy and said, "I'll wait for you by the car. I'm going to go and say good-bye to Joci." With a wave she was off.

Tammy's cheeks flamed bright pink as she looked at the ground and Danny's shoes.

Placing his finger under her chin, Danny gently pulled Tammy's face up catching her gaze with his. "I look forward to seeing you tomorrow. Thank you for everything."

Tammy swallowed the large lump in her throat and willed the wild butterflies in her tummy to slow down. Tilting her lips at the corners she whispered, "I look forward to seeing you, too."

Wrapping one arm around her shoulders and one around her waist, Danny pulled Tammy in for a hug. He just couldn't let her go without at least this.

Feeling his heart hammer next to hers Tammy wrapped her arms around Danny's waist and hung on, because her knees were shaking and she didn't know if she would be able to stand on her own. His warmth surrounded her and his scent, part Danny and part the wood they'd cut all afternoon and wholly sexy. His muscles contracted under her arms and she could feel how firm he was. She laid her cheek on his chest and listened to the strong heartbeat beneath his impressive chest muscles and she let out a sigh. This felt good. No, great. This felt great. Who knew a hug could feel so...right.

Pulling away she looked up at him and smiled. "See you in the morning."

Danny swallowed as the loss of her heat against his body left him cold. He watched her perfect lips form the most beautiful smile and she told him she'd see him in the morning, and all he could do was nod because his stupid mouth wouldn't form words.

CHAPTER 8

"**DID YOU ASK HER** out?" Paul asked Danny as he reached forward and filled his taco shell with meat.

Grace busied herself sprinkling cheese on her taco as she discreetly looked through her lashes at Danny, waiting for him to respond.

Danny chuckled. "Yeah." He wasn't entirely comfortable with this conversation.

"So why aren't you with her now? When are you going out?" Grace couldn't stop herself from asking.

Danny set his beer bottle on the table and sat back in his chair. He looked into Grace's beautiful blue eyes and saw excitement in them. "Grace, don't get too excited about this, okay? I don't even know why she said yes. She was probably just feeling sorry for me. She may change her mind and cancel."

"What on earth are you talking about, Dan? That's crazy. She looked positively smitten with you today. Every time I looked over at the two of you she had 'dreamy eyes' on you." She emphasized 'dreamy eyes' with air quotes.

Paul burst out laughing. "Dreamy eyes? What the hell are dreamy eyes, babe?"

"You know, she looked all…" trying to find the words Grace batted her eyes at Paul and folded her hands together under her chin. "Like all lovey-dovey and sweet."

"She wasn't doing that, Grace. That's bullshit," Danny admonished.

"Was too. I saw it. She's definitely got it for you. Did you kiss her?"

"What the fuck, Grace?" Danny asked, face burning bright red to the tips of his ears.

"What? Gosh, Dan, you're touchy on this subject. I'm just sayin'."

Paul laughed again and, leaning across the table, smacked his lips against his wife's. "Leave it alone, babe. Apparently this is a hot button."

Danny swiped his hand down his face and grabbed his beer. He downed the majority of it, swallowed, and downed the rest. He stood and threw the bottle in the garbage basket next to the cabinets. Running his hands down his thighs he walked to the refrigerator and grabbed another beer. Stepping back he peered around the fridge door and looked at Paul. Paul shook his head no. Danny closed the fridge door and resumed his seat at the table. Suddenly, his stomach was knotted up.

"Sorry Danny. I wasn't trying to make you mad."

"I'm not mad at you, Grace. I just..." looking past Grace out the window Danny's mouth formed a straight line. "It's just, you know. I'm trying not to read too much into it. It'll take someone super special to want to be with me now. I have PTSD, phantom pain, nightmares, the works. I'm not exactly whole," he said motioning his hands toward his leg. "You know?"

Grace's eyes glistened with unshed tears as she looked at Danny. She blinked and a lone tear slid down her cheek.

"Fuck. I didn't mean to make you cry. Christ, Paul, what am I supposed to do with this?"

Paul reached over and took Grace's hand in his. "Babe, don't cry. It's okay."

Paul gave Grace's hand a squeeze causing her to look over at him. He raised his eyebrows and Grace nodded.

"Stupid hormones. I swear I can laugh one minute and cry in the next. Sorry."

Grace wiped her cheeks and looked at Danny. "You're whole. A missing limb or part of a limb is overcomable, if that's a word. You have nightmares, I have raging hormones. You have PTSD. I pee every ten minutes. We all have something. Did you ever think that maybe she has something she's worried about you finding out about?"

"No, she's perfect."

"Ha. See, you're smitten too."

Grace picked up her taco and bit down, causing a loud crunching sound. Danny grabbed his taco and looked at Grace, just before taking a bite, he said, "Am not."

* * *

"Molly has a date tonight and I was outside working all day, so, I'm going to soak in the tub and go to bed early tonight. I'm going back tomorrow to work again."

"Don't get too wrapped up in this guy until you know he's good, okay honey? I know I don't have to tell you to protect yourself." Tammy's mom, Denise, said on the other end of the phone, while swiping her hand through her short brown hair.

Tammy, walking toward her bathroom froze when her mom brought up the painful subject of 'protecting herself'. Letting out a long breath, she whispered, "Mom. Don't. Please."

"I'm not lecturing. I just want you to be careful. Not everyone is who they seem to be."

Tammy walked into her bathroom and looked at herself in the mirror. Her nose was rosy from being outside all day. Her eyes looked tired and her hair was a mess from blowing in the wind. But, overall, she looked…happy.

"I know you're not lecturing, but, please stop reminding me. I've worked so hard to forget, though, I never will. I…just…please."

Denise's lips turned down into a frown. "I'm sorry. I won't bring it up again. But, if you continue this relationship with Danny, you'll need to tell him. It hurts to hide things like this and it usually comes out when you don't want it to. Promise?"

Softly Tammy said, "Yes."

"Okay, babe. Go soak in your tub and I'll talk to you tomorrow. Goodnight."

"Night, mom." Tammy tapped her phone to end the call and set it on the bathroom counter. She turned to the tub and twisted the faucet to start the water. She sprinkled in her favorite bath salts and undressed. Gently easing herself into the warm water, Tammy leaned back and smiled to herself. Taking a deep breath and letting the tension float away on the water, she closed her eyes and smiled when visions of Danny floated into her mind.

CHAPTER 9

"**WANNA TELL ME** about your hot date last night?" Tammy smirked as she climbed in Molly's car.

"Nope. We were both tired and didn't go out. I made pizza at home instead." Molly smiled as she stared out the windshield.

"Really?" Tammy looked over at her friend and waited for her to say something. Respond. Look at her. Nothing. "Really? That's all?"

Molly's cheeks bloomed bright red. She looked over at Tammy and they burst out laughing.

"Wow. Hot, right?" Tammy asked.

Molly put her car in gear and swallowed. All she could do was nod and smile. "What about you? Are you excited to see Danny today?"

It was Tammy's turn to turn red. "I am. He asked me out for next week. It feels like it'll take forever for next week to get here." She sighed and turned slightly in her seat. "I just loved working with him yesterday, Mol. He's precise, caring, and easy to talk to. We chatted little bits in between cutting boards. He's smart, but not arrogant or full of himself." Tammy sat back in her seat and stared straight out the windshield. "He's…I've never met anyone like him, Mol. Never."

Molly glanced over at her friend and saw the dreamy look on her face. She smiled and glanced back at the road. "Are you going to tell him about the video?"

Tammy curled her lip down and wrinkled her nose a bit. "I don't know. It's…ugh, I don't know. It's hard and I hope we can get to know each other a bit before I have to say anything. After all, maybe he'll change his mind and not want to go out with me and then I won't have to say anything at all."

Molly bit the inside of her lip as she let those words roll around in her head. "I get it; after all, I'm doing the same thing."

"It's a different scenario Molly. What happened to you wasn't your fault. Lancaster's a pig."

"What happened to you wasn't your fault either. You didn't know Scott was videoing you. Scott's a pig, too."

Both girls nodded and stared straight ahead.

* * *

Molly pulled her camera equipment out of her trunk while absently looking for Ryder in the crowd of people at Danny's house again today. Things looked very different than they had yesterday, all the way around. Molly's night with Ryder last night was, well, remarkable really. They fit together in a way she never dreamed she'd ever fit with anyone.

Tammy closed the car door and zipped up the hoodie she was wearing. She looked over the crowd finding Danny almost instantly. He stood next to Dog and Gunnar and he was watching her. Her heart fluttered and the butterflies in her tummy were flapping furiously to get out. Tammy walked toward Danny, leaving Molly to follow. As she approached Danny, Tammy's lips quivered and then blossomed to a full blown smile. She thought she heard him huff out a breath, but wasn't sure. But she did see him swallow a large lump in his throat, which gave her a thrill.

"Hi," she said softly.

Danny smiled at her. "Hi."

Two pair of brown eyes locked on each other, each feeling as though they were the only ones on the planet. Until they heard a throat clear and a male voice. "Ah, we'll just run along and do something."

Tammy blinked and looked over at Gunnar, who was smirking at her. She blushed profusely and tucked her hair behind her ear. "Sorry. Good morning, Gunnar. Dog." Tammy leaned forward and shook hands with each of them.

"Morning, Tammy. Nice to see you again. Thanks for helping Joci out yesterday. We all appreciate it," Dog said.

"Oh, I was happy to help her. She's great. The interview at the end of the ride DVD is going to be awesome." Tammy looked over at Danny, a broad smile splitting her face.

Danny ducked his head as he rubbed his hands down his thighs.

"She mentioned how much she enjoyed the interview. She's very excited about the DVD. I am, too." Dog smiled as he looked across the crowd at the food table where Joci was talking with some of the folks who were there to help out for the day.

"Okay, let's get to it. See you guys around." Gunnar waved and turned to walk toward the side of the house where the work was commencing.

Dog walked beside Gunnar, the two of them talking to each other as they walked.

Danny cleared his throat as he looked at Tammy. "Um, did you have a good night last night?"

"Yeah. I didn't do anything. I stayed home, soaked in the tub and put together some drawings for a mural I'm painting. How about you?"

"Yeah. I had dinner with my brother and sister-in-law." Danny said pointing to a beautiful petite blonde woman with a very round baby bump and a man who looked very much like Danny standing with his arm around her shoulders speaking with Danny's mom, Janice.

"Oh, that's nice. Do you get together with them often?"

"Yeah. I guess a couple of times a week. The past few weeks, not as much, but…you know."

"Sure. I have a brother, but we aren't that close. Molly's my sister as far as I'm concerned. We grew up together. I see her about three to four times a week. I get it."

Danny nodded. "So, if you haven't changed your mind about going out with me, I thought we could go out to dinner and then maybe go to a bar and shoot some pool. Do you like shooting pool?"

Tammy giggled. "I do like it, though I'm not that good at it."

"Neither am I, but I'm willing to try if you are."

"Absolutely. Okay, now what do you want me to do today?"

They worked side-by-side all day, chatting when they could between jobs. By mid-afternoon, they were working inside, painting the bedroom walls a beautiful cocoa brown. Dog and Joci walked in, Dog explaining to Joci what was going where.

"Wow, the color is perfect. Do you like it Danny?" Joci asked.

"I love it. I never would've thought about this color, but, it's perfect. Thank you for all of your designing. It's better than I could ever have imagined."

Joci smiled and glanced at Tammy. Tammy's smile widened as she spoke. "It's the perfect color with the light coming in the windows. You're fabulous at interior design."

"Well, I understand you're the perfect person to paint this room, though, I understand we're under-utilizing your talents," Joci said.

Danny looked down at Tammy, eyebrows raised in question. Tammy blushed flicking her gaze to Danny and then to Joci. "Thanks. You should come to the home and see the mural I'm doing. It's coming together nicely. Did Molly tell you about it?"

"What home? What are you talking about?" Danny asked.

Before she could answer, Dog said, "I hope you don't mind, but I wanted Joci's ideas on a couple of things in the bathroom. Will you excuse us?"

"Of course." Tammy said, with a slight wave of her hand. She leaned down to refill her roller with paint.

"What home, Tammy?" Danny asked.

"Oh, I work at Stateside Home for Retired Veterans."

Danny froze in mid-motion of laying paint on the wall. He looked over his raised arm at Tammy, a frown creasing his features.

"You work at a Veterans' Home?" he asked.

"Yeah. I'm an administrative assistant there. I work for the Director. She's grooming me to take over for her when she retires in a few months. But, I'm also painting a mural on a wall in the activities room. I have all the wars depicted except this last one."

Slowly lowering his arm, Danny looked at Tammy full on. Softly he asked, "Why haven't you painted this war yet?"

Tammy, feeling uneasy, put her roller into the paint pan and stood facing him. "I don't have a frame of reference for this war. I've spoken to each of the veterans in the home regarding each of the wars so I can get the mural correct. They help point inconsistencies out so the mural is accurate. We don't have a veteran there who's been in this current war."

Danny's breathing became choppy and his heart hammered in his chest. He just knew it was too good to be true. She only wanted to spend time with him so she could finish her damned mural. Fucking figures. He took a step back and then a second one. He gave his head a quick shake and turned and left the room without another word.

Tammy stared after him, confusion on her face. "Hey, what's wrong?"

Dog and Joci walked out of the bathroom and seeing Tammy's face, Joci asked, "Tammy, are you alright?"

Tammy's bottom lip trembled. Her eyes were bright with tears. She looked at Joci, but she couldn't say anything.

"Honey, are you okay? What on earth happened?" Joci wrapped her arms around Tammy and hugged her. The caring in Joci's voice opened the flood gates and Tammy began crying. Joci looked at Dog over Tammy's head and nodded slightly. Dog got the message. He turned and walked out. He never knew what to do with a crying woman.

When Tammy had composed herself, Joci walked her over to a bench and they sat side-by-side. Tammy wiped the tears from her face and swallowed.

Pulling Tammy's hair over her shoulder Joci quietly said, "Are you ready to tell me what happened?"

Tammy nodded. "I don't know to be honest. I told Danny I work at Stateside and he seemed angry and turned and walked out. He didn't say anything and I don't know why my working at the veterans' home would make him mad. I don't know what happened."

"Okay." Joci took a deep breath. "Well, maybe it hits close to home for him or maybe he knows someone who had a bad experience at a home or something. You need to go find out. If you want to forge a relationship, you need to talk things out, honey."

Nodding Tammy wiped her cheeks with both hands and dried her hands on her thighs. She tucked her hair behind her ears and took a deep breath. "Okay. I'll go see if I can find him."

Tammy stood up and took a couple of steps before turning to Joci. "Thanks, Joci. I appreciate you talking to me."

Joci smiled as she stood, her hand automatically rubbing her baby bump. "Any time, honey. Go find your man."

CHAPTER 10

WALKING ONTO THE front porch, Tammy looked around the yard, finding Danny talking to his brother Paul. His posture was rigid, his jaw tight. As she watched them speak to each other, Paul looked up and saw Tammy watching them. He said something to Danny, who turned and looked at Tammy. She saw sadness. What on earth had caused such sadness? Rubbing her hands on her thighs, she stepped off the deck to walk toward Danny and Paul. Her stomach was rolling and she was sweating, though the temperature was cool today.

As she approached, she swallowed and saw Danny do the same. She glanced at Paul and smiled. Holding her shaking hand out to Paul, she said, "Hi. I'm Tammy."

Paul took her small hand in his and smiled at her. "I'm Paul, this lug's brother. Nice to meet you."

Tammy's smile quivered and she nodded. Slowly turning to Danny, she said, "May I speak with you?" She looked into his eyes, though he didn't move. "Alone. Please?"

Taking the cue, Paul said, "Great idea. I'm going to see what Grace is up to. Nice meeting you, Tammy." With a squeeze to Danny's shoulder, Paul walked away.

Tammy placed her hand over her stomach to try and stop the rolling. "Danny, is there somewhere we can speak privately?"

Danny huffed out a breath and looked around. There were about a hundred and fifty people milling about. Hard to find a private place to speak. Taking a deep breath, he said, "We can go sit in my truck. It's about the only private place around right now."

They turned and walked toward the garage, not holding hands, for the first time since the build had begun. Anytime they'd walked anywhere together, Danny always took her hand; her mood plummeted. Danny opened the service door on the side of the garage and opened the passenger door for Tammy to climb in. A running board dropped down to assist her.

Danny closed her door and walked around to the driver's side. After climbing in, he placed his hands on his knees and looked straight ahead. So, he wasn't going to just tell her what made him mad, she was going to have to drag it out of him.

"Danny. What happened back there? Why did you leave? Why are you mad?"

"You're kidding, right? You only want to be with me because you need to finish your damn mural. You just need someone to talk to you about this war. That's why you're here, with me. I knew you weren't interested in me for me. I was an idiot to think you could be. Look at me. I'm a cripple, for fuck's sake."

Tammy's eyes grew wide. She stared at him in disbelief. Not able to form words she simply stared. After a long silence Danny turned his head to look at her. "Aren't you at least going to admit it?"

Now she was getting angry. "You think I'm so damned shallow that I would go out with you to finish painting a stupid mural? That's what you think of me? Thanks a lot. I've never, ever, been called shallow before. I'll have you know, I'm a good person. I've never used anyone for anything. EVER!"

Tammy turned her head and grabbing the door handle, pulled it up unlatching the door. Turning quickly back to Danny, she said, "The only person who thinks of you as a cripple is you. I happen to look at you and see a smart, handsome, fascinating man who I enjoy talking to and working with. I see someone who has sacrificed for our country and the freedoms we enjoy. Honorable. That's what I see. When I close my eyes at night, I see someone I can't wait to see the next day. I see someone who, quite frankly, has taken my breath away. That's what I see. I never even thought to ask you to help me with the mural. When I see you, I'm not thinking about the mural or Stateside. I'm thinking about…You!"

Tears slipped down her cheeks as she turned to leave. Her breathing was ragged and she was wrecked. Mostly she was pissed.

Danny reached out and grabbed for her arm, but she was out the door too fast. She slammed the door of his truck and stomped off toward Molly's car. She'd had enough for today. She was crushed. Tammy climbed into the car and sat staring straight ahead. Dammit. Hitting the steering wheel a few times for good measure, she let her tears flow. She laid her head against the headrest and closed her eyes. Dammit, she liked him so damn much. She let herself dream he could be the one. Dammit, dammit, dammit.

The passenger door to the car opened and Molly slid inside. Worry marring her pretty face, Molly softly asked, "What's wrong Tammy. What happened?"

Tammy, first surprised and then relieved, wiped her face. "That stupid son-of-a-bitch said I was shallow and using him."

"What? Are you kidding me?" Molly looked out the window, searching for Danny. She saw him walking out of his garage and into the house with his head down.

"He looks sad," Molly absently said.

Tammy looked out the window and saw Danny just as he closed the front door. "He has no reason to be sad; I do. I'm so angry right now I could spit cotton."

"Tell me what happened."

Tammy and Molly sat in the car as Tammy relayed the conversations with Joci and Danny. Molly's jaw continued to drop open and then close again. She sat quietly, giving Tammy the time to cool down. Molly reached into the console and pulled out a tissue. Tammy wiped and blew her nose. Pulling the visor down, she checked herself in the mirror.

"Fabulous. I look fucking amazing," she said sarcastically.

Molly looked over at her and giggled. "At least you aren't swearing anymore."

Tammy couldn't help it, she burst out laughing and Molly laughed right along with her. When they'd composed themselves, Molly turned in her seat and looked at Tammy.

"I remember you telling me when you first started working at Stateside that some of these veterans have so much to overcome. Especially losing a limb. Ryder told me that a week after Danny came home his girlfriend dumped him. He's dealing with a lot of stuff and naturally, after that, he would assume he isn't good enough for a little hottie like you." Molly smirked and Tammy rolled her eyes in dislike. "I think you need to cut him some slack, Tammy. Try and see things from his point of view. He's probably not sure what to do from here."

Tammy huffed out a breath. "I can't today. I need some time. I'll just sit here until you're ready to go."

"Don't be silly. Take my car, I'll catch a ride. Joci or Ryder will take me home. Okay?"

Sniffing, she said, "Okay. Thanks Mol."

Molly leaned over and hugged Tammy. "It's going to be alright. I promise."

Tammy nodded. Molly pulled her car keys out of her pocket and handed them over. "Drive safe. I'll talk to you later."

Tammy watched Molly climb out of the car and walk across the lawn to speak to Ryder. She saw Ryder lean down and kiss Molly's lips and then the tip of her nose. Molly turned back toward the car and waved, signaling all is good. Tammy started the ignition and drove home in a funk.

CHAPTER 11

THE LOUD RAPPING *of gunfire drowned out the yells of his team. He could see them talking to him, yelling, the chords standing out in their necks, eyes wild, darting back and forth. The odors of sulfur and gunpowder burning his nostrils, the dust burning his eyes. Danny's heartbeat was wild, sweat covered his entire body. Mortars hit close by causing the ground to vibrate beneath his feet. He felt a bullet whiz by his ear, so close he felt the heat. He dropped his head and scrambled to find cover. They were under attack and this time, it was bad.*

Barely able to catch his breath, Danny scrambled over to Lex, who'd found cover under a boulder that jutted out from the hills. It felt like he crawled miles; no matter how far he crawled, he couldn't get there. Lex looked at him with eyes wild, quickly ducking as gunfire rained off the top of the boulder. Lex yelled something at Danny but he couldn't hear. He couldn't get there. Muscles straining, sweat dripping into his eyes the loud crack of another mortar caused his ears to ring. Nausea was creeping into his stomach. He couldn't get there. Lex floated further away and Danny felt helpless. Another loud crack rang the air, Danny rolled to avoid the incoming blast. He fell with a thud so forceful all the air whooshed from his lungs.

He lay still, trying to command his lungs to take in air. Ears ringing, sweat coating his skin, his eyes started adjusting to the dusty light filtering into his bedroom. He lay on the floor, his shoulder sore from the fall. Danny slowly rolled over on his back to get his bearings. He stared at the ceiling until his breathing evened out. Fucking nightmares. Third one in as many nights. Since his fight with Tammy, they were coming every day. He went to bed each night with a heavy heart and it played terrible tricks on his mind.

Wiping the sweat off his brow and throwing his arms over his face, Danny groaned at his miserable life. Allowing himself a few minutes to calm down, he hoisted himself up and sat on the side of his bed. His sheets were wet with sweat again. Heaving out a deep breath, Danny reached over and rolled the compression stocking over his leg. Smoothing it in place, he reached for his prosthetic leg and pulled it on, fitting it just right. He pushed himself up and turned to grab the sheets off his bed. Taking his dirty laundry and sheets downstairs, he threw them in the washer, added soap and turned the dial beginning the wash cycle.

He poured himself a cup of coffee and walked outside to sit in one of the rocking chairs on his front porch and watch the sunrise. The light peeking over the horizon rained sparkles in the dew across his front lawn. His mind wandered to the first time he saw Tammy and Molly walking up to his house. A smile spread across his face. *She's a little beauty. She makes my heart flutter and feel.* It'd been so long since he felt anything but pain and frustration. She made him feel...hopeful.

Yesterday, his counselor told him that he needed to reach out more. Talk to her, talk to others. Be more social. He'd holed himself up outside of having hundreds of people converge on his property to help him out. He was so damn grateful, but, he didn't venture out himself much. He needed to pull himself together and be the man Tammy said she saw. He wanted to be that man...for her.

* * *

Tammy stood from her desk as her boss, Sally, walked into the office. "I have the trip planned for next month's honor flight. I'm working with Old Glory this time and it's all come together nicely. I'm finished for today. I'll see you tomorrow unless you need anything before I go."

"No, go on home, Tammy, and try to get some rest. You look so tired this week. Is everything alright?"

Tammy rearranged the paperwork on her desk one more time. She never left work unless her desk was organized. Straightening and smoothing her cream-colored pencil dress, she said, "I'm fine. Thanks. Just a tough week. I'll be fine."

"Well, it's going to get tougher. I just got word that there's a benefactor interested in Stateside. He'll be here tomorrow afternoon. We'll be showing him around, going over some of the financials, and then taking him to dinner. As my successor when I retire, I'll need you there, okay?"

"Okay. Do you need me to make reservations anywhere?"

"No, I've got it covered. He's a wealthy trust-fund baby, so I'm not expecting much. He's probably a privileged, self-serving egomaniac who's used to getting his way, but we need the money to stay open, so we're going to pamper him and laugh at all his stupid jokes." Sally pointedly looked at Tammy.

"Message received. Do you need me to stay tonight?"

"No, go on home, but why don't we start early tomorrow and pull some things together for his visit?"

"Sure. I'll be here at six-thirty."

Sally nodded and continued on to her office. Tammy sighed as she pulled her purse out of the bottom drawer of her desk and threw the strap over her shoulder. Still pulling her coat on as she walked toward the exit door, Tammy heard, "Hey, Tammy. Leaving so soon?"

Tammy turned and smiled as Gerry pushed himself toward her in his wheelchair. "Hi, Gerry, yeah, I'm finished for today. How are you?"

Gerry chuckled. "I'm good, real good. I've noticed you haven't been working on the mural. Are you stuck?"

A faint upturn of her lips was the only visible sign of pleasure in her features. Usually when Tammy saw Gerry, he raised her spirits immeasurably. Today, however, it would be a monumental task to cheer her up. Her heart was heavy.

"Yeah. Stuck. I guess I needed a break from it." Tammy sighed. "You know how we artists are. Moody." A genuine smile formed for the first time in days.

"I'd never say that about you, girl. You're never moody. Now…" Leaning forward so as not to be overheard, he said, "That Gladys in three sixteen, she's a moody one. OooWee, she's moody."

Tammy genuinely laughed. "Don't let her get you down, Gerry. She's having a difficult time. There aren't many women here and she's still new. Getting to know people can be a challenge. Especially when you're dealing with so many other issues. Cut her some slack; you may find she can be a true friend. Maybe just go sit and talk to her." Tammy froze as the last of her words fell from her lips. Straightening her spine, she realized, for the first time in days, that she should take her own advice.

Chuckling, Gerry spun around in his chair. With a quick wave, he said, "Okay, girl. You have a good night. I'll see if I can get the old bat to speak to me."

Tammy watched as Gerry rolled down the hall and turned right, out of sight. Pursing her lips, she nodded once and turned toward the exit door, resolved to lighten the burden on her heavy heart.

CHAPTER 12

WHILE WALKING TO HER CAR, Tammy's phone rang. Digging it out of her purse, she tapped the *connect call* icon and answered. "Hello."

Clearing his throat, Danny said. "Hi. Um, I wondered if we could talk." Rushing before she could tell him off, he said, "I'm sorry. I had no right…I shouldn't have…It's…not…" Huffing out a breath, Danny said. "I'm sorry. I'd like to tell you in person. Will you talk to me?"

Tammy leaned against her car, back to the driver's door, staring down at her nude heels. Her 'pity purchase' from yesterday to try and cheer herself up. It worked for about fifteen minutes. "Yeah. I'll talk to you. I'm just leaving work. Should I run by your house?"

Quickly looking around to see that things were mostly in order, Danny said, "Yeah. That'd be good. I'm making lasagna. Will you eat with me?"

Tammy smiled. "Yeah. Eating's good." Turning and opening her car door, Tammy slid into the driver's seat and inserted the key in the ignition. "I'll be there in about twenty minutes."

"Yeah. Good. Okay, see you then."

Danny tapped his phone screen to end the call. He finished sprinkling the cheese on the lasagna he'd been preparing in hopes Tammy would come over and have dinner with him. Danny had honed his cooking skills since he'd been home. His counselor had encouraged him to try new recipes and play with his cooking. Every time he made something he enjoyed gave him a sense of accomplishment. This was the first time making this recipe, but so far it smelled amazing. His mouth watered as the aroma of garlic-laced marinara sauce wafted up to his nostrils. Sliding the pan into the oven, Danny began cleaning up the dirty dishes.

Drying the last dish, he heard the knock on his door. Neatly folding the towel in his hands, he laid it on the counter and went to open the door. Taking in a deep breath, he opened the door to the most beautiful sight he'd ever seen. Tammy stood in an unbuttoned, long brown leather jacket, showing him a cream pencil dress hugging her body masterfully. The thin brown belt at the waist only accentuated how tiny she was. A breeze lifted her brown curls, making Danny realize he was staring and it was cool outside.

Quickly stepping back, Danny held the door open, "Hi. Come in."

Tammy smiled as she stepped through the door. Seeing him again made her stomach quiver. On the ride over she'd been nervous. What would she say? How would she say it? She held the strap of her purse like it was a lifeline.

"Can I get you something to drink? I have water, tea, wine and a couple types of sodas. What would you like?"

"Supper smells amazing. Since we're having lasagna, I'll have a glass of wine, if you're joining me."

Danny smiled, running his hands down his thighs. "Yeah. I'll join you. Red or white?"

Walking to the cupboard in the kitchen, Danny pulled two wine glasses off a shelf. Turning to look at Tammy, he watched as she pulled her coat off her shoulders. Danny shook his head. "Sorry. I've forgotten my manners." He swiftly walked toward her and helped her remove her coat. "Let me pour our wine and we can sit in the living room and talk for a few minutes."

He hung her coat on the coatrack and went to pull a bottle of wine from the cupboard. "You didn't answer. Red okay?"

A sweet smile spread her kissable lips and Danny was transfixed. "Yeah. Red is good."

Their eyes locked for several moments before Danny nodded once and tore his eyes away from hers. Pulling a bottle of red from the wine rack and keeping his hands busy opening the bottle helped to calm him a bit. He poured their wine and turned to hand Tammy her glass. Their fingers brushed and both felt the shock of contact.

"Thank you," she said, voice quivering, still unsure of what to do and where to start. The tension in the room was tightening the muscles in her neck.

Danny held out his hand in a gesture for her to precede him into the living room. She walked ahead of him, taking in every detail. The far side of the room had the doorway to Danny's new bedroom cut in it, but the door and trim hadn't been put in yet. From what she could see, the painting had been completed, but the room was still bare. No carpeting on the floor, but it'd been swept and was as clean as a construction zone could be. His living room was the same. A few things sitting around from the construction, but they were all neatly placed against the wall. It seemed Danny liked things neat and tidy.

Taking a seat on the end of the sofa, Tammy leaned forward to set her wine glass on the coffee table. Smoothing her dress with her hands she looked up at Danny. He leaned forward and set his glass on the table next to hers. He reached forward and took her hands in his. Looking straight into her eyes, he said, "I'm very sorry. I shouldn't have jumped to conclusions. If you haven't noticed, I'm still dealing with...things." He looked down at his leg. "It's been...difficult."

He smiled at her and she felt her core tighten and her panties dampen. Damn, the man was simply gorgeous. Breathtaking. Mesmerized by the sight before her, all Tammy could do was stare. Danny gently squeezed her hands, waiting for her response.

Her lips quivered into a soft smile. Tammy said, "I'm sure it has." Moistening her lips with her tongue, she continued. "I think it's fair to say I overreacted a little. I'm sorry, too."

Nodding, Danny said, "Great." He continued, "Okay." Releasing a long-held breath, he said. "So, a couple weeks after I came home...like this." Looking at his leg again, "My girlfriend broke up with me. She said we'd just grown apart, but I know differently. I don't think she could handle me like this. Handle being with me...like this. It's shaken my confidence. All of this has."

"I'm sorry you were with a shallow, selfish woman. Believe me, I've been there. Not with a woman, I mean with someone who's shallow and selfish. It can be devastating. It's ..." Huffing out her own breath, Tammy said, "Is it fair to say we both have scars? Some outside, some inside?"

"Definitely fair to say."

Never taking his eyes from hers, Danny's heart pounded in his chest. He could feel his pants tighten as his nervousness ebbed and desire flowed. He stared into her eyes. The deep brown had little flecks of gold which held his attention. He leaned forward an inch, waiting for her to react. He needed to kiss her, he'd thought of it so many times over this past week. When she inched forward he made his move.

Their lips touched and a fire raged through his body, instant, and consuming. The softness of her lips touching his was everything and more than he'd imagined. Releasing her hands, Danny held her head between his hands, his thumbs gently rubbing her cheeks. He deepened the kiss, allowing his tongue to explore her mouth, taste her, feel her warmth. She sighed and he breathed it in like she was breathing life into him. His heart hammered in his chest and his breathing quickened. Needing air he pulled away and touched his forehead to hers. He heard her whisper, "Wow."

He smiled. "Yeah."

Tammy placed her hands over his, still holding her head. His skin was warm, the slight roughness of his hands felt fabulous under hers. She rubbed up and down enjoying the texture of his skin against hers. After a few moments Danny pulled away and looked into her eyes. He opened his mouth to say something when the oven timer went off.

His smile grew. "I guess the oven's telling us supper's ready. Are you hungry?"

Unable to speak just yet, Tammy nodded, enjoying the beautiful cocoa of his eyes. He had full, long, absolutely envious lashes. Noticing for the first time the soft lines around his eyes, a smile formed on her lips.

"Tell me what you're smiling at," he said, teasing slightly.

"Your face holds so much character and all of my girlfriends will be positively jealous of your eyelashes."

He shook his head and stood, holding his hand out to her. She grabbed his hand and he led her to the kitchen.

He stopped behind a chair and pulled it out for her. "Sit here and let me pull the lasagna out. Do you need anything else?"

"No. Thank you."

Danny busied himself cutting the lasagna while the bread was in the oven. He used the time to get his emotions and his penis under control. The girl had a way of making his body hard at the sight of her. Interesting.

As they ate, Danny broached the subject that'd started this crazy argument in the first place. "Are you interested in telling me about your job?"

Tammy watched his eyes for signs this could go bad. He looked into her eyes from across the table. When he sensed her hesitation, he smirked. Tammy visibly relaxed.

"I work for the director, Sally, as her assistant. I'm involved in the day-to-day management of the home and Sally is grooming me to replace her when she retires in a couple of months. We're privately owned by a small company out of Texas, FMS. Recently, we've lost some of our funding from the government and we're in the process of finding a benefactor to keep us afloat. There are several residents I enjoy speaking to and I've been painting a mural in the activity room for the past year and a half. That's the fifty-cent version."

"How did that come about, you painting the mural?"

Tammy set her fork down and dabbed her lips with her napkin. A soft smile spread her lips as she remembered. "I've always loved drawing and painting, since I was a little girl. One day, about a year after coming to work at Stateside, I was sitting in the activity room eating my lunch. The wall across the room was blank, dull, unexciting. I always have a tablet with me, so I started drawing pictures of soldiers and scenes. Gerry, one of my favorite residents, rolled over in his wheelchair to see what I was doing. He looked at my drawing and we started discussing it. He pointed out a couple of things from the war he'd been in. He left and at the end of the day he came to the office and showed me some pictures he had from his days in Vietnam. He said I could borrow them, but instead, I made copies of them and spent the next couple of nights drawing out my mural. Word spread through the residents and a couple others stopped by the office here and there with pictures or drawings or ideas. That's how the idea popped into my head of the mural depicting war through the years. It begins with the war of 1812 and travels through Desert Storm, now, but someday, will travel through to Operation Enduring Freedom."

Danny reached across the table and rested his hands over Tammy's. He needed to touch her. Looking into each other's eyes, both felt the stirrings of desire, the previous tension having vanished.

"That's..." his voice cracking, he cleared his throat and tried again. "That's amazing."

She saw the moisture gather in his eyes as he swallowed several times. Turning her hand over so their palms were touching, she curled her fingers around his hand.

"We don't have to talk about this if it's painful." A faint smile formed on her lips.

"No. It's...fine." Wiping his eyes with his other hand caused Tammy to squeeze the one she held.

When he had composed himself a bit more he said, "I'm supposed to talk about it. My counselor said I should. Doesn't make it easy. He also said that. It's just imagining all that war on the wall so soon..." He swallowed. "It's tough."

Tammy nodded slowly; choosing her words carefully, she said softly, "It is. It's brought me to tears more than once as the guys...and ladies, tell me about their experiences. So many have lost friends and family. So many have lost parts of themselves. Physically and emotionally. I debated for a long time on whether it was the right thing to paint on the wall, but Gerry told me it was so much better to honor what they've all done than to pretend it never happened. Many of the others agreed and were excited to share their experiences. Sometimes they'll sit in the room with me while I paint and tell me their stories. Sometimes, I go into the room and see them sitting there staring at the mural, lost in the memories of the days and years they served. It feels good. They tell me it's good for them to see it memorialized. I've painted the faces of some of their lost friends in the mural. To honor them. So they aren't forgotten."

"That's incredible. What you're doing is incredible. What do the veterans there do for counseling?"

"We have counselors come in. But mostly they talk to each other. That seems to help the most, talking to other veterans. You should come and talk to them. They don't have anyone from this current war to talk to and it would help. It would help you too, Danny."

Danny stared into Tammy's eyes. Who was this woman? She hadn't seen the brutality of war, yet she felt it. She had the compassion of a woman who'd lost so much, yet she didn't have the crusty shell one erects to protect herself from the ravages of life. She was warm and beautiful and absolutely was stealing his heart.

The thought jolted him. He quickly pulled his hand away. Busying himself with the dirty dishes he jumped up. "Can I get you anything? More wine?"

Tammy, shocked by the sudden change in atmosphere shook her head quickly, forcing her mind to catch up with the dizzying pace of this evening. "No. I'm fine. Thank you."

She stood and carried her plate to the dishwasher, placing it inside as Danny packaged up the leftover lasagna.

Not sure what to do or what'd just happened, Tammy continued clearing the table. When she finished she looked over at Danny, who'd stopped placing the lasagna in a plastic container and stood staring down at the empty pan before him. His breathing was ragged and his shoulders bunched and stiff.

Nervously, she said, "Well, I'll go then. Thank you for supper. It was delicious."

CHAPTER 13

DANNY LOOKED OVER at her and saw the nervousness in her face. Her posture was rigid and her jaw tight. He stepped towards her and saw her lips quiver. Taking another step, he stood directly in front of her. He wrapped his arms around her and pulled her to him. The feeling of her body pressed tightly to his sent a shiver up his spine. He slid his hand into her hair and reveled in the feel of it between his fingers. Soft and silky yet thick and full. The color of the richest light oak. The curls catching the light and showing off the multi-colored highlights in a kaleidoscope of color. Sexy!

He felt her nipples pucker through her little dress and push against his chest. He claimed her mouth with full force. Her moans rippled through him, creating riotous emotions deep inside. His dick hardened, his breathing shuddered through his body and his knees weakened. He couldn't think of a time in his life when he'd felt like this about a woman before. Scary!

His tongue explored her mouth and dueled with hers. She was giving as good as she was getting. One of his hands skimmed along her back and rested on her ass, pulling her tight to him. When her body created a fabulous pressure against his hard-on he grunted and thrust forward, showing her what she was doing to him. The response was Tammy wrapping her arms around his waist and squeezing him tighter to her. She rotated her hips against him and he tore his lips away from hers. "Fuck…that feels good."

Tammy's lips didn't stop. She rained kisses around his neck and, up the side of his jaw, until she reached his earlobe, which she sucked into her mouth and then nipped with her teeth. She heard him rasp out, "Jesus." She released his earlobe but laid her head on his shoulder, breathing in his scent. Her heart was hammering away in her chest and her nipples were puckered so tight they hurt. The wetness and throbbing between her legs increased when Danny thrust his hips into her another time. Wow.

She felt his cheek rubbing back and forth into her hair and she heard him sniff and then felt him kiss the top of her head. She could feel him shaking, his heartbeat strong and rapid. The heat emanating from him felt cozy and safe.

"Tammy. Do you know what you're getting with me?" He spoke into her hair, his voice lightly shaking.

Tammy pulled away to look up at him. Their eyes locked as she spoke. "I do. I'm getting a fabulous man who's served his country with honor. A man who loves his family and obviously has a community who loves him as well. A man who is strong, incredibly sexy and…" taking a deep breath, she said, "Smells fabulous."

Danny chuckled which made Tammy chuckle in return. "I smell fabulous?"

"Did you hear the incredibly sexy part?"

She felt the rumbling in his chest as he growled out, "Yeah. I heard that, too. You haven't seen me naked."

"Yeah, about that. When do we get to that part?"

"I'd like to get to it right now. You?"

"Yeah. Now's good."

Danny kissed the top of her head again and pulled away. Taking her hand, he led her to the steps leading to the second floor. Pulling her forward to walk up the steps in front of him kept her from seeing his discomfort while climbing the stairs and gave him the added advantage of watching her sweet ass sway as she went before him. Spectacular.

At the top of the steps Tammy turned to face Danny. He smirked and stepped in front of her, taking her hand again and leading her a few steps down the hall and into his bedroom. Entering his most intimate space gave her a thrill. This room, like the others in his home was neat and tidy. His bed was large, king-sized, with a deep oak flat panel headboard. Matching bedside tables framed the bed on each side. The comforter was deep tan suede. It looked warm and inviting. The pictures in his bedroom were a collection of his parents, his brother and sister-in-law and vintage motorcycles. Her shoulders relaxed and she inhaled the deep scent of...Danny. The spicy, fresh unique scent she now associated with him. This room was clearly his.

Danny stood back and watched Tammy's face as she looked his bedroom over. He saw her smile when she spotted the pictures of his family, which made him smile. He'd been nervous coming up here with her, excited, but nervous. Standing here now watching her relax, made his heart squeeze in his chest. He was falling for this woman. She pulled at him like no other. He walked up behind her and wrapped his arms around her. Resting his cheek against the side of her head he whispered, "You look perfect in here."

Tilting her head back so it rested against him she said, "I feel like I belong here. Is that stupid?"

"No. It's...perfect."

Tammy turned in his arms. She pulled the bottom of his t-shirt out of his jeans, eager to touch his skin. Once the shirt was pulled free, she ran her palms under the shirt, against his warm skin, enjoying the ridges of muscle. Her fingers danced across his chest and stomach, not leaving any portion of his abdomen, sides, back, untouched. Excitement taking over, Tammy pulled his shirt up and over his head. With the faint light of the waning day still filtering through the window, she saw the multitude of scars smattering across his chest and stomach. Glancing up into his eyes, she saw his fear. His beautiful eyes warily watched for her reaction. Her lips formed a sweet smile as she whispered kisses on each scar, not missing a single one. He rested his hands on her head and she heard his breath catch in this throat.

Tammy whispered, "Magnificent."

Danny pulled her shoulders so she was standing. He reached down, unbuckled the thin brown belt at her waist and pulled her dress up and over her head. After pulling it off her, he gently laid it across the bench at the foot of the bed. Tammy smiled as she watched him take care of her clothing. He turned back to her, his eyes roaming down her entire body. He slipped his fingers under the straps of her bra and dragged both down her arms, reaching in to lift her heavy breasts from the cups. As each dusty pink nipple peeked out of its hiding place, he huffed out a breath. "Beautiful."

Leaning down, he sucked one puckered nipple into his mouth while gently rolling the other between his thumb and forefinger. Tammy held his head in place as he laved attention on her breasts. He sucked one into his mouth, creating a beautiful pressure that ran straight to her core. She felt the moisture pool between her legs, eliciting a shiver throughout her body.

Danny felt her shiver and mistook it for a chill. He stood immediately and lifted her in his arms, carrying her the few feet to the bed. Pulling down the comforter, he laid her on the cool sheets and quickly covered her with his body. Instinctively, Tammy spread her legs, cradling his body between her thighs. It felt so right. Danny claimed her mouth again while his hands roamed everywhere, exploring every aspect of her beautiful body. He kissed his way down her jaw, across her breasts, down her flat tummy to the little strip of lace covering what he wanted. He looked up into her eyes. With one swift flick of his wrist, he ripped her panties, throwing them over the side of the bed.

The surprise registered on her face. Her voice suddenly raspy, she said, "That's sexy."

Danny immediately captured her clit between his lips and flicked it with his tongue. Closing her eyes, she moaned, grabbing his head and thrusting her hips up into his mouth. His hands slid around between the bed and the cheeks of her ass, gently kneading as he licked and sucked her.

Tammy bucked and writhed and quickly exploded around him. The man was simply intoxicating. Everything about him. He made her feel more like a woman than any man ever had. It was heady.

Danny softened the pressure but continued to lick around the lips of her pussy. He hummed appreciatively a few times as Tammy's heartbeat began to slow. She kneaded his scalp with her fingers and gently pulled his head, urging him to move up her body.

He wiped his mouth on the inside of her thigh and looked up at her. "Damn girl, you came fast. Is it always that way with you?"

"I don't know. I mean…no. It's different with you. I can't explain it."

Danny worked his mouth up her body, kissing, licking and nipping up to her breasts. He paid particular attention to one, then the other. Meanwhile, Tammy reached down and unbuttoned and unzipped his jeans. Reaching in, she palmed his erection. He hissed out a breath at her touch. He laid his forehead on her chest and thrust his hips forward into her hand. She pumped him up and down, enjoying the feel of the satiny skin over the steely hardness. She felt him bob in her hands as she touched certain areas, memorizing the spots for future reference. She pulled her hand away to push at his jeans.

Danny froze. Here it was, that moment. He rolled over and shimmied his jeans down to his knees. He looked over at her waiting for a response. Within seconds he had it. She sat up and tugged at his jeans. Danny closed his eyes and said, "I'll need to help you with this part."

Tammy whispered, "Okay."

"Take my shoes off first sweetheart."

Tammy untied his shoes and pulled the first one off his foot, dropping it to the floor next to the bed. Reaching for the other shoe, she looked up at Danny for approval. When he nodded, she gently pulled the shoe off his prosthetic foot. She dropped the shoe to the floor and looked to Danny for instructions. He leaned up on his elbows and said, "I can just take care of it, hon."

"No. I want to do it." She smiled at him.

Danny's lips formed a straight line across his sexy face. "It's easier if you pull my jeans down to just below my knees."

Tammy crawled up his body, gently pushing him down so he was on his back. She kissed across his chest, flicking his nipples with her tongue. She kissed her way down his abdomen swirling her tongue around his navel several times. She leaned up and ran her hand over his tightly stretched briefs. Hearing him suck in his breath, Tammy added pressure as she lovingly caressed his cock. Tucking her fingers into the waistband of his underwear, she began pulling them down, revealing what she wanted more than anything at this moment. His cock bobbed up as she released it from the tight confines of the cotton. She wrapped her fingers around it and pumped him a few times, watching the moisture pool at the tip. Danny thrust his hips forward as Tammy pumped. Groaning loudly at the feel of her small hands circling his cock, Danny had to fight not to come in her hands. Fuck. She felt fabulous.

Danny watched Tammy. She was staring at his cock, watching her hand slide up and down his length as the precum formed at the tip. Slowly, she leaned down and licked the dew off the head and he thought he would blow his wad right then and there. Watching her little pink tongue slide across the head of his painful dick and feeling the warm wetness soothe the heated tip was almost more than he could take. Then. Fuck. Then she hummed and slid her mouth over his whole cock. Fucking most beautiful site he'd ever seen. She added pressure and sucked, hollowing her cheeks as she rose up. Magnificent.

Danny's breathing was heavy, his body quaking. Tammy leaned up and released his cock. She looked at him and smiled while she pulled his briefs down his legs, stopping at his knees, where his jeans were bunched up.

"Help me out, baby, so we can help you with that raging hard on you have there."

"Slide my jeans off my good leg, darlin'."

Tammy worked his jeans off his leg. Danny sat up. When it looked like she was going to protest, he grabbed a fistful of her hair at the back of her head and slowly pulled her forward to taste her mouth. He claimed her with a ravenous hunger, his tongue bursting into her mouth and tasting her fully. His soft lips devoured her mouth and he heard her whimper and moan. He released her mouth and looked into those perfect brown eyes. She smiled at him.

"I love the way you kiss me, Danny."

He was able to growl out, "Good. I plan on kissing you a lot."

Danny slid his thumbs into each side of his prosthetic leg and released the vacuum, pulling it off his stump along with his jeans and briefs. He let them fall to the floor to rest next to his shoes.

He looked back at Tammy just as she slid her hand across the bottom of his stump and caressed his leg up to his still fully erect cock. At his intake of breath, she smiled as she pushed him back against the mattress.

He looked up at her and swallowed. She reached down and pumped his cock a few times causing Danny to hiss and throw his head back.

His voice husky, he said, "Ride me. Let me watch you."

Gladly. Tammy straddled him, positioned his cock with one hand and slowly slid down his length. His eyes never left hers. She began riding him, up and down. He squeezed her breasts as he pumped up into her. The fire shooting through his balls was about to explode out of his cock with the force of Hades. He grabbed her waist and pumped into her hard. She cried out her orgasm just as his hit. Arching up into her, he pulled her down hard on top of him, sending his release into her.

Danny pulled Tammy down so she was lying on top of him. He anchored his arms around her as both of their hearts beat wildly from the exertion. And the emotion. Holy hell, that was…no words. No words for what that was.

Just as Danny was dozing off Tammy sprang up, "Danny. Oh my God, Danny. We didn't use protection."

Danny's eyes popped open. He saw the panic on her face. He reached over to grab tissues off the bedside table and handed her one, grabbing another for himself. Tammy rolled off to the side and they both cleaned themselves up silently.

Tammy spoke first, "I'm sorry. I wasn't…I didn't know I was coming over here this morning. I didn't plan…I'm sorry."

Surprisingly, Danny wasn't all that concerned. He shook his head, "It isn't your fault sweetheart. Don't worry, it'll be fine."

"How do you know?"

"Well, I'm not psychic or anything, but, it'll be fine."

"Why aren't you panicked?"

Danny's eyebrows drew together. He shook his head. "I don't know. I'm…just…not." Lying back down, he held out his arms to her.

She swallowed and snuggled in, nestling her head on his shoulder as he wrapped his arms around her. She pulled the covers up over them and had to admit, it felt nice. It probably would be okay. But, just in case, she was going to the doctor tomorrow to renew her birth control.

Danny lay with Tammy in his arms. His mind was racing a mile a minute. He should've thought about the condoms. He didn't have any here, a situation he would rectify tomorrow. She felt good in his arms. No, great. She felt great in his arms. They fit perfectly together. He wanted her to sleep here with him, but the nightmares were still so strong. He didn't want to scare the shit out of her. He didn't want her to go either. He had a dilemma here.

CHAPTER 14

DANNY LISTENED to Tammy's soft, even breathing. She'd fallen asleep with her head on his shoulder and her arm around his waist as he cradled her soft, warm body in his arms. Taking a deep breath to draw in the clean fresh scent of her hair, he kissed the top of her head and slowly slid his arm from under her head. He gently moved to the edge of the bed and slowly leaned down to pick up his prosthetic leg. He slipped it over his stump, ensuring the vacuum was in place to hold it on. He stood, softly walked to his dresser and pulled a t-shirt and pair of shorts from the second drawer. He picked up his phone and turned to see Tammy still sleeping, a soft smile on her lips, the moonlight caressing her curves. One of her legs was on top of the covers, revealing her creamy skin, which captured the glow from the light streaming in. Unable to turn away, he captured the moment to replay later. Beautiful.

After making his way downstairs, Danny sat in his recliner, watching out the window as the neighbor's dog sat proudly on the front porch, keeping watch over the street. He leaned his head back and reclined the chair and closed his eyes.

"Danny, what's wrong?" Tammy whispered as she ran her fingers through his hair. "Danny?"

Slowly opening his eyes, Danny smiled when he saw the face of the woman he was quickly becoming addicted to. Sleepily he said, "Hey. What's up?"

He reached up and pulled Tammy into his lap and wrapped his arms around her. When she snuggled in, he kissed the top of her head and sighed. He pulled his head back and looked down at her from the faint light streaming in the window.

"You wearing my t-shirt?"

"Yes. Why are you down here?"

Danny chuckled, "You were snoring."

Tammy softly smacked his arm, "I don't snore. Why are you down here?"

Taking a deep breath, Danny let it out slowly. With a quake in his voice, he said, "I still have nightmares, hon. I didn't want to scare you. They've been bad recently. I wanted you to sleep."

Tammy lifted her head and looked into his perfect brown eyes. "Danny, I'm so sorry. Are you getting help? There are things they can do to help you."

Danny leaned up and softly kissed her lips. "Yeah. I'm seeing my counselor. They were getting a little better until a few days ago." He looked away, staring at nothing. His heart hammering in his chest as he let little pieces of himself out of their hiding places.

Tammy laid her hand on Danny's cheek and pulled his face toward hers so she could look into his eyes. Whispering, she asked, "Because we fought?"

Danny swallowed but held her gaze. Finally he said, "Yeah."

Tammy kissed him, softly at first, but increased the pressure quickly, showing him her emotion. When she ended their kiss, she pulled away just an inch. He could see the silvery tears shimmer in her eyes and her lip quiver. "I'm sorry Danny. We shouldn't have fought. It was stupid."

Danny wiped the tear that made its way down her cheek with his thumb. "It was stupid. But, it's over now."

He kissed the tip of her nose as she burrowed into his body. He wrapped her up in his arms and took a deep breath. Exhaling, he allowed himself to relax and enjoy the feeling of her weight on top of him, her musky scent surrounding him and her soft breathing lulling him to sleep.

* * *

"So? Are you going to tell me about it?" Tammy said as she swirled the straw around in her drink. She smiled at her friend as the smile grew on Molly's face.

"I'm not going into details. But, he's pretty great. I enjoy spending time with him and his family is fantastic."

Tammy nodded. "You tell him about Lancaster yet?"

"No. I can't. Not yet. I just want to make sure we have something before I say anything. I don't want him to think I'm soiled."

"I don't know, Mol; I think you need to say something."

"Right. Have you told Danny about Scott and what he did to you?"

Tammy groaned and rolled her eyes. "Touche'."

Molly smiled as she picked up her sandwich and took a bite. Tammy continued swirling her straw in her iced tea, watching tiny bubbles float to the top and pop. Studying her friend from across the table, Molly watched Tammy's face for signs of distress. She seemed concerned.

Setting her tuna melt on her plate, Molly wiped her hands on her napkin. She reached across the table and grabbed Tammy's hand. "Hey. What's up with you?"

Tammy looked up and held her friend's blue gaze with her own. "He's been through a lot, Mol. I don't want to bring more on him. We just got over that misunderstanding I told you about, which was a stupid fight, but we didn't speak for days afterwards. He said he had nightmares after that. If I tell him about Scott, I'm worried the nightmares will come again. I can't do that to him."

Molly squeezed Tammy's hand. "Keeping this from him could be worse. I would imagine, more than anything right now, he needs honesty and trust. Maybe you need to show him that stupid video and get it out there. Explain how it affected you and move on from there. Before you fall in love and you each get hurt."

"That's just it, Mol. My feelings..." Taking a deep breath and twisting a clump of hair around her finger Tammy softly said, "I like him. I mean, I really...LIKE him. Like sounds stupid. I don't know if I love him, but I more than like him."

Molly nodded. She watched her friend signal the waitress for a box to package up her partially eaten sandwich. Sometimes, life is just too damn hard to figure out.

CHAPTER 15

"OKAY, I HAVE everything you asked for. Did you see him, Sally? Crap, he's...holy hell, he's sexy. He's probably a dick, but he'll be nice to look at over dinner."

Laughing, Sally shook her head. "Let me see." She reached for the printout Tammy handed her. Her eyebrows rose under her gray-blonde bangs and she let out a slow whistle. "Damn. I see what you mean."

"Right?"

Tammy flipped through documents she'd recently printed and stacked them neatly on the edge of Sally's desk. Ordering her pile of documents from most important to least, Tammy looked up and opened her mouth to say something when she saw Sally still staring at the picture of their hopefully, new benefactor.

Smiling, Tammy crossed her arms and said, "Staring at his picture isn't going to get this work done."

Abruptly sitting back in her chair, Sally lowered his picture and looked Tammy in the eyes. "Right." Clearing her throat and sitting forward once again she waved her hand over the pile of papers. "Where do you want to begin?"

Laughing Tammy lifted the first stack of documents. "Zeke Hamilton was born in – get this Hamilton, Massachusetts, in nineteen seventy-seven. He has one younger brother, Isaiah and two sisters, one older, Jacqueline and one younger, Celeste. His family owns the world; lumber mills, paper mills, trucking companies, newspapers, real estate holding companies, tech companies and more. Last accounting the Hamilton family was worth over three billion dollars. Billion with a B. Holy crap. Why the hell would he want to invest in Stateside?"

Sally, still staring at Zeke's picture, softly said, "I don't know."

"It doesn't make sense. We aren't profitable, obviously. We need repairs and the Hamiltons don't have any other nursing type facilities that I could find. Of course, they could be hidden under other umbrellas."

Sally finally set Zeke's picture on the desk and looked over the documents Tammy had placed in front of her. Sally read through a few of them while Tammy sat across from her in one of the two soft brown leather chairs, crossing her legs and swinging her foot while she read. "It looks like this might be something." Sally pushed a document across the desk towards Tammy.

"They purchased the Farnham Real Estate Holdings in two thousand and twelve. Farnham held about forty nursing-type facilities. Nursing homes, assisted living, and senior housing."

"And we still have them."

Tammy swung around as Sally's mouth fell open. And there he was. Zeke Hamilton in the flesh. Six foot three, broad shoulders, dark hair, steel-gray eyes and a Van Dyke graced his upper lip and jaw. Tammy was at a loss for words. He was simply gorgeous. He stood with the arrogance of a man who knew he was handsome and wealthy and the effect he had on women. He bore into Sally's blue eyes but made no further move to introduce himself. Sally swallowed the large lump in her throat and slowly stood to her full five foot five height. Briefly wiping her hand against her thigh she rounded the desk and moved toward him. Her mouth quivering to a smile she held her hand out. "Sally Garrison. I'm the director here."

"I guess you know my name, however, I'll clarify just in case. Zeke Hamilton."

Sally nodded and Zeke turned his gaze to Tammy. Realizing she was staring, Tammy slowly rose from the chair and smoothed down the front of the tan and black dress she was wearing. Her black heels made her three inches taller, but she still had to tilt her head up to meet Zeke's eyes. Pushing her long brown hair over her shoulders she smiled and held out her hand to Zeke. "Tammy Davis. It's nice to meet you, Mr. Hamilton."

He took her hand in a firm shake and as Tammy moved to pull her hand away, he clamped down tighter, holding her hand a bit longer than was comfortable. Tammy's eyebrows creased then smoothed quickly and Zeke released her hand.

"Call me Zeke." Looking over her shoulder at the pile of papers on the desk he smirked. "I see you're studying my family businesses. No need, I'll tell you anything you need to know."

Tammy felt embarrassed and looked over at Sally, who quickly tucked her graying blonde hair around her ears as she motioned toward the door. "Why don't I give you a tour of the building while Tammy cleans up these papers."

Tammy looked at Sally, her forehead creased. She was Sally's successor and should be included in the conversations. Sally didn't look over at Tammy, keeping her eyes securely focused on Zeke. Tipping his head slightly toward Sally, he looked at Tammy. "What's your position here, Tammy?"

Smiling quickly, Tammy folded her hands together in front of her. "I'm Sally's assistant and working to become her successor when she retires in a couple of months."

Sally's quick intake of breath caused Tammy to look at her. "Well not retire per se, but I was intending to travel for a few years." Looking Zeke in the eye her smile quivered.

Tammy frowned and looked at the floor. Sally had never mentioned traveling. Though she was young to retire, she'd saved like a demon after her husband died and said she wanted to retire at fifty years old, which was in January, two months away.

Zeke, noticing the change in the room, gracefully slid both hands in the front pockets of his impeccably tailored suit trousers. Firmly but quietly he said, "Tammy should join us if she's to be the director next year."

Sally briskly walked toward the door with a rushed, "Of course."

Zeke turned to the side and motioned to Tammy to walk before him out the door. Tammy smiled as she walked toward the door, desperately wanting Sally to look at her. This sudden change in mood was downright mind-boggling.

Touring the home Tammy felt like an outsider. Sally spoke only to Zeke and only made eye contact with Zeke. She was actually making an ass out of herself at the way she behaved towards him. Clearly she was thinking like a woman and not like the director of this home. Her interests in Zeke seemed personal in nature. Pathetic.

Stopping outside of the activities room Sally motioned with her hand, "Oh, and this is the activities room, but I think they have a counseling session going on in there, so we don't have to disturb them."

She turned to walk away when Zeke's deep voice stopped her in her tracks. "I'd like to see it if you don't mind." Turning to Tammy he said, "Tammy, why don't you show me the activities room?"

Working to hide the surprise on her face, Tammy nodded once and stepped forward to open the door to step inside. Three veterans were sitting at a table having coffee and talking. They all looked up and waved. "Tammy, look at this." Donald, the oldest of the three said pointing to a picture lying on the table top.

Smiling brightly Tammy walked over to look at the old photograph of a soldier from long ago. "Wow. Who's this, Donald?"

"That's my brother, Dennis. This was taken during the Korean War in 1951. He served with the 352nd Communications Recon, Army Security Agency. My daughter found this picture while going through some boxes in the attic."

Tammy picked up the picture and studied it closely. She smiled as she set the picture on the table and looked at Donald. "I see the resemblance but he isn't as handsome as you are."

Donald laughed and pointed to the two men sitting at his table. "I told you she liked me better than you two old cusses."

"She's just being nice, Don. Don't get all full of yourself," one of the others said.

"Tammy, can you paint him on the wall?" Donald asked pointing to the mural.

Sally's quick intake of breath caught Zeke's attention. He looked over at Sally and then to the wall Donald had pointed to. His brows rose as he studied the mural. Sally quickly said, "Well, if you'll follow me I'd like to show you the nurse's area in the back, we don't need to linger in here."

Tammy's spine grew rigid as she watched Sally try to ignore all she'd painted on that wall. These men sitting here found that wall a comfort. How dare she belittle what it signified to them? Zeke walked toward the wall across the room, studying the painting. He knelt and studied some of the faces of the soldiers painted there. After long moments he stood back and studied further. Sliding his hands in his front pockets he turned and locked his eyes on Tammy. "You painted this?"

Tammy wasn't sure how to answer. Of course she painted it, but Sally clearly didn't want this to be a focus of this tour. When she didn't immediately respond, Donald spoke for her. "Damn right she did. We come in here and sit and help her with it. We've given her pictures and told her our stories so she can paint those scenes."

Donald smiled up at Tammy. "Damn good job she did, too." The others nodded in unison. Tammy cheeks flushed bright red at the praise. She watched the grimace form on Sally's face. Then she noticed Zeke's mouth twitch at the corner slightly. He looked at the mural again, seemingly disturbed and proud at the same time. Hard to describe.

"It's a beautiful mural. You've done a fabulous job with it. What's going on the far side?"

Tammy swallowed while flicking her gaze to Sally then back to Zeke. "I'm going to paint this current war in that section."

Zeke studied her face. It didn't even seem as though he blinked. Feeling nervous Tammy balled her fists at her side which caught Zeke's attention. He watched as she relaxed her fists and then his eyes slowly caressed her body as he dragged them up to her eyes. Tammy could barely breathe. That was a blatant sexual overture if she'd ever seen one. The man simply exuded sex.

CHAPTER 16

"HEY, SEXY, how's your day going with Mr. Moneybags?" Tammy smiled as she heard Danny's voice.

"It's probably the most stressful day I've ever had here. Mr. Hamilton is very intimidating and Sally's behavior is just weird. She's clearly attracted to him, but she's trying to leave me out of every conversation and ignores anything I have to say. She'd be happy if I begged off dinner tonight, but, frankly, I'm afraid to do that. I don't know what she'll say when I'm not there."

"For what it's worth, I would be thrilled if you begged off for dinner tonight. I'd like you to myself."

Smiling, Tammy leaned back into her desk chair. "I'd like that too. Hopefully tomorrow. I don't know how late it'll be tonight. Hopefully not too late, not sure how much more of this tension I can handle."

"Okay, I'll wait until tomorrow, but I'll be thinking of you non-stop until then."

Oh, the man simply made her tummy quiver. Her smile growing larger, she said, "Me, too" while tucking her hair behind her ears. "How did your meeting with Dog go today?"

"Well, you're speaking to the new Parts Manager of Rolling Thunder Motorcycles. Ricky and Bear are still there, but neither of them wants the manager's role, so that's me."

"That's awesome, Danny. Congratulations. I can't wait to celebrate in person with you."

"Me, too. I start tomorrow since I don't have to give notice anywhere. It'll help me pass the time until I can see you again."

"How should we celebrate? Did you want me to cook?"

"Nope. I want to take you out like I promised last week. We never went on our date."

"That's right, dinner and pool." Tammy began twirling her hair around her finger.

Heaving out a heavy breath, Danny said, "I can't wait to see you, Tammy. I'm hard as rock thinking about it."

The rapid flush rushing up her body as his raspy voice crooned into her ear hit Tammy hard. Her nipples puckered and the instant moisture between her legs made her squirm in her seat. Softly she said, "Danny." Nothing else would come out.

That feeling you get when someone's watching you floated over Tammy. She looked up and saw Zeke lounging in the doorway to her office. Straightening quickly, eyes locked on his, Tammy said, "I have to go, Danny. I'll see you tomorrow."

"Yeah," Danny said before the line went dead. Rubbing his hardening penis through his jeans Danny, huffed out a breath as he set his phone on the table next to his recliner. Woman had him all knotted up. And horny, she had him horny as hell.

"Looks like I interrupted some phone sex." Zeke smirked.

"No you didn't. I don't...I've never..." Clearing her throat Tammy swirled her hair around her ear and stood. "I was just talking to my boyfriend."

Tammy fidgeted as Zeke made his thoughts clear, raking his eyes down her body once more and sensually sliding them back up,.

Sally walked out of her office and watched as Zeke mentally fucked Tammy and straightened her spine while clearing her throat. "Would you like to discuss anything further Mr....Zeke?"

Removing himself from the doorjamb he'd been lounging against, Zeke stood and walked the few steps toward Sally. "Yes, as a matter of fact I would. I would like both you and Tammy to go over the financials and show me where the issues are. Then, we'll have dinner at the Washington, where my brother Isaiah will be joining us."

The drive over to the Washington, an upscale restaurant in downtown Green Bay was the first time in hours Tammy had been able to relax. She had to fight the urge to turn her car toward Danny's house. Zeke Hamilton made her nervous and had eye-fucked her all afternoon. Sally was incensed that he didn't pay that same attention to her.

Picking up her phone at a stop light, she swiped her thumb across her phone and located Danny's picture. Smiling wide, she tapped his nose and put her phone on speaker, waiting for him to pick up.

"Hey, beautiful, on your way to dinner or did you change your mind?"

"Ugh, I'd love to change my mind, but I can't. Just wanted to hear your voice before I suffer through a couple more hours of this slow torture. How was your day?"

Chuckling he said, "My day was good. I met with my counselor this afternoon and I want to come to Stateside and speak with the veterans there. Is that still good with you?"

"Oh, Danny, that would be fabulous."

Chuckling into her ear he said, "I'm happy you approve. Who do I line that up with?"

"I can help you with that. You just need to tell me when your schedule will allow it and I'll set it all up." For the first time all day, Tammy's mood lightened.

"Okay. How about I look at my schedule and tomorrow night after I've had my way with you, we can discuss it, 'cause for the life of me, I can't concentrate on anything else but you right now."

Tammy's heart beat rivaled the wild beat of the AC/DC song playing on her radio, fast, hard and pounding. "Stop it. You'll have me walking into a dinner meeting with wet panties and hard nipples."

Listening to him groan through the phone indeed made her panties moist. She pulled into a parking space, throwing her car into park. She started to perspire and the thoughts racing through her mind right now were definitely carnal.

"Geez darlin', what you do to me is sinful. Come over after dinner, I can't wait."

CHAPTER 17

"AH, THERE SHE IS."

Tammy heard this as she walked into the bar area of the Washington. Seeing Sally, Zeke and another man, who looked like Zeke, Tammy walked toward them while letting out a slow, soothing breath.

Zeke stood and motioned for her to join them as the other man, presumably Isaiah, also stood. "Ms. Tammy Davis, meet my brother, Isaiah Hamilton. Isaiah, Tammy Davis."

As Tammy shook Isaiah's hand, she noted the smirk on his lips as his gaze bored into hers. "It's nice to meet you, Mr. Hamilton."

Isaiah laughed. "Isaiah, please."

Tammy nodded and looked at Sally, deciding to throw her a bone and change the atmosphere from earlier, Tammy smiled at her. "As usual, Sally, you look beautiful." She'd changed into a beautiful cocktail dress and was wearing heels. A new look for her. Tammy felt a bit uncomfortable still wearing the same black and tan dress she'd worn all day; there simply was no time to change. She wondered when Sally found the time.

Sally actually preened. "Thank you, Tammy."

Of course, there was no in-kind offering of platitude. Oh well. A waitress appeared and Tammy ordered a glass of Riesling as she removed her jacket.

"Tammy, we were just discussing some of the issues at Stateside with Isaiah. We've heard very little today on your ideas, and as I understand you'll be taking over the directorship from Sally early next year, Isaiah and I are both interested in your thoughts."

Trying to hide her surprise and at the same time, calculate the danger in entering into this conversation, Tammy sipped the wine that was just placed before her. Licking the sweet taste from her lips, she said, "Until recently, we weren't having financial issues. Unfortunately, Stateside is just another casualty of the recent government budget cuts, which seem to happen all too regularly to veteran related initiatives. Once the government is finished with its soldiers and Marines, it seems to be more than willing to wash its hands of the fact that these men and women risked life and limb to protect what the very politicians, who readily cut them out of their budgets, hold so dear. It's a grand idea to support veteran causes while running for office, but, once elected, it seems as though the usefulness of the cause is no longer valid."

Isaiah raised his eyebrows, while Zeke narrowed his eyes. Sally sat stone silent, surprise registering on her face.

"So, you're a true supporter of veterans' rights are you?" Zeke all but growled.

"Yes, I'm a staunch supporter of veterans' rights. Until you spend day after day with the men and women who've fought at great risk, I think it's hard to understand. The bureaucrats who thought nothing of cutting our funding never even came to Stateside to see what we do there. Not a phone interview, not a request for budgets, nothing."

Isaiah started laughing. "Wow, you're a spirited little thing aren't you?"

Zeke sat in stony silence as Sally seemed to fume. Setting her wine glass on the table, Sally jumped into the fray. "You'll have to excuse Tammy's exuberance in this area; her boyfriend is a disabled veteran."

Tammy's narrowed eyes focused on Sally, her lip curled. "He's not a label. He's an amputee, but willing and able to work and is a contributing member of society. While you so quickly want to label him or anyone else as disabled, please remember what he's given up for you and yours."

Sally blanched. Tammy's breathing was rapid, her nails digging into her tightly-curled fist. It was simply too much. A whole day of this crap was more than she could tolerate. If she lost her job, so be it. Sally's sudden change in demeanor because of a wealthy pretty face was a hard enough blow. But no one was going to dis Danny or anyone else she loved and get away with it. Tammy's spine straightened. She stared at the slightly beige color of the wine and the simple shape of the glass it was in.

Isaiah chuckled. "Nothing wrong with being passionate about your job." Taking a drink, he set his glass on the coaster before him and said, "Or those you love."

Tammy's eyes flicked up to Isaiah's and she watched his steely gray eyes as he watched hers. Isaiah's eyes were lighter in color to Zeke's but just as disconcerting. Both men seemed to be trying to look into her soul and find her secrets.

Zeke finally seemed willing to enter into the conversation. "So, the sole issue is the government funding. You're able to continue until either the end of February, which is what, four more months? Or if you find a benefactor or possibly a new owner to take over. Is that how you see it?"

"Yes. We do a phenomenal job with budgeting. We've always been on a tight budget. Many of our nurses volunteer several hours per week to ensure our veterans have adequate care. Our visiting doctors are voluntary in many ways, only getting paid what Medicare or Medicaid will pay them, which is much less than they normally make in private practice. Our cafeteria manager does a remarkable job shopping for bargains and making do with what's available. The major concern moving forward, financially, is that we're now in need of new windows and doors and the roof will need replacing in the next year or so. We can probably find volunteers to help with labor costs, and maybe even some of the supplies could be donated, but it will still be a huge expense and money we don't have. I've looked at moving to a different building to try and manage our expenses better, but that would be a costly undertaking as well. I couldn't see a way to manage the expense of moving and justify it to staying and repairing."

Zeke looked directly into Tammy's eyes, "Why don't you raise the rates on your residents?"

Tammy's sharp intake of breath caused them all to stare at her. "Many are living only on Social Security or Disability. They couldn't afford a raise in rates."

"Then they should find another place to live."

"There aren't other places to live for these folks. Nothing habitable. Those low cost nursing facilities are horrible."

"You aren't running a home to afford a cushy lifestyle just because these men and women served in the armed forces. No owner owes them anything. Good business sense and compassion simply don't mix." Zeke's voice took on the sternness of a father chastising his errant child.

Tammy's hackles were raised. She heard Sally chuckle under her breath and Isaiah sat with a smirk on his face.

"It appears you're an idealist, Ms. Davis," Zeke said with sarcasm dripping from his voice. "Idealists do not make good business partners."

And there it was.

CHAPTER 18

"**THERE'S MORE TO LIFE** than making money. Sometimes, just doing the right thing is much more important."

At Zeke's raised eyebrow, that stupid perfectly groomed insolent arrogant arched eyebrow, Tammy realized she may be making the biggest mistake of her life. She could blow this whole thing.

"Your table is ready. If you'll follow me, please." Saved by the waitress. Tammy slowly stood, smoothed her dress, set her purse strap on her right shoulder and reached forward to grab her drink. As she did Sally leaned in, piercing Tammy with her eyes. "You'd better get your temper under control, girl. We need the money these men can provide. Got it?"

Breathing deep and letting it out slowly, Tammy nodded. The men stood back and allowed Tammy and Sally to precede them into the dining room. As they reached their table Zeke stepped forward and held Tammy's chair for her to sit. "Thank you," Tammy whispered.

Watching Isaiah help Sally with her chair Tammy rotated her stiff neck. She just wanted to get home to Danny. For the second time tonight, she realized how much he meant to her already. Losing herself in her menu offered her a few moments to calm down and redirect her thoughts. They needed this money. Stateside would close without it. But working with Zeke on a daily basis would be awful.

"So, allow me to tell you a bit about our ideas for Stateside," Isaiah offered. "As you're aware, we have several nursing type facilities but nothing like Stateside. However, we aren't in the business of not making money." Watching Tammy's reaction seemed incredibly interesting to Zeke.

"We're mostly interested in Stateside because, as you know, we have nursing facilities under our Farnham Real Estate Holdings, now Hamilton Real Estate Holdings. A variety of assisted living facilities and other nursing type facilities. We aren't in the Green Bay area as of yet and the location appeals to us. With our current holdings, we've been able to negotiate contracts with food vendors, toweling, and bedding vendors as well as medical staff and supplies to make it more affordable to run these types of facilities. The condition of the building is a bit of a concern, but as with all of our other ventures, we can negotiate reasonable costs for windows, roofing, etcetera, and we own construction companies. Sending one of our crews here isn't as costly as you having to hire it out."

Tammy cocked her head to the side while addressing Isaiah. "So, you want into the area and you're looking at a facility that's not making money because?"

Isaiah briefly glanced at Zeke before continuing. "Quite simply, the price is right."

"So you intend to purchase it, not just become a benefactor."

"Yes."

Tammy sat and mulled this over. Something didn't quite seem right. It still didn't make sense. Even with their holdings, they probably could offer cost savings in places she couldn't negotiate, but not enough to make it a fabulous investment.

The remainder of the meal was quiet small talk which Tammy didn't participate in. She smiled when appropriate, nodded when addressed and said very little while the other three chatted amongst themselves. Wondering if she would still have a job in a few months, her mind wandered often.

As their meal ended Tammy stood slowly and said, "Good night and thank you for dinner."

She turned and left the dining room when Zeke caught up to her. "Please allow me to walk you to your car."

"No thank you, that isn't necessary."

"I insist."

Closing her eyes for a moment Tammy straightened her posture and allowed Zeke to help her with her jacket. He rested his hands on her shoulders much longer than appropriate. Tammy quickly pulled away and began walking to the door, Zeke in step with her.

"There's no need in fighting this, Tammy. Take it for what it is. While your ideals are admirable, they aren't realistic in this world. We want you to stay with Stateside for the time it has left and then we'll find something else for you in one of our other companies. We'll make sure you're taken care of, provided your work is good and we can count on you."

"What do you mean by 'the time it has left'?"

Zeke took a deep breath. His eyes never wavered from hers. Looking into his eyes, noticing the steely gray had light flecks of deeper blue, surrounded by dark lashes and dark brows, she also saw coldness. When he spoke, she noticed the tightening of his jaw and realized he was working to maintain some control. Apparently, he was used to getting his way.

"These places come and go, I'm sure you're aware of that. You're smart, succinct, and level-headed. Even you must know that as times change, so must places such as Stateside."

Pushing through the door and allowing the cool night air to clear her head and wake her up, Tammy bit her lip to fight the tears threatening to fall. As they reached her car, she hit the key fob button and unlocked her door. Zeke quickly reached forward to open the driver's door for her. "Goodnight, Tammy. It was nice seeing you. I'll be in the office first thing in the morning."

"Yes. Thanks." Tammy climbed into her car and inserted the key in the ignition. Zeke still stood in her open door, watching her every move. When he made no attempt to step back, she looked up at him. "Is there anything else you need?"

Pressing his lips together for an instant Zeke looked deep into her eyes. "You have no idea do you?" He stepped back. "Have a good night, Tammy. I'll see you in the morning."

Zeke closed her car door. Tammy turned the key in the ignition, and reached across her chest to pull the seatbelt in place. She looked behind her to see that the coast was clear and slowly backed out of her parking spot. As she put her car in drive, she looked up to the left and saw Zeke standing on the sidewalk, hands in his pockets watching her drive away. Tammy could have sworn she saw regret on his face, but then again, it was probably her imagination.

On the drive to Danny's house, she fought the tears that threatened. How could she go to work tomorrow and face Gerry or any of the residents, for that matter, knowing in a few short months, these men and women would be uprooted to God only knew where? Her back and neck were so tight she thought she would break in two with the wrong move. What a shitty day.

Pulling into Danny's driveway felt…great. Just as she put her car in park, the garage door opened. Surprised, she looked up to see Danny walking toward her. Damn, he looked good. The t-shirt stretched tight across his chest accented the ridges beneath. He was wearing gray sweatpants and no one wore them like he did. Barefoot… sexy! She pushed the button to roll her window down. Danny reached in, grabbed the back of her head and pulled her toward him while instantly claiming her mouth. Realizing she was white-knuckling the steering wheel, Tammy reached up with both hands and held his head. Accepting his kiss fully and giving him as much as he was giving was like a salve to her wounds.

Breaking the kiss Danny leaned back and between short breaths said, "Pull your car into the garage, babe."

He stepped back as Tammy pulled ahead, turned the ignition off and removed her seatbelt. Danny had her door open before she could grab her purse from the passenger seat.

As she turned to step out of the vehicle Danny reached down and pulled her up and against him, instantly wrapping his arms around her and holding her close. He grabbed a fistful of her hair and ravaged her mouth once more. "I missed you," he managed to say between kissing her and nuzzling her neck.

Tammy giggled as her body began trembling. "I missed you, too." Holding him tighter she inhaled his scent and her mind began releasing the horrors of the day.

"Hey, you okay? You're shaking."

"I know…I can't…ugh, Danny, it's been a horrid day and just being here with you is so overwhelming and at the same time, comforting."

He looked into her eyes, his brows dipping down in worry. "Babe. Let's get inside and talk."

They walked hand-in-hand into the house. Danny slapped his palm on the garage door button to close it and stepped aside to let Tammy walk into the house ahead of him. She set her keys on the little table next to Danny's and laid her purse next to them. She smiled as she realized what she'd done. She felt him lifting her coat from her shoulders and closed her eyes as she breathed in his scent again. Peaceful.

Danny hung her coat as Tammy walked further into the kitchen. He came up behind her and wrapped her in his arms. "Wine?" he whispered in her ear.

"Yes, please."

He kissed the side of her face and squeezed before walking to the cupboard to retrieve two wine glasses. Pulling a bottle off the wine rack he busied himself uncorking and pouring while Tammy leaned against the counter and watched him. She smiled as she noticed the smoothness of his movements. He was self-assured without being arrogant.

Danny looked up as he handed her a glass of wine and cocked his head to the side. He *clinked* his glass with hers and walked past her, grabbing her hand in his as he went by. Pulling her into the living room, he set his glass on the table next to his recliner and turned to sit. He pulled her down onto his lap and wrapped her in his arms. Tammy took a drink of her wine, set it on the table and snuggled into Danny's warmth. He kissed the top of her head wrapped his arms tighter. "You're safe here with me. I'm happy you're here."

Tammy burst out crying. She turned her face into Danny's neck and let the tears flow. He held her and crooned into her ear. "It'll be okay, babe. I've got you. Don't worry sweetheart."

After long minutes Tammy calmed, Danny's voice soothing her like no one ever could. Wiping the tears and makeup from her eyes, he leaned forward and grabbed a tissue from the table and handed it to her. She noticed his furrowed brow and smoothed it with her fingers.

"Sorry," she whispered.

He shook his head, "No need to be sorry. Can you tell me what happened?"

"Something isn't right with this situation. They kept talking about it not making money and while they can offer assistance in some cost savings, they also insinuate that there's no future for a home that doesn't make money. All day today I've been ignored, treated as if I don't matter and Sally treated me as if I were a pariah."

"I thought you and Sally got along well."

"We do. We did. But she fell in lust with Zeke and he eye-fucked me all day and it set her off."

"What?" Danny's heart was slamming in his chest. The rage building in his body was over-powering. "What exactly do you mean he 'eye-fucked' you all day?"

Tammy swallowed. Realizing her error she sat up, but Danny held her tight. She looked into his eyes, no longer loving and sympathetic, but angry. Her lip quivering she swallowed. "You know. He looked me up and down every time I stood up. When he helped me with my jacket, he put his hands on my shoulders and squeezed. He made it perfectly clear that if I wanted to tumble into bed with him, I would be welcome."

Danny swallowed. Through clenched teeth he said, "Did you?"

Tammy raised her brows. "Did I? Fall into bed with him? How dare you?"

She tried getting up but he held her in place. "I didn't mean did you sleep with him. I meant did you want to."

"God, no. Of course…how can you even ask that shit?" Pushing off his lap she stood. She walked a few steps and turned and walked back. She raised her finger to say something, but words wouldn't come. She pivoted and walked a few steps again. Danny jumped out of the recliner and caught up to her.

"I had to know. I'm sorry. I had to ask."

CHAPTER 19

"WE'RE SO NEW and he's wealthy, I'm not. And, of course... you know." Danny let the rest of his sentence hang in the air.

"Stop it. Stop worrying about the fact you lost a limb. I don't care about that. I don't know how I can make that clear to you. Money isn't the attraction here." Standing with her hands on her hips, Tammy's body was vibrating with emotion.

Danny watched her lip tremble and worried the tears would flow again. Running his hand through his hair and down the back of his neck he let out a breath. "Sorry. I'm sorry for all of it. I'm trying to get over it...all of it. I just think you deserve so much good. I can't shower you with gifts, only kisses. I can't buy Stateside and ensure it'll be there. I would do anything to be able to give you everything."

Tammy looked down at the floor between her shoes. Fuck this day!

Her body was encased in warmth the instant he wrapped his arms around her. He pulled her to him, kissed the top of her head and held her to his chest. She could hear the strong rapid beat of his heart. Slowly she wound her arms around his waist and reveled in the feeling of being pressed against him. She heard his whispered, "I'm sorry, baby," and closed her eyes.

As soon as she knew she could speak without crying, Tammy pulled her head away from his warm firm chest and looked into his beautiful brown eyes. "Danny, all day long all I wanted to do was be here with you. That's the truth of it all. Not because you have money or two legs or for anything you can give me, except this. What I want from you, or rather with you, is this feeling. My heart is soothed when you're holding me. When you kiss me, I feel transported to another world. I think I even hear birds sing." They both chuckled.

"Birds singing?"

"You know what I mean." She patted him on the arm. Danny pulled her into him again and squeezed her tight. He laid his cheek on the top of her head and breathed deeply. Would he ever tire of the way she smelled? It was a fragrance he longed for during the day when she wasn't around. But holding her close and feeling her while breathing in her aroma, was perfect.

Pulling away just a bit, Danny tilted her chin up to him and covered her lips with his. He tasted her fully, he feasted on her lips until he needed to breathe; still he kissed her. He fisted her hair and held her close. He felt Tammy pull his t-shirt up and slide her hands up his torso, kneading his muscles as she moved up his chest. The heat from her touch warmed him everywhere. The thickness in his pants was becoming uncomfortable. He groaned as Tammy started walking them back to the recliner. When the back of his legs hit the chair she gently pushed. He pulled her on top of him and they both laughed. He reclined the chair and began pulling her dress up over her head. She reached behind her to unhook her bra, Danny froze. Watching her strip for him was hot. Slowly lowering the straps she smirked as she saw the look in his eyes. A quick glance at his bulging sweat pants and she knew the effect she had on him. Leaning forward, she palmed his erection through his pants and he huffed out a breath. Tammy rocked back and forth a few times, moaning. She leaned forward and nipped his lips.

"Gonna be kind of tough in this chair, big guy," she growled.

Danny smirked and nipped her bottom lip. "Turn around babe. Show me your ass. Pull them panties off first."

Climbing off the chair, she first bent down and nipped lightly at his cock, forcing a groan from deep in his throat. She stood and turned her back to him. Wiggling her ass side to side as she slid her panties down her thighs, reaching her calves she halted her movements and allowed him the full view. What she felt was a thick finger sliding into her very wet pussy. Danny sat forward as Tammy started to rise.

"Nope, stay just like that. Grab your ankles, darling and hold on, got me?"

"Yes," she whispered.

"Ooo, you like that don't you babe? I can tell 'cuz your little pussy just oozed juices. Damn girl, that's fucking hot." Watching his finger slide in and out of her a few times had him throbbing with need. Listening to the moisture she was creating was even better. He could smell her arousal and that just about sent him over the edge. He pulled his finger out and quickly slid his tongue into her. Holding her thighs with both hands, he pulled her to him and buried his face into her. Lapping and licking and tasting her was outstanding. He heard her moan and couldn't take anymore.

In one swift movement he stood, pulled his sweatpants down his thighs and slid his cock into her. He held her firmly so she wouldn't fall over and began pounding into her. He'd thought of being in her all day. She lifted just a bit and placed her hands on her knees as he slid his hand around and found her clit. She huffed out a breath as he worked her from the front and behind. He feverishly swirled fingers around her clit and she exploded, crying out his name. He gripped her thighs once again and slammed himself into her a few more times before releasing himself with a loud groan. Weak, he pulled her back with him as they both fell into the chair his, arms instantly around her waist, both of them panting.

"Wow."

"Yeah, wow."

Heart beating wildly, breathing ragged but fully sated Tammy felt like she was home.

Danny kept his arms around her as he inhaled her scent and slowly closed his eyes. Soon he heard Tammy's slow even breathing and he allowed himself to drift to sleep.

CHAPTER 20

LOOKING THROUGH her emails and addressing those that needed an immediate response, Tammy tried keeping her thoughts on her work. So many swirled through her head. Danny, Zeke, Stateside, on and on.

"You look perfect sitting in this office." Zeke's smooth voice rolled over her. Fighting the goose bumps that skittered across her skin Tammy looked into his steel-gray eyes. Once again, he was lounging against the frame of her door watching her. She wondered how long he'd been standing there. Minimizing her email she cleared her throat. "Thanks. Good morning."

Zeke pushed off of the frame with his shoulder and strode toward her desk. Pulling out the brown leather chair in front of her desk, he sat and crossed his ankle over his knee, steepled his fingers under his chin and stared into her eyes. Tammy fought the urges to clear her throat again, fidget, and run. Meeting his steady gaze she silently waited for him to speak first. The corner of his mouth hitched up as he nodded once. "I trust you're feeling better this morning."

"Yes, thank you."

"Wonderful. So, I wanted to take the time to speak with you before everyone else gets here. "

Tammy's mouth formed a straight line, but she didn't say anything. Let it come she thought.

Realizing she wasn't going to offer anything, he forged ahead.

"We realize yesterday was quite the shock to you and we're sorry for that. It wasn't our intention to do that. Isaiah and I thought Sally had shared with you our initial conversation with her."

"No. Sally didn't share anything with me. May I ask what that conversation was and when it took place?"

"Several weeks ago Isaiah and I had a telephone conference with Sally and your management company, FMS and the corporate owners."

Several weeks ago. What the heck? Suddenly Tammy felt like she didn't know Sally at all. She simply nodded at that bit of information. Zeke continued.

"Our purchase was discussed. Our Letter of Intent had been submitted and we were actively vetting the business and working through our due diligence. This is the last phase of due diligence, viewing the property and the area. We wanted to see firsthand the potential of this area."

"And what do you think of the potential of this area?"

Zeke studied her for a few moments. He noticed her swallow. "I think the potential is phenomenal."

The slight tick of her cheek was the only thing that moved on Tammy. She was determined to not look nervous around him. She simply couldn't figure him out. Why was he always making passes at her? He could have any woman he wanted; she had no intention of being a notch on his belt.

"I don't understand what you need with me. You've clearly made up your mind. You don't need me here for anything. So, I would appreciate it if for once someone around here would actually tell me what's going on and my part in all of this."

"There we go. I assumed there was some spirit in there."

Huffing out a breath, Tammy shook her head. She was tired of these games.

"Sally will be leaving here in a few weeks and instead of retiring, she'll be coming to Seattle to work in our corporate office. She'll be working with Isaiah in the management of the nursing homes we have."

"And this all had to be secret, even from me?"

"Not at all. It was Sally's decision to keep you out of the loop. We gave her cart blanche to handle all of this in her own way." Pushing himself forward and resting his arms on the edge of her desk, he watched her expression. "I can however, admit that I don't like the way she handled this situation. I'm not sure of her motivations. Is there something going on between you two?"

"No, I thought we got along very well. Until yesterday, I'd never felt Sally had anything against me." Tammy sat back in her chair, pushing her hair over her shoulder. Zeke watched every move she made. His eyes traveled from her face to her waist and back up, very slowly.

"Would you have dinner with me tonight, Tammy?"

Surprise registered on her face until she reined it in. Pursing her mouth and then biting her lip, Tammy shook her head no. "No, thank you."

"Why not? I think you can tell I'm attracted to you. You're a very beautiful woman and I'd like to get to know you a bit better."

"Thank you, but I have a boyfriend and I'm not interested in replacing him."

"Ah, yes, the boyfriend." Standing Zeke walked around the chair he'd been sitting in. "I have a few calls to make, but you should know, I can be very persuasive when I want something."

Holding two fingers to his brow, he saluted her as he walked out the door. Tammy sat motionless for several minutes mulling over their conversation. He is incredibly arrogant and sure of himself. When you look like that and have money falling out of your pockets, it's probably easy.

"What are you daydreaming about?" Sally breezed past Tammy's office and into her own, not even stopping to hear Tammy's answer. Mustering up the courage to see what she was up to, Tammy stood. She looked down at the outfit she'd chosen this morning, gray slacks with a wide black belt, a white cami and bright yellow cardigan. Dressing down to keep Zeke from lusting after her; the man was positively in heat all day long. Danny was as well. Last night was mind-blowing. He took her by surprise, in a good way. She shivered and grew moist just thinking about it. She felt her nipples pebble and fanned her face as she walked around the desk to face the music this morning.

She tapped on the open door of Sally's office and then froze. Sally sported a shorter but very stylish bob, which had been colored the hue of honey. She was wearing a tight fitting light blue dress with a scoop neck and a chunky blue necklace and matching bracelet. Standing over her desk and straightening the paperwork that'd been left strewn around, Sally looked up and smiled brightly at Tammy. Not expecting that, Tammy snapped out of her surprised muteness and decided the best tactic was to complement Sally. Clearly, she was intent on snaring Zeke while he was here.

"Wow, your hair's beautiful. That color looks perfect with your skin tone, Sally."

Beaming Sally stood and touched the back of her hair. "Thank you, I absolutely love it. I don't know why I waited so long."

"I'm curious why you didn't tell me what was going on here. I thought we got along great and that you trusted me. I don't understand."

Tammy's intent hadn't been to blurt that out, but, there it was.

Sally stopped fussing with the papers and faced Tammy. "I don't know really. I've always admired your work and you've been dependable and reliable more than I ever dreamed. You've taken on the tasks of running this home with such love and fervor that I couldn't see anyone else running this home. But, then the video came out, and my confidence in you was shaken. I just couldn't comprehend that someone as smart as you seemed would put herself in that situation. Then FMS started talking about selling because the funding was falling through. So, I decided to play it out and see how things went."

Sliding her hands into the pockets of her slacks, Tammy's brown eyes, which now shined with the tears that threatened, clashed with Sally's blue eyes. "I didn't know he was videoing me and I never would've allowed it. I'm the victim here. I can't believe you'd throw that in my face and hold it against me. You know how hard it's been this past year getting over that. Trying to get the damned thing removed from the Internet is a non-stop endeavor."

"Yes, I'm aware it's been difficult for you. That's the other reason I didn't say anything. You were dealing with enough as it is. I didn't want to add more to it."

Sally almost looked sorry for Tammy, almost. Then she straightened and preened and Tammy knew Zeke was standing behind her.

"What did you have on your plate that was so heavy?"

Tammy froze. Her heart beat wildly. Thank God she wore slacks this morning to hide her shaking legs. Clenching her hands into fists in her pockets, Tammy held her breath waiting to see what Sally would say. She watched Sally's face as she smiled brightly at Zeke.

Glancing briefly at Tammy before speaking, Sally tucked her hair behind her ear and louder than she needed she said, "Last year

Tammy had a bad breakup with a boyfriend. But she got over it. Look at her, she has a new boyfriend now and life is grand."

Tammy slowly exhaled and immediately felt light-headed. Waiting for Zeke to respond she stared at the painting of the ocean behind Sally as Sally watched Zeke move into the room and stand beside Tammy. Tammy heard him chuckle and then, clearing his throat he said, "Okay, let's get down to business. Today I want to go over some ways we can make Stateside more profitable."

*   *   *

Are the days getting longer or does it just seem that way? Tammy practically dragged herself to her car. Spending another day watching Sally trip over herself to get Zeke's attention was exhausting and kind of embarrassing. Most of the day Tammy's mind drifted to Danny and last night. Holy hell…amazing. The man positively did it for her. He listened to her, he talked things out with her, after they made love last night she'd drifted to sleep and woke an hour later wrapped in Danny's arms, feeling completely safe and warm. She laid and listened to his soft even breathing. She stared at his handsome face and gave in to the urge to touch him. Her fingers softly fluttered over his handsome features, tracing his lips, his nose and his brow. She leaned forward and placed a soft kiss on his lips and intended to nestle back into him and sleep, but he woke and they sat and talked for two hours. Tammy shared her day, he shared his. When they were exhausted, they went upstairs to bed, for the last time. Today, the Rolling Thunder guys were all coming over to move Danny's bedroom downstairs. Tammy couldn't wait to see it all finished. She'd tried leaving at lunch, but ended up having to stay and have lunch with Zeke and Simpering Sally.

*   *   *

"It's perfect, just perfect. Thank you for all you both have done for Danny." Janice Schaefer hugged first Joci Sheppard, then Jeremiah. Standing in the living room, after spending the day getting his bedroom furniture set up, clothes and the bathroom supplies moved down, the rest of the men who helped had gone back to Rolling Thunder. Joci, Jeremiah, and Janice Schaefer were the only ones from the hoard of men and women who'd converged on Danny's house to help get him situated.

"We're happy to help him," Joci said as she touched Danny's arm. Smiling brightly, Joci continued, "Jeremiah's thrilled to have you working with him at the shop. I hope you like it there, Danny."

"I love it. I know it's only been a couple of days, but everyone's been great to work with. I appreciate the opportunity."

Jeremiah wrapped his arm around Joci's waist and said, "Great, we've been expanding faster than my mind can get around and it helps having good people I can depend on. Your knowledge of bikes and the mechanics certainly is a boon to us. Welcome aboard."

Hearing the door from the garage open, Danny turned his head in time to see Tammy round the corner into the living room. "Hi. Come on in and see what we've accomplished today." Walking the few steps to greet her, Danny wrapped his arms around Tammy and hugged her close. He lightly kissed her lips, smiled and winked. Pulling her to the group he said, "Mom, you remember Tammy don't you?"

"Of course. It's a pleasure to see you again, dear. I think you'll like how everything turned out."

"It's nice seeing you again as well. Hi, Joci. Jeremiah."

Joci leaned forward and hugged Tammy. Stepping back she said, "You look tired, sweetheart. Long day?"

Tammy smiled. "Yeah. We're being bought out by a new company and it's been long days getting through this preliminary stuff. It'll get better."

"That's brutal. I'm sure it'll turn around in no time. We'll leave you all to it then. I'm about to fall asleep standing up." Joci chuckled and Jeremiah squeezed her again.

Danny's eyebrows pushed together. "Thanks again. Sorry Joci, I keep forgetting about your accident. You shouldn't have been working so hard, especially being pregnant."

Joci waved off the worry. "I'm fine and honestly, Jeremiah doesn't let me overdo it. It's just been a long day today. I'm starting to have to get up and pee at night, so, sleep isn't that great lately. Only about three months left now." She patted her baby bump as Jeremiah smiled down at her.

Jeremiah waved and pulled Joci toward the door. "See you tomorrow, Danny. Bye ladies."

Tammy waved then looked up at Danny. "Show me."

He smirked; he'd show her alright, later. In the meantime, he took her hand in his and walked her toward the bedroom door.

Her eyes grew large as she took in the beautiful chocolate-colored walls and light tan carpeting. The cream-colored trim and crown molding set off the dark color perfectly. The dark wood bedroom set showcased the beautiful brown suede comforter. It was rich and dark and cozy.

"Oh, Danny, it's absolutely beautiful." She slowly walked into the room. She twirled around, looking at everything. They'd hung the pictures from upstairs down here. The orange glow from the setting sun shone through the windows, creating a mellow glow in the room.

"It's better than I could've imagined. You've got to come and see the bathroom." Taking her hand he pulled her toward the bathroom and flicked on the light. The large jetted tub sat along the far wall, candles placed on either end of the decking around the top. The glass shower allowed the elegant tiles in tans and browns to show. The rainfall shower-head and multiple water jets gleamed. The double sinks sitting in front of individual oval mirrors set the room off perfectly.

"Wow. I'm simply speechless. It's the most elegant bathroom I've ever seen." Looking around in awe Tammy caught Danny watching her in the mirror. She smiled and turned to face him. "You deserve this and so much more. I'm so happy for you, Danny." She flung her arms around his neck and kissed him. He kissed her right back.

When they needed air, he chuckled in her ear. "My mom is still here or we'd be climbing in that tub and relaxing together. But, we will later."

Remembering Janice in the other room Tammy tried pulling away, but Danny held her firm. "Don't pull away from me. She wants me happy. You make me happy."

"I just don't want to be rude or look like a slut."

"You don't look like a slut." Kissing her again, he whispered in her ear, "Though I'd like you to be slutty in a little while."

Tammy's face burned bright from the flush of emotion that raced through her body. She'd be slutty all right. He turned them and took her hand to lead her out to the living room. Janice was in the kitchen wiping down the counter. When they entered the room she smiled at Tammy.

"What did you think?"

"It's fabulous. They did a knock-out job on the rooms, the decorating, everything."

Janice nodded. "They sure did. I told Danny he should get Molly over here now to take some after pictures for him."

"That's a great idea. We could invite her and Ryder over for dinner. Would you like that?" Tammy looked up at Danny.

His face splitting into a big grin, "I'd love that. I'll let you set it up."

Tammy nodded and clapped her hands. "I can't wait."

CHAPTER 21

"**BECAUSE I WANT** to meet him, Tammy. I'm your mother, I want to know who has you giddy one minute and pensive the next."

Tammy watched her mom as she continued making the fruit salad for supper. Denise Davis was a beautiful woman. Her short brown hair glowed with tiny streaks of caramel-colored highlights that wisped around her face. Green eyes concentrated on the task at hand, her brows slightly pinched with concern. Tammy leaned over the sink and rinsed her hands, watching the water, tinted pink from the strawberries she'd been cutting, swirl down the drain.

"I'll see if he's up to it. This is all fairly new, you know. It's kind of early to meet the family. I don't want him thinking I'm pushing him down the aisle or anything. Besides, he doesn't make me pensive, this situation at work makes me contemplative. It's been a tough week."

"Oh for crying out loud, I'm not asking him to come over here and get fitted for a tux. We would just like to meet him. Have you met his family?"

"Well, yeah, but it's a little different."

"How is it different?"

"It isn't like I went to their house and had a meal or anything. They were at the build and it was a brief meeting. Then I saw his mom at his place when they moved his bedroom downstairs. That's it."

Denise put both of her hands on her hips as she turned to square off with her daughter. "Do you like him?"

"Of course. Geez, mom."

"Do you love him?"

Tammy folded her arms across her chest. "No. I don't know." Ramming her hands into her hair on either side of her head and holding them at the back of her head, she softly said, "I think I'm falling in love with him."

Denise walked forward and wrapped her arms around her only daughter. She kissed the top of her head and whispered. "It's scary isn't it?"

Tammy nodded slightly as she let out her breath. "Yeah."

Giving her daughter a squeeze Denise stepped back, her hands on Tammy's shoulders and said, "Call him and ask him to come over tonight. And all you can do about work is play your cards and see where they land. If things go bad, dad and I are here for you."

Tammy's brown eyes bored into her mother's green ones. Seeing no end to the argument, Tammy huffed out a breath and pulled her phone out of her pocket. Walking down the hall to her old room, she swiped her finger over the face of her phone and upon seeing Danny's handsome smile she smiled back as if he could see her and tapped his nose to connect the call. She sat on her old bed, leaning her back against the headboard. Staring at the picture on her childhood dresser of her and Molly on graduation day, smiling and hugging each other, Tammy's smile grew.

"Hey. I was hoping I would hear from you soon. What are you doing?"

Tammy giggled. "I'm at my parents' house and apparently won't be allowed to eat if I don't present you to the family this evening. Please tell me you don't have dinner plans or I'll starve."

Danny pushed open his front door and stepped into the living area. He dropped his keys in the bowl on the little wooden table his mom had given him. "Ha, well with an invitation like that, how can I refuse?"

Tammy twirled a lock of hair around her finger. "I don't mean it to sound like I don't want you here myself, I certainly do. I just don't want you to feel weird or like it's too soon to meet my family."

Danny let out a breath as he sat in his recliner. "I'll tell you what. Why don't we stop tip-toeing around each other and let things fall where they fall? We aren't children and I'm thrilled they care enough to want to meet me."

Tammy smiled as she dropped the lock of hair she was worrying around her finger. "Yeah. They care, a lot. My brother can be a pain, so I'll just apologize now and tell you I warned you."

Danny smirked. "Consider me warned. So, did you tell them we're sleeping together?"

The blush raged up Tammy's chest and bloomed into her cheeks. "Oh, my gosh, no." Tammy's voice softened. "Danny, don't you dare say anything."

Danny laughed on the other end of the phone. "I'll bet your cheeks are the perfect shade of pink. They probably match the color of your nipples. And I love that color."

Tammy groaned as the thrill of his voice talking dirty to her zinged through her body and landed between her legs.

Danny heard her groan and said, "Did that make you wet?"

Tammy, finding it difficult to speak croaked out, "Yes."

Danny rubbed his thickening cock, listening to her voice become raspy as she became excited. It was making him horny as hell. It'd been two days since they'd seen each other. Tammy heard his clothes rustling and his breathing become ragged.

She whispered, "Are you touching yourself, Danny?" She softly padded to her door and closed it. Her nipples pebbled and her panties grew moist with her desire. She was making him hard talking to him over the phone. Erotic.

She heard him grunt. "Fuck yeah. I'm hard as a rock listening to your voice and thinking about your nipples all puckered and wet from me sucking on them."

Tammy huffed out a breath. Gawd, this was sexy.

"Touch your nipples, darlin'. Pretend I'm rubbing them between my fingers. Sucking them into my mouth."

Tammy's breath hitched. "Danny." It was all she could say as she reached under her t-shirt and into her bra. She rolled one of her nipples between her fingers and he heard her breath catch.

His voice gravely, he said. "Touch your pussy, baby. I bet it's dripping wet. Tell me. Is it?"

Whispering Tammy said, "Yes."

"Tell me. How wet?"

A sob escaped from her throat. "Danny. I shouldn't do this here."

"Tell me baby. How wet are you?"

Tammy's heart was pounding away, her throat was dry, her body heated as she skimmed her fingers down her tummy and into her jeans. She leaned against the headboard and slid her fingers into her pants and under her panties. Feeling the wetness and the sensitive bud she rolled her fingers over her clit and huffed out a shaky breath.

Hearing her arousal, Danny said, "Fuuuuck. Baby, that sounds good."

Movements jerky, Danny quickly unzipped his jeans and pulled his aching cock out of the tight confines of clothing. He fisted it in his hands and began pumping listening to her heavy breathing.

Tammy whimpered and Danny said, "Make yourself come for me, doll. I want to hear you come."

Tammy's fingers worked feverishly around her clit. Running circular strokes over and around, she felt her climax raging through her body. She huffed into the phone a moan escaping her lips. "Danny. Oh...Danny," she whispered as her body spasmed when her release hit. She choked out a moan, trying to be quiet.

Danny feverishly worked his hand up and down his cock. Listening to Tammy get herself off on the phone with him was sexy. He ground out, "Keep going. Tell me what you feel like now."

Coming around from her daze and hearing Danny's need, she whispered huskily, "My fingers are dripping in my juices. I just came listening to your sexy voice and thinking about that hard cock of yours sliding into me. Are you pumping it, Danny? Is it hard and hot and ready to blow?"

Danny grunted and pumped. His breathing staggered he tightened his grip and exploded with a loud groan. He watched as the milky ropes of cum shot out of the head of his cock and landed on his t-shirt and his hand. They continued to flow out of him with each pump of his hand, each one causing his body to jerk and convulse.

Tammy listened to Danny's moans as she moved her fingers gently around her sensitive clit. The images in her mind of him stroking himself off were sexy as hell. She closed her eyes as she thought about sliding herself over the top of his dick and sliding down on top of him.

A few breaths later she heard Danny huff out a breath. "Damn, babe. That was fucking hot. I've never done that before."

Tammy's voice quivering, she said. "Me either. It was sexy thinking about you touching yourself and sexier listening to you. Damn."

Danny let out a long breath as he laid his head back against the recliner. "Shit, baby. I have no words."

Tammy sighed, "Me either." Taking a deep breath to calm herself, she said, "Can't wait to see you."

His heart calming, Danny husked, "Me too. I have to clean up a bit. I'll be there in about a half hour. That good?"

"Yeah. I'll tell mom you're coming." Tammy giggled at the pun. Growing more serious she said, "Danny..."

"Yeah, babe."

She couldn't say it. Her heart was hammering away; it was getting quite the work out these days. The man simply excited the shit out of her. She closed her eyes, thinking about his lips on hers. She sighed.

"Babe?"

Realizing she'd started to say something, she said, "Can't wait to see you."

"Yeah. Half hour, okay?"

"Half hour." Tammy ended the call. She straightened her clothes and walked into the adjoining bathroom to wash her hands. As she looked at her flushed skin in the mirror a smile spread across her face. No doubt about it, he got her juices flowing. She looked like a woman who'd been thoroughly fucked and all she did was have phone sex. Nice. But nothing like the real thing.

*   *   *

Laying the last plate on the table, Tammy looked up when she heard Danny's truck pull into the driveway. She glanced over at her mom, who was pulling the salad out of the refrigerator.

"He's here. Please don't completely fry him with questions."

Walking into the kitchen from the direction of the master bedroom, Tammy's dad, Steven, bent down and kissed the top of her head.

"Please, at least give us credit for having some manners."

"I didn't say you didn't have manners, I just don't want Danny run through the wringer."

Denise set the salad on the table and turned to Tammy. "We've done this before. We're not idiots."

Tammy's mouth turned down slightly at the corners as she turned to walk towards the front door. As she stepped out of the kitchen, Denise said, "We'll only lightly grill him to make sure he's worthy."

Tammy's steps faltered as she tossed a glance over her shoulder to see her parents standing together, her dad's arm around her mom's shoulders and both of them smirking at her look of frustration. Tammy bit back a terse comment when she heard Danny knock on the door.

Just as she pulled the door open, Tammy's brother Jeff started stamping his feet on the floor, causing her parents' stupid dog, Wiener, to run circles around the sofa, barking his fool head off. Tammy looked over at Jeff, who was sitting in a chair in the living room, grinning at the look on her face. She looked back at her parents who both wore grins on their faces.

Shaking her head, Tammy opened the door. Amid the incessant barking and running and her brother's stamping feet she looked at Danny and shrugged. Her voice slightly louder than it needed to be, she said, "Welcome to my world. May as well get this over with."

Danny hesitated at the look on her face. Tammy shrugged her shoulders and reached forward to grab his hand and pull him into the house. She looked back at her parents and said, "Paybacks are a bitch." Which caused her mom to giggle. Tammy's dad looked over at Jeff and said, "That's enough, Jeff. Behave now."

As Weiner ran past, Jeff leaned down and scooped him up. With Wiener tucked under his arm, Jeff walked over and held out his hand to Danny.

"I'm Jeff and this is Wiener. And, no, it isn't an original name for a wiener dog, but he isn't all that original. What you saw there is about the only trick he can do."

Danny looked slightly down as Jeff was only a couple inches shorter than him. "Nice to meet you. Both." Danny said glancing down at Wiener. "Danny." Taking Jeff's hand in his, Danny offered him a firm handshake.

Tammy's parents came forward. Tammy looked up at Danny and smiled. "These are my parents. Denise and Steven Davis. Mom, Dad, this is Danny Schaefer."

Danny leaned in and shook both of their hands. When he stepped back, he automatically put his arm around Tammy. After their phone conversation, he was so damned excited to see her in person it seemed like time slowed just to punish him. Danny hesitated and then thought, tough shit. He leaned down and kissed her lightly on the lips.

He looked into her eyes and softly said, "Hi."

Tammy's face burned bright red, but not from embarrassment. From the memory of their phone sex not an hour before. She held his gaze as she said, "Hi back."

"Well, you don't have to stand in the doorway. Come on in. Dinner's on the table, so let's go in and eat," Denise said as she and Steven turned to walk into the kitchen. Jeff followed close behind, allowing Tammy and Danny a few moments alone.

Danny kissed the top of her head and breathed in her scent. There, that felt better. "I've missed you," he croaked out.

Tammy snaked her arms around his waist and squeezed. "I missed you to."

"This week has sure been a trial. How's Mr. Moneybags? He still eye-fucking you?"

Tammy's face scrunched a bit. She looked into Danny's eyes, a soft smile forming on her lips. "A little. But I'm only interested in you. And he left town to head back to Seattle today, so I don't have to deal with him for a while."

Danny's heart thundered in his chest. "Good. It's been killing me thinking of him there with you."

Lost in the emotion of his eyes and finding her mouth dry, Tammy nodded. "I know. It's been hard for me, too. But, we're going in tomorrow and you're going to have your first session with the vets. They're so excited to meet you."

"I'm pumped to meet them. Thanks for setting it all up."

Danny squeezed her shoulders once and whispered, "Let's go eat so I can drag you home and properly satisfy you."

Tammy groaned as she fisted his shirt in her hands. "Gawd. Yes."

Entering the kitchen Tammy pulled out her chair as Danny quickly leaned forward and finished pulling it out for her. She smiled up at him and motioned with her hand to the chair next to hers. He winked and sat next to her, allowing his thigh to press against hers.

Having the same need, Tammy wound her leg and foot around Danny's leg. Better.

CHAPTER 22

"SO, DANNY, TELL US about yourself. Of course Tammy has told us about your service to our country and we thank you for it. But tell us where you work. What you like to do in your spare time. You know, all that," Steven said between bites of food.

Danny looked up from his plate. He felt Tammy clench her leg around his for support. He looked down at her and smirked. Turning to look her father in the eye, he said, "I work for Jeremiah Sheppard at Rolling Thunder. I've always been mechanically inclined and it was a natural fit at Rolling Thunder."

"That's impressive. Do you like it?" Denise asked.

"I do. Before I went into the Army, I finished tech school in engineering. In the Army, I was a Bradley engineer. When we were deployed, they put us where we were needed but we didn't bring our Bradleys."

"What about fun stuff? What do you do, besides my sister?" Jeff smirked.

Tammy's mouth dropped open. Gaining her composure quickly she leered at her brother. She opened her mouth to tell him off when her father jumped in.

"Jeff!" Steven chided. "That's enough."

Jeff shrugged and shoveled a large forkful of mashed potatoes into his mouth.

"I bike. I'm working with Dog right now on making some alterations on my bike so I can ride it again. My right leg is my rear brake on the bike. Not much is needed. A larger brake pedal and an adjustment to the position of it. Come spring it'll be ready to go."

"How long have you been riding?"

"Since I was seventeen. I'm twenty-eight now."

* * *

"That wasn't so bad." Danny chuckled as he walked Tammy to her car.

"True. I was expecting it to be much worse. Thank you for answering my parents' questions and dealing with my shithead brother."

Danny laughed and oh the sight of his face when he was happy. His eyes actually sparkled and that smile. Oh. My. God. He had dimples. Dimples! Absolutely mesmerizing. Not being able to tear her eyes away from him, Tammy stood motionless and actually gaped.

"What? That was funny," he said.

Shaking her head to bring herself back to earth, Tammy said, "Well, he's a shithead."

Danny grabbed the lapels of her jacket and pulled her close to him. Staring into the depths of her big brown eyes he dipped his head, never losing eye contact. When they were nose to nose he whispered, "You're stunning when you blush, when you talk and when you sleep."

He lightly kissed her lips and stood to his full height. Tammy smirked at him. "You don't know what I look like when I sleep."

"Of course I do. I've been looking at you for a couple of weeks or so."

Looking back to make sure her parents weren't looking out the window, she tossed her head and said, "We've only slept together a few times. You couldn't see me."

Danny smirked. "Do you mind coming to my place?"

"No. Of course not."

"Okay." He swatted her on the ass and opened the driver's door of her car. "I'll follow you there."

Tammy climbed into her car, a slight frown marring her pretty face. *What the heck did he mean?*

She pulled into his driveway and the double garage door opened up. She looked up into her rearview mirror and saw Danny waving her forward to pull into the garage. Slowly navigating her car off to the right, she put her car in park and gathered her things as Danny drove his truck in next to her. He pulled his keys out of the ignition and stepped out of his truck. He looked over and saw Tammy getting out of her car, her expression serious.

"Hey. You okay?"

Tammy looked into Danny's eyes. "I don't know what you meant by 'looking at me for a couple of weeks.'"

Danny took her hand and pulled her toward the door. Walking into the back entryway, he set his keys on the counter in the kitchen and pulled his jacket off. He hung it on a hook next to the door and turned to take Tammy's jacket.

He leaned forward and kissed her lips softly. He pulled his phone out, swiped his thumb a few times over his phone and smiled when something came up. He turned the phone around and showed her the picture he'd taken of her while she was sleeping.

Tammy looked at the picture and swallowed. Before she knew what she thought of the picture, tears rolled down her cheeks. Danny's brows pinched together as he watched the tears stream down her face. She turned to leave but he caught her arm.

"Hey, what's wrong with this picture? I think you look sexy as can be. Every time I look at it I'm amazed you wanted to be with me. Can't get over it, you're fucking beautiful."

Tammy swiped the tears off her cheeks and huffed out a long breath. Lifting one corner of her mouth she looked at Danny just as another tear snaked its way down her cheek.

"I guess we need to talk," she whispered. "Do you have a computer?"

Pinching his brows together, Danny replied, "Sure."

Tammy opened her mouth to say something, but nothing came out. She cleared her throat just as Danny's phone rang.

He huffed out a breath as he looked deep into her eyes. "Hold that thought."

Pulling his phone out of his pocket he tapped the screen to answer the call. "Hey Paul, what's up?"

CHAPTER 23

DANNY HELD TAMMY'S HAND as they walked into the hospital, neither saying a word. It'd been a very emotional day, he was feeling exhausted and wrung out, now this.

"The elevators are over there," Tammy stated softly, pointing to their right. Danny squeezed her hand and turned in the direction she'd pointed. They reached the elevators at the same time as another couple. Danny leaned forward and pushed the up button, looked at the couple and nodded. The doors slid open and three little kids came bursting out, one little boy around six-years-old crashed into Danny's legs. He felt the prosthetic under Danny's jeans and looked up at Danny with fear in his eyes. Danny smiled at him as he leaned down and grabbed the boy's shoulders to keep him from falling.

"What's wrong with your leg?" the little boy asked.

"Jason. That's not nice to say. I'm telling dad." Turning her head, Jason's sister yelled into the elevator, "Dad."

"Sarah, don't yell, we're right here." Presumably Sarah's mom said.

"Jason asked this guy what's wrong with him. That's not nice. You said we had to be nice to get ice cream."

A harried woman with short blonde hair stepped out of the elevator, pushing a stroller. Seemingly her husband behind her, looking worn out and ready for bed followed carrying a large diaper bag, which was too small for all of the items to fit inside. Coats and sweaters were spilling out of the top. The man was fishing in his pocket and relief washed over his face as he pulled out his keys.

Danny smiled at the man and the woman and nodded. He looked down at the little boy and said, "I lost my leg in Afghanistan. So, I have a prosthetic leg."

"Cool. Can I see it?"

Danny smirked and looked up at the little boy's mom and dad. Dad quickly nodded at Danny, giving permission. Danny leaned down and pulled up the leg of his jeans showing the bottom portion of his prosthetic leg. As his prosthesis came into view the little boy exclaimed, "Cool. Do you have super powers? Can you jump real high?"

Danny chuckled. "No, buddy, I don't have superpowers and I can't jump all that high."

Reaching forward the little guy touched the prosthetic with the tips of his fingers. He looked back at his dad and said, "Dad, look. I want one of these. Only, I want superpowers in mine."

His Dad looked at Danny. "Sorry. Clearly he doesn't understand."

Danny dropped his pants leg and stood to his full height. "No worries."

Mom began ushering the kids away. "Okay. Let's go kids. Grab your jackets."

Jason's dad leaned forward and extended his hand. "Thank you for your service. It's much appreciated."

Danny shook his hand and swallowed the lump in his throat. It choked him up every time someone thanked him.

Danny took Tammy's hand in his and pulled her into the elevator when the coast was clear, the other couple stepping in just behind them. Tammy looked up at Danny, a soft smile forming on her lips as she watched the emotions play across his face. Humble. He was humble. Sexy, too. She watched him swallow a few times all the while back rigid, eyes forward, looking at nothing. She squeezed his hand, which prompted him to look down at her. When their eyes met her smile grew. He winked at her and looked ahead as the doors opened.

Stepping out of the elevator, Danny saw the sign that directed them to the rooms; higher numbers to the left, lower numbers to the right. Danny pointed to the sign showing Tammy which direction they needed to turn. Walking down the corridor his spine tingled. Those hospital smells brought back all the days and nights he laid in one, pain gripping his whole body and the horror of what'd happened to him pounded his brain. Days turned into weeks and weeks into months. Three months, three weeks and two days to be exact.

"Here it is. Do you want me to wait out here?" Tammy said as she searched his face with her eyes. He'd been too quiet and she worried this was simply too much today.

"No," he croaked out. Clearing his throat, he said, "No. I want you with me."

He lifted her hand in his and kissed her knuckles. He smirked at her as her eyes grew large. She watched his eyes as she pulled their hands toward her and kissed his knuckles.

Taking a large breath she said, "Let's do this."

Danny rapped on the door twice and pushed the door slightly open as he said, "Ready for company?"

"Of course."

They walked into the spacious hospital room to see Danny's mom sitting in a glider rocker holding a precious little bundle in her arms, eyes wet with tears. Danny slowly walked over to his mom and kissed her forehead. Then he looked down at the baby in her arms. All he could say was, "Wow."

Danny reached down and gently smoothed the baby's cheek with the back of his forefinger. Janice looked up at him and said, "Isn't he beautiful?"

"He? It's a boy?" Danny smiled. He stood and looked over at Paul who was propped on the edge of Grace's hospital bed. "You had a boy?"

Paul's smile was wide reaching up to his eyes. "Can you believe it? I have a son, Danny."

Danny dropped Tammy's hand and walked over to Paul. They wrapped their arms around each other and hugged tightly. It seemed like minutes, but was actually just a few seconds. Watching them hug pulled at Tammy's heart like nothing else had ever tugged. Suddenly feeling out of place Tammy nervously pulled her bottom lip between her teeth and tucked her hands in the front pockets of her jeans. Grace caught her attention and smiled as she said, "Nice to meet you, I'm Grace," as she extended her hand to Tammy.

Tammy smiled at Grace and walked over to the bedside and shook Grace's hand. "It's nice to meet you, Grace, I'm Tammy. Congratulations."

Danny pulled away from Paul and looked across the bed at Tammy, a broad smile stretched across his face. "Tammy, I'm an uncle. I have a nephew."

Tears pooled in Tammy's eyes at the awe and love in Danny's voice. She smiled at Danny. Looking deep into his eyes she said, "You're going to be a great uncle."

Danny nodded quickly then leaned down to hug Grace. "Congratulations, momma. How are you?"

Grace chuckled and wiped the moisture from her eyes with the tips of her fingers. "I'm good. It's all surreal to be honest."

They all looked over at Janice holding her new grandson. Tammy looked back at Grace and asked, "What's his name?"

Grace looked up at Paul, a soft smile on her lips. Paul's gaze rested on Tammy and then he looked Danny in the eye and said, "Noah. Noah Daniel Schaefer."

Danny's head snapped back, his brown eyes full of so much emotion. He and Paul locked eyes for long moments while Danny gained control of his emotions. He opened his mouth to say something then promptly closed it swallowing the large knot in his throat. He opened it again and the words wouldn't come. Instead he grabbed his brother in a bear hug and squeezed with all his might.

As they pulled away from each other Danny turned and walked over to Janice who was dividing her attention between her sons and her new grandson.

"You want to hold him? I'm warning you, I won't offer to hand him over very often."

Danny smirked, "Yeah, I want to hold him. Figure I better take you up on your offer."

Janice stood and stepped aside as Danny sat in the rocker. She laid Noah in his arms and straightened. She looked over at Tammy and smiled, which Tammy promptly returned.

Danny looked up from his bundle and locked gazes with Tammy. "Come and meet my nephew."

Tammy walked over and knelt in front of Danny and Noah. She reached up and pulled the blanket back from his face and admired the beautiful baby. It wasn't lost on her how perfect Danny looked holding a baby. His babies would be perfect. She was now almost regretful that she wasn't pregnant from their first time and the forgotten condom. Her period had started a couple days later.

She breathed in the smell of fresh clean baby and Danny. Perfect.

CHAPTER 24

WALKING HAND-IN-HAND into Stateside, Tammy led Danny through the front entrance and down the hall to her office. The nurses and aides as well as many of the veterans were out and about and she introduced him to everyone they met. Entering the suite that housed her office, Sally's office and the accounting department, Tammy stopped at her door and reached in to flip on the lights. Stepping in, she looked at Danny and said, "Welcome to my world. My other world."

He stepped into her office and looked around. She had a picture of her and Molly at some Festival, each with a drink in their hand, both smiling beautifully. There were pictures of her family and on a credenza were various pictures of soldiers lined up along with the family pictures.

"Who are these men you have in such a prominent place in your office?"

Tammy smiled as she walked forward. She picked up the first picture, which was an older photograph and lovingly looked down at it for just a moment. She turned the picture around and handed it to Danny.

"Meet my grandfather, Duncan Davis, my father's father. He was a radio technician in the Army. He lived here in this home until he died about nine years ago. I used to come here and visit him as a little girl. He's the reason I wanted to work here so badly. I saw a place that normally older people dread living in and he thrived here. He had friends, they did activities, they played cards but mostly, they had their service to our country, and many times war, in common."

"Nice to meet you, Mr. Davis." Danny looked at the old photograph a bit longer and set it back in its place. Tammy picked up the next picture and smirked as she handed it to Danny.

"Guess who this is."

Danny looked down at the soldier, clearly a Boot Camp photograph, the day the Army has recruits all lined up for hours in their uniforms to snap their "first photo". It was easy to recognize Steven Davis. Though he was much younger in this picture, he looked very much the same.

"Your dad hasn't changed much. Other than the stiff uncomfortable look in this picture, that is."

Tammy giggled as she looked at the next picture.

"This is my grandfather, Jeb Sanders, my mom's father. He served in the Army as well and actually, Grandpa Sanders was Grandpa Duncan's superior in the Army. They served together. That's how my parents met, at a reunion with some of the men they served with and their families. Mom was seventeen and dad eighteen, just before he went into the Army. They connected and then, obviously, stayed in touch while dad was serving. When dad came home, they married."

"Wow. That's amazing."

"Yeah. I love their story. When I was younger and getting ready for bed, I would ask mom to tell me their story to relax me. It always worked."

Turning to face Danny, she looked into his eyes. "Are you ready to go meet the guys?" Inhaling his scent and feeling his hands seek hers between them made her mind go to places not suited for this environment.

"Yeah, I'm ready. I'm a bit nervous, but I'm ready."

"Nothing to be nervous about." Holding his hand in hers, Tammy led Danny to the door and out towards the meeting room. "You just talk to them. They'll probably want to ask you all kinds of questions about this war and what you did and you ask them. You're just talking to them."

Walking into the meeting room, the first thing Danny noticed was the smell of coffee and the chatter. The men were sitting around a couple of big tables, about twenty of them, chatting away and drinking coffee. There was laughter and joking, not the depressed, down-trodden group Danny expected. As the first of the men noticed them a couple of the men smiled brightly at Tammy.

"Hello, Tammy, nice to see you on a Sunday. Come on in and introduce us. As you can see we have a record crowd today."

Tammy's smile spread across her face. "I'd like you all to meet Danny Schaefer. Despite being here to talk to you all, Danny's also my boyfriend." Her cheeks bloomed a pretty pink.

Some chuckles and snorts were heard, but then again, they were in a room full of men. Tammy started making introductions when Gerry spoke up. "Tammy, we can do the introductions if you don't mind. He isn't going to remember us all this way. We like to give our names as we tell a story, it helps to associate the story and the name."

"That's right. Okay, then I'll leave you all to it. Be gentle on him, guys."

She turned and looked into Danny's eyes. He gazed deeply into hers and then lightly kissed her lips. He stood back and smirked at her as he watched the color rise up her cheeks and ears. Leaning in he whispered, "Go on now before you catch fire. I'll come back to your office when we're finished here."

Tammy nodded and, braving the looks of the men in the room, she turned to them and waved once while adding, "Have fun." She promptly turned and walked out.

* * *

"Hey, sexy."

Tammy looked up from her computer screen and into the eyes of the sexiest man in the world to her.

"Hey, how did it go?"

Danny all but bounced into her office and walked around the desk. Leaning his butt on the desktop, he watched as she pushed away and faced him.

"It was fantastic. It's exactly what you thought it would be; we just talked. You have some great men here."

Laughing Tammy said, "We do. We have a few women here as well, but only about fifteen of them. They usually don't sit in the groups with the guys. Are you coming back?"

"Absolutely. Next week and every week if they want me to. They asked all kinds of questions about the Bradley and our current weapons and technology. I'm going to see if I can set up a tour for them at the base here. They'd like to see an MRAP and some other vehicles. I wish I had a Bradley here to show them."

Danny excitedly told her about their visit. Tammy was lost in the look on his face. As he talked about the men, his dark brown eyes glowed with happiness. His full sensual lips took on a softness as they spoke and the smiles were frequent. His hands, so strong and large, gestured with emotion as he told her the things he wanted to do with these men. And she was lost in him. In his excitement.

CHAPTER 25

"SO YOU HAVEN'T told him yet?" Molly asked as she swirled the wine in her glass, watching the slightly amber liquid glide down the inside of her glass.

"No. I started to tell him, then his phone rang and we went to the hospital to meet his new nephew. When we went back to his place that night, we were both exhausted. The following day he was nervous in the morning about going into Stateside the first time and I didn't want to say anything then. I know in my heart he'd never do anything like Scott did. But he took a picture of me while I was sleeping and it creeps me out."

Tammy pushed her hair over her shoulder as she leaned forward to pick up her wine glass from the coffee table. Taking a sip, she snuggled into the corner of her sofa and trained her eyes on Molly.

"We haven't been able to see each other that much lately, I missed you."

Molly's lips formed the prettiest smile, her bright blue eyes crinkling at the corners. "I know, I missed you too. So, I have big news and I'm freaking out."

"Well, don't keep me in the dark any longer. Spill."

"At Gunnar's adoption party we were looking at old pictures he has from his biological dad's wife. One thing led to another and Joci thinks Gunnar and I are brother and sister. Can you believe that shit?"

"What?" Tammy's brows pinched together as she let the words roll around in her head. "How can that be? I don't understand."

Molly tucked her hair behind her ear and relayed the entire story to Tammy as they continued to sip their wine.

"So, tomorrow we're going to see mom and ask if she remembers anything."

"Holy crap, Mol. How do you feel about all of this?"

"Well, it's weird, I'll give you that. But, when I look at Gunnar, I see it. We have the same eyes, the same hair, the same basic features. After looking at a picture of Keith, that's Gunnar's and maybe my dad, we look like him."

Molly looked at a picture on the television stand of the two of them last summer at a concert. "I'm kind of excited, actually. I've never had a brother. You know?"

"Yeah, wow. Will you call me as soon as you know?"

"Of course. I've been busting about not telling you sooner, but things have been hectic and I knew you were dealing with work stuff."

"That should never stop you from talking to me, Molly. We tell each other everything. Right?"

"Right. So tell me how things are going at work. What's with this Zeke character?"

Tammy's lips turned down and her nose wrinkled. "I don't know what's up with him. He and his brother Isaiah are interested in purchasing Stateside but I don't know why. We're not profitable now that we've lost government funding. We have costly repairs that need to be completed on the building. They don't seem to be in it for the satisfaction of helping men and women who have served our country. So, what am I missing?"

Molly sat in thought for a moment, watching Tammy's expression. "I don't know, Tammy. What else could there be?"

"I don't know, but I'm going to find out."

*   *   *

Singing at the top of her lungs Tammy sat at a stop light in traffic. Tapping the steering wheel with her fingers and bobbing her head side-to-side, she allowed the music to wash over her. As the light turned green, traffic inched forward through the intersection. A For Sale sign caught Tammy's attention as she drove passed the building that used to be a boutique clothing store. Craning her neck to see as she moved down the road, another For Sale sign caught her attention at the little coffee shop next to the clothing store. "When did this all happen?" she softly said.

Her mind wandering as she walked into Stateside, Tammy didn't see the tall dark figure watching her from the inner office where the nurses gathered. As she entered her office, switched on the light and padded her way to her desk, she was lost in thought. She pushed the button to start her computer and tucked her purse away in her bottom drawer.

"You look lost in thought."

Whipping her head around. Tammy saw Zeke lounging against the frame of her office door.

"What are you doing here?"

Pushing off with his shoulder, Zeke sauntered into the room with his hands in the front pockets of his impeccably designed dress pants.

"That's hardly the reaction I was hoping for."

Closing her eyes and swiftly shaking her head, Tammy opened her eyes and said, "Sorry. I'm just surprised to see you. I thought you went back to Seattle."

Sitting in the chair in front of her desk, Zeke crossed his right ankle over his left knee as he settled into the leather. "I did go to Seattle and now I'm back."

"For how long?"

"So, you're eager to get rid of me then, are you?"

Taking a deep breath, Tammy sat back into her chair and folded her hands across her stomach. Partly to try and quell the churning and partly to try and match Zeke's look of being totally comfortable.

"I simply thought you had finished your due diligence and would certainly need to pull everything together to make your decision."

Zeke's steely gray eyes captured Tammy's brown one and didn't waiver. He didn't even seem to blink. "I have unfinished business here."

"There you are; you beat me here this morning. Can I get you anything before we begin?" Sally narrowed her eyes at Tammy before training them on the side of Zeke's head.

"If I need anything, I'm certainly capable of getting it myself, Sally."

Sally's voice rose what seemed like an octave as she giggled like a school girl before saying, "Of course you can, I just thought I would offer before I go grab my coffee."

Spinning on her heel, Sally all but stomped out of the office. Zeke's attention never wavered from Tammy.

Leaning forward Zeke tapped twice on the front of Tammy's desk with his forefinger then stood. "I'd like a word with you later. First, I have a couple of things to discuss with Sally."

Without another word, he sauntered out the door and disappeared in the direction of Sally's office.

Tammy sat for a moment staring at the empty doorframe wondering what on earth was up. Glancing at her computer, seeing that it was booted up, she entered her password and immediately upon being granted access, pulled up her internet browser. She typed in 'Melon Real Estate'. Browsing the site she found the two buildings she'd noticed up the block for sale as well as a couple others. It seemed as though the whole neighborhood was for sale. Pulling her cell phone out of her purse, Tammy entered the number of Melon Real Estate into her phone. Closing down her internet browser, Tammy sent Danny an email.

From: Tammy Davis
To: Danny Schaefer
November 09, 2014, 8:13 a.m.
Subject: What do you think?
Hey there, hope you're having a fantastic day, I missed you last night. On my way to work this morning I noticed a couple of the businesses about a block from here were for sale. I looked up Melon Real Estate and found a few more buildings in this general area for sale. What do you think that means? I wonder if that's why Mr. Moneybags and his brother are interested in Stateside? See you later?
Tammy

From: Danny Schaefer
To: Tammy Davis
November 09, 2014, 8:34 a.m.
Subject: What do you think?
I missed you last night as well. Did you and Molly have a nice time? You bet I'll see you tonight. Let's finally have our date, I believe I'm a couple of weeks behind on that. 6:00?
I think you should call Melon Real Estate and see if anyone will talk to you about what's going on. I'll ask Dog if he's heard anything.
Danny

From: Tammy Davis
To: Danny Schaefer
November 09, 2014, 8:57 a.m.
Subject: What do you think?
Okay. Mr. Moneybags is back again today. He's in meeting with Sally right now, but I wasn't invited in, so I'm not sure what that means. Anyway, I don't want him to hear me call them, so I'll do it on my lunch hour.
6:00 is great, should I come to your place?
Tammy

From: Danny Schaefer
To: Tammy Davis
November 09, 2014, 9:05 a.m.
Subject: What do you think?
Yes, come to my place and we'll go out. Gotta go, babe, getting busy here. Later.
Danny

* * *

Tammy answered a few of her emails, checked in with the nursing staff for updates, checked over the weekly reports in her inbox and worked valiantly to keep her mind on her work and not on what Zeke wanted to talk to her about. At ten forty-five her cell phone belted out "Shake It Off," her ring tone for Molly.

"Hey, Mol, so do you have a brother?"

"I do. Gunnar is my brother. My mom thought he was Keith as soon as she saw him. She said she promised she didn't tell Joci she was pregnant and begged him not to leave her. Oh my God, Tammy, I have a real life brother. And the best part of it is, I really like him."

"Congratulations, Molly. I'm so damn happy for you. Are you guys going to go out and celebrate?"

"We haven't discussed that at all. I think we're all a bit overwhelmed at this revelation. We'll see."

Hearing a knock on her door Tammy looked up to see Zeke standing in the doorway.

"I've gotta go, Mol. I'll call you later, okay?"

"Sure. Talk to you later."

Tammy tapped the 'End Call' icon on her phone and set it aside. Looking up at Zeke she noticed he'd made no move to sit. "How can I help you?" she managed without her voice shaking.

"Let's take a walk, shall we?"

Tammy nodded, hit the ctrl-alt-delete on her computer, clicked once with the mouse and slowly stood. Taking in a deep breath, she rounded her desk and walked toward Zeke, keeping her pace even and steady. As she neared him, she noticed once again the clean scent of his aftershave and the impeccable cut of his suit. The deep blue silk jacket he wore set off the steel blue of his eyes. She saw that his jaw was firmly set and his hands, which were usually in his front pockets, were hanging loosely at his sides. As she neared, he held his hand out toward the hallway, beckoning her to walk into the hall ahead of him.

He stepped into stride next to her and they slowly traveled down the hall of Stateside. Her strappy black heels lightly clicked on the shiny smooth floors, her knee-length cream skirt whispered against her thighs. She was suddenly warm and pushed at the long sleeves of her black knit shirt. Zeke remained quiet, which made Tammy's heart begin beating wildly in her chest. Suddenly she wished she'd taken the time to eat something this morning. But, she and Molly had downed a few glasses of wine last night and her head and stomach weren't one hundred percent this morning.

Zeke steered them to the front doors of the building and Tammy had to fight the panic rising in her stomach at the thought that he was walking her out. Was she being fired? She braved a look up at him and saw that he'd been watching for her reaction. With a quirk in that arrogant mouth of his he said, "I want to have a private conversation with you and I've arranged to use the nursing office." He nodded at the door of the office, which was just to the right of the front doors. Tammy's mouth quivered into what she thought might be a smile, but actually looked more like a sneer. Zeke's brows rose in question.

Tammy entered the nursing office to find it empty. She walked across the room and stood near the window that looked out over the dining room. She watched as the cleaning staff wiped down the tables from breakfast, getting ready for lunch. Zeke cleared his throat.

"I wanted to speak with you about your job here. It's apparent you're very passionate about Stateside and that it means a great deal to you. Isaiah and I have told you how we feel about the need to be profitable. One of the things we intend to do immediately, even though Stateside isn't officially ours yet, is to lower the overhead. That's where you come in."

CHAPTER 26

"**MELON REAL ESTATE,** how may I help you?"

"Hi. My name is Tammy and I'd like to talk to someone who can tell me something about the buildings you have for sale on Washington Street."

"Sure. If you can hold, I'll put Sandra on the line for you."

Tammy tapped her turn signal lever to make a right turn while she waited. Navigating the corner, she pulled into the lot in front of the boutique and parked in a spot where she could look at the front of the building. The red brick showed little sign of wear. The building had been there fifty years or so, and the little coffee shop next to it a few years longer. Both were single story buildings, big front windows, perfect for retail type businesses. Traffic on the road in front was busy. What on earth?

"Hello this is Sandra, how can I help you?"

"Hi, Sandra, my name is Tammy and I'm calling about the buildings on Washington Street. All of a sudden, there are a few of them for sale and I wondered if you could tell me what's going on? I checked the tax records today and they're all different owners."

"Well, the recent discussions at the City level of turning this area into a mall have speculators putting their businesses up for sale."

"Mall? I hadn't heard about that. If a developer was coming in to build a mall, the businesses wouldn't need to put their buildings up for sale, the developer would purchase them anyway."

"Correct, however, many of them are hoping to entertain higher offers to bump the price of their buildings so they have negotiation power with the developer."

"Okay. Thank you."

"You're welcome. Is there anything else I can help you with?"

"No. Thanks. Oh wait! Do you know who the developer is?"

"I believe the City of Green Bay is talking to several developers and haven't selected one yet. All developers would have to submit plans and have them approved. The City Council will select the developer based on the plans. From there, the developer will come in and purchase the buildings they need."

"Thank you, Sandra."

Ending her call Tammy looked at the buildings again. Biting her bottom lip, she put her car into gear and headed toward Danny's house and their date.

"Hey there." Pulling her into a big hug, Danny's arms encircled Tammy in a cocoon of warmth and comfort. She breathed in deeply and let his scent consume her entire being. She loved the way he smelled. She loved the way he felt. She loved the way she felt in his arms. Sliding her arms around his waist, she pulled him tight to her chest and willed herself to relax.

"I missed the hell out of you, babe," Danny said into her hair. Holding her tightly, he could feel her body slowly relax in his arms. Dammit, only one night away from her and he felt like it'd been weeks.

"I missed you, too. Damn, you feel good," she said into his chest, her cheek firmly resting over his heart. She could hear and feel the strong steady beat.

Pulling back a bit, he lifted her chin with his fingers and looked into her eyes. "You okay?"

"I am now."

"Okay. So, that sounds like you had a day. So let's go to the restaurant and while we wait for our food, we'll talk. Good?"

"Yeah? Good."

Danny led Tammy to his truck. He opened the passenger door and helped her step up into it. Walking around to the driver's side, he slid in and looked over at Tammy, a slight frown on his face.

"Are you sure, babe? You look worried and tired."

"I am; both. But I don't want either of us to have to cook and we'll talk when we get there, okay?"

Danny nodded, turned the key in the ignition and pushed the garage door button.

After ordering their food, the waitress came with their drinks. As she walked away, Danny reached across the table and held Tammy's hands in his. "Tell me what's up."

"Okay, let's see, where to begin. Oh...I guess you already know that Gunnar and Molly are brother and sister."

"I do. That's all anyone was talking about today. He's so damned excited to have a sister. Isn't that the freakiest thing? To think Joci and Molly were friends only to find out that Molly's mom was Joci's friend first. Weird."

"Yeah, it sure is. So then, work. Zeke talked to me today. He freaked me out because he wanted to have a 'private' conversation with me." Private in air quotes. "He told me that they need to get the overhead down on Stateside. In order to do that, Sally is done as of tomorrow. She'll be moving to Seattle to work in the Hamilton corporate office with Isaiah, overseeing their nursing home properties. Apparently, she'll be making some great money and of course, she's positively embarrassing over her attraction to Zeke."

"Where does that leave you?"

"I'll be taking over Sally's duties, but, they aren't going to replace me. So, that means, at least for the time being, I'll be doing double the work, though some duties can be shifted to others."

"Wow. So, is this congratulations?"

"I don't know Danny. FMS still owns us...Stateside. They had a conference call with us this afternoon and they're going to sit tight and wait to see if the Hamiltons are ready to move forward with the purchase. They must feel confident that it'll go through. After that though, my position is a bit uncertain."

Danny nodded as his mouth formed a straight line across his face. He didn't take his eyes from Tammy's.

"Okay. So, Dog said the City is planning on tearing down some buildings by Stateside and building a mall."

"Yeah. I called Melon on my way to your place. That's what they said, too. They don't know who the City will select as the developer, but some of the business owners are speculating that their buildings will be bought out. What do you think the odds are that the Hamiltons are drawing up plans to be the developers?"

Danny nodded. "That's what I was thinking."

Tammy sat back in her seat and tucked her hair behind her ear. She watched Danny's eyes focus on her and she couldn't help but smile. When he smiled back, she leaned forward and once again took his hands.

"I don't want to talk about work anymore. How was your day?"

Danny genuinely smiled again and it was brilliant. "My day was awesome. Dog invited Lex, Coop and Dirks to Green Bay to talk about joining us for the Veteran's Ride next year. I've already called Lex and he's coming. I'll call Coop and Dirks later tonight. I'd like to bring them by Stateside to talk to the guys while they're here, do you think that will be okay?"

"Oh, my gosh, yes. The guys will absolutely love it. Thanks, Danny, it means so much to them." Tears welling in her eyes, she wiped the corners with her fingers. "It means so much to me, too. Thank you."

Danny reached across the table and smoothed her cheek with the back of his forefinger. "Don't cry, babe. This is all good."

Smiling she put her hand over his. "I know. Too much emotion lately. I never would've guessed four weeks ago all that's gone on. It's a bit overwhelming. Tell me about Lex, Coop and Dirks."

Danny regaled her with stories. "Lex was the first guy I met when I went to Boot Camp. I walked into the receiving room and Lex was already there. He looked up at me with a great big smile on his face and said, 'Hello. Name's Charlie.' His southern drawl brought a smile to my face. He's exactly what you'd expect of a southern gentleman. I told him my name was Danny and he held out his hand and said, 'Well, damn, it's nice to meet you, Danny.' From that moment on, we were together all the time. We cheered each other on when we needed to. We helped each other when it got rough. We had each other's backs. We managed to be deployed together, which we were grateful for. When we first got to Afghanistan, we met Coop and Dirks. We've been tight since then."

Tammy watched the emotion play on his face. When he spoke of his friends, his eyes sparkled, his smile was a sight to behold. But, then, the tough times played across his face, too. "They were with me when I lost my leg. I looked up and Lex was yelling at me, but I couldn't hear him because of the ringing in my ears. I saw Coop and

Dirks standing there covered in blood and dirt. They looked so damn scared, but my brain couldn't get around why. After I'd been in the hospital in Germany for a couple of weeks, they let me call them. That's when Lex told me it was the worst thing that'd ever happened to him. He was so damn scared he'd lose me. He said he was yelling at me to get up. To be tough, to make it."

Danny wiped the bit of moisture from the corner of his eyes and swallowed several times to get his emotions under control. Smoothing his hand down his face, he smiled slightly at Tammy and croaked out, "He suffers so badly right now from PTSD. That's why I want him to meet the guys at Stateside."

"Aww, that's so nice of you, Danny, and so sad. I'm sorry he's suffering right now, but I've no doubt that seeing you and spending time with you will help. When he sees how well you're doing, he'll know your body is different, but you're fine, better than fine."

"That right? Better than fine?"

Tammy laughed, "I think you're better than fine. I think you're smokin'."

Danny burst out laughing. Unable to look away, Tammy sat back in her chair as she feasted her eyes.

"You ready to get out of here?"

"Yes. Where are we going?"

"I thought we could go to The Barn. They have pool tables and Ryder said it's a great crowd there. Sound good?"

Tammy nodded and stood up. As they drove to The Barn, she checked her phone and, seeing an alert in her email, her shaking fingers swiped the email open and she gasped at the image on her phone.

Concerned Danny looked over at her, "Everything okay?"

Tammy began shaking uncontrollably. "Can we go home?"

Danny's brows drew together. "Talk to me, babe. I need to know what's going on."

"I need to go home." Tammy laid her phone in her lap and folded both hands over it. She stared straight out of the windshield and began breathing deeply, trying to calm herself. Her stomach began to lurch violently and she worried she wouldn't be able to keep down her amazing supper.

Danny drove carefully but quickly worry marring his brow. He reached up to the buttons on the overhead panel on his truck and pushed the button to open his garage door. Pulling in, he shifted into park and turned off the ignition. He turned his head, worried at the paleness of Tammy's face and how deathly still she was.

"Babe," he whispered, afraid he would startle her. When she didn't move, he slowly reached over and slid his fingers into her hair at her nape and gently massaged the back of her head. Tammy swallowed and closed her eyes.

"We need to talk."

"Okay. Let's go into the house."

Tammy slowly opened the door and stepped out. Danny waited at the front of the truck and slid his arm around her when she reached him. He opened the kitchen door and stepped back to let her walk before him. Setting her purse on the little table by the door, Tammy entered the kitchen and stopped at the counter.

"You're going to need your computer."

Brows furrowed, Danny nodded and walked into his bedroom to grab his laptop. He came back into the kitchen and set it on the table.

Watching Tammy closely, he said, "What do you want me to do, babe?"

Tammy swallowed the emotion in her throat and walked over to the table. "I tried telling you this the day Noah was born. It's why I was concerned when you took that picture of me while I was sleeping the first time we had sex."

Taking a calming breath she slowly explained. "A year ago I dated a jackass who videoed us having sex without my knowledge. He uploaded it to all of his friends and the internet. It's been the most humiliating year of my life. It took months for people to stop staring at me when I went out. His group of friends had shared it over and over and over. I felt like everyone I knew had seen it. My parents hired an attorney and we got an injunction and then a restraining order on Scott. But, once something like that is out there, it's impossible to completely eradicate it. People save it on their computers and you simply never know when it will resurface."

Danny swallowed and clenched his teeth. His heart was hammering away in his chest, his stomach was so tight he thought it would twist him in two. Before his knees gave out, he sat across from her and waited.

Tammy pulled open his laptop and pushed the button to power it up. Danny watched her and then said, "What are you doing?"

"I just got an alert that someone else just viewed and commented on that video. I'm going to pull it up and show you."

"Show me? I don't want to see that fucking video."

Danny's fists clenched on the table top as he watched Tammy's eyes fill with tears.

"You don't?"

"Fuck no. I don't want to watch you having sex with someone else. What the fuck do you think?"

Shaking her head she blinked a few times, her voice quivering she said, "I thought you'd..."

"No," he yelled. When she jumped he took a deep breath and loudly exhaled. He shook his head as he flexed his fingers a few times to relieve the tension.

"No," he said, quieter. "I...can't see that. I can't watch you with someone else. I can't."

CHAPTER 27

OUT OF BREATH, Danny's chest hurt with the overexertion of running. Breathing was becoming difficult and the dust flying through the air made it damn near impossible to bring any good oxygen into his lungs. Trying to see through the smoke from the burned out buildings, he couldn't see any of his brothers. Where the hell was everyone? Afraid to call out, he lowered himself to a sitting position next to the remains of a wall and willed his lungs to fill with clean air and his heart to calm. As his breathing slowed to normal, he heard his men laughing and cat-calling. He turned his head to the left and listened. "That's fucking hot," he heard Lex say. A few more whistles from Coop and the others. Danny slowly raised himself to his feet and walked around the wall. There they were, all his brothers, no one looking scared or as if they'd been running. They were all standing around a table laughing. As Danny neared the table, the hairs on the back of his neck prickled. His shoulders bunched up, bile forming in his stomach. He peered over Lex's shoulder to see his brothers watching a video of Tammy having sex with some fucker. Her beautiful face twisted in ecstasy, her naked body bared for all to see. Lex yelled, "Fuck her hard man," as his brothers all laughed.

Danny flew bolt upright in bed, his heart slamming in his chest, his body coated in sweat. His breathing coming in short raspy spurts. Looking around he slowly realized he was in his bedroom at home. He wiped his eyes with is shaky fingers as he felt the first soft touch of a hand brush across his back.

He jerked his head to the left and saw Tammy. Her sleepy eyes were clouded with worry, her hair was tousled from sleep and her breathing was rapid.

"Nightmare," Danny croaked. How was he going to overcome this? They hadn't had the time to work through this revelation, so much had happened recently. They'd been hit with one thing after the next.

Tammy scooted behind Danny and smoothed her hands up his back, then down. Adding pressure, she started massaging the bunching muscles into submission. His neck muscles were tightened cords and she could feel the pulsing as she gently pushed the pad of her thumb into them until they relaxed. Danny moaned and she smiled softly. Tammy scooted to the side and said, "Lie on your stomach and let me massage your back."

Silently, Danny did as he was told. Tammy crawled over him and sat on his legs, just behind his mighty fine ass. Unable to resist, she ran her hands over the taught muscles, rubbing circles with her thumbs and easing the tension as her hands floated up his back to his neck. As she felt him relax, she lay on top of his back and kissed his neck, his ear, and finally his cheek.

He reached his arm back, cupped her head with his hand and pulled her forward to kiss her lips. He rolled under her until he was on his back and she was on top of him. He drove his fingers into her hair and fisted it, bringing her mouth to his, hard and possessive.

His heart began pounding again, only different this time. His cock swelled between them and Tammy moaned. He reached his hand down between her legs and felt the moisture and heat. Her scent circling them in a cocoon, he was overcome.

Twisting quickly, bringing Tammy to the mattress in one swift move, Danny reared above her and plunged in without a thought. Tammy responded by wrapping her legs around his waist, allowing him to slide in further. Groaning, Danny began a sweet assault on her body. Pounding into her fast and furious, they moved in unison, each grunting and groaning. Tammy cried out her orgasm just seconds before Danny huffed out his. He jerked and spasmed a few times until he'd spilled himself completely into her. Spent, he laid his head next to hers while their hearts pounded in unison.

Boneless. That's the only way to describe it. As their breathing slowed Danny pulled out of Tammy and rolled over. He stared at the ceiling as Tammy snuggled into his side. He wrapped his arm around her, lost in thought.

"Can you tell me what your nightmare was about?" she asked softly.

Danny stared at the ceiling as if it was the most interesting painting he'd ever seen. When he didn't respond, Tammy began smoothing her hand along his chest, gently soothing his warm skin. She could still smell his cologne, him, and their lovemaking. All mingled together, it made her quiver. When he still didn't respond, she lifted herself up on an elbow and looked down at him. Finally his eyes found hers and quietly they took in the sight of the other. "Tell me," she whispered.

Danny looked away and sat up. Twisting to the edge of the bed, he reached over and grabbed his prosthetic leg and stocking. Pulling them on he stood and pulled on the t-shirt and boxers still laying on the bench at the end of the bed.

"Hey. You can talk to me. Did you have a nightmare about when you lost your leg?"

Danny shook his head as he headed for the door. "I'll get coffee going."

"Danny?"

He stopped in the doorway and watched as she scooted to the edge of the bed and stood. Beautiful. Her soft brown hair tumbling in waves down her back. Her slim body and creamy skin perfect. She walked to the end of the bed and pulled her t-shirt and panties on. Turning, she smirked as she saw him watching her. She reached up and tried running her fingers through her hair, making it behave. Still he watched her.

"You're beautiful," he rasped out.

She stilled for just a moment then continued trying to untangle her silky tresses. Pulling it over her shoulder, she wove it into a messy braid, securing it with a band she pulled out of her jeans pocket. She walked to the door where Danny was rooted and softly touched her lips to his before preceding him into the hallway.

Occupying his hands with making coffee helped Danny to pull his thoughts together. Tammy pulled mugs down from the cupboard and pulled creamer from the refrigerator. She looked at the time on her phone and figured she had enough time. Looking across the room at Danny, she sat in a chair, listening to the coffee gurgle through the maker and begin filling the pot. Danny wiping the counter seemed nervous and uncomfortable.

Taking a deep breath, Tammy said, "What would your counselor tell you about your dream?"

"Nightmare."

"Okay, nightmare."

Tossing the dishcloth into the sink he turned and leaned against the counter, crossing his arms across his chest. He held her gaze and finally said, "Talk about it."

Tammy nodded. She patted the table – an invitation to come and sit. Danny nodded once and grabbed the coffee pot, poured them each a cup and returned the pot to its place under the again steady stream of steaming coffee. He took the seat across the table from her and wrapped his big hands around his cup. He locked eyes with her, took a deep breath and said, "I had a nightmare about the video."

Tammy closed her eyes and fought the nausea rising from the pit of her stomach. Figures.

"Hey."

She opened her eyes to look into his. His hand cupped hers on the table top and softly he said, "We didn't have enough time to deal with everything. I'm fine. I'll be fine. I just need time to get my head around it. Okay?"

A lone tear raced down her cheek as she swallowed the bitterness in her mouth. She nodded her head and searched his features for signs of distance or untruth. She saw neither. He gave her hand a quick squeeze and then lifted his cup to his lips and sipped.

"Terrible timing, but I have to get ready for work. We'll talk later, okay?"

Tammy sat up a little straighter and nodded. "Yeah. Later. I need to get home and get ready for work too."

* * *

"Good morning. To what do we owe the pleasure of your company so early this morning?" Molly's smile was bright, she looked happy.

"We? Shit. I'm sorry, I didn't realize Ryder was here. I'll just go."

Tammy gathered a fistful of her jacket in her hands on either side of her and bit her lip.

Molly pulled her into the house and hugged her before Tammy realized what was happening.

"You'll do no such thing. Ryder's getting ready for work and I have the day at home to go through pictures and put some DVDs together, so you'll come in and have some coffee and talk to me."

Molly walked into the kitchen, Tammy following her. Molly grabbed three coffee cups from the cupboard and set them on the counter next to the coffee maker. Tammy watched her from next to the table. Molly looked over at her friend, sensing her unease.

"Tam? Sit and tell me what's up."

As Tammy sat at the table she said, "I had to tell Danny about the video. I got an alert that someone commented on it last night. He didn't want to see it, but while he was in the shower this morning, I looked at the comments. There were three of them. They were gross of course."

Molly's lips formed a straight line. "Tammy, we've discussed this before and I know you've had conversations with your attorney and your parents. You knew the day would come when you fell in love and would have to tell the man you love about the video."

"I don't..."

Molly raised her eyebrows and cocked her head.

Tammy quickly slumped back in her chair like she had been socked in the stomach. She loved him. She loved Danny. Holy crap.

"I told him all about my feelings about the video, just how much my family and our attorneys have gone through to get it removed from the internet. I told him everything and then last night he had a nightmare about it. I did that to him."

"You can't take the responsibility of his nightmares."

"It's my fault. He was doing well, we were doing well. He hasn't had a nightmare in a couple of weeks." She raked her hands through her hair on either side of her head. "Last night he did."

"Go tell him you love him."

"It's bad timing. It'll look like I'm just saying it to make up to him for the video."

"You don't owe him anything because of the video. It wasn't your doing. You don't owe him."

CHAPTER 28

DANNY SAT IN THIS favorite recliner on Saturday morning and watched the bare branches on the trees quiver in the frigid wind howling outside. He looked down at Noah, peacefully sleeping in his arms, and felt almost content. When Grace called him this morning and asked him to watch Noah for a couple of hours, he was scared. He'd never watched a two-week-old baby before. It was one thing holding him while someone else was there to help him; it was something altogether too scary to be here all alone with him.

Noah stretched and cooed as Danny watched, wondering if he was waking up. His sweet little lips puckered and sucked a few times but he stayed blissfully asleep. He heard the garage door opening and a smile creased his face; she was home. Tammy came walking in from the kitchen and peeked into the living room to see Danny in his recliner. He looked up at her and held his forefinger to his lips, signaling for her to be quiet. Tammy raised her brows and slowly walked toward him. When she spotted Noah in his arms her smile rivaled the sun.

And, damn she looked good. Tight jeans and a deep gray button-up shirt with a lighter gray sweater over the top. Casual yet sleek, da-am!

Tammy bent down and kissed Danny's lips, first softly then adding a bit more pressure, he held the back of her head with one hand. As she began to pull away, he held her in place to kiss her a few more times. She smiled softly and whispered, "I missed you."

Danny chuckled, "I missed you to. I'm so damn glad you're home."

"Because you're afraid to watch Noah alone or…" She stopped and looked at him as his words finally sunk into her brain.

Quietly he said, "Move in with me. Live here with me."

"Danny…"

"Hi, sorry I'm late," Grace softly said as she opened the front door and stepped inside. Tammy pulled away and moved over to the sofa as Grace walked in with a smile on her face.

"Hi, Tammy, it's great to see you again."

"You, too. You look fabulous, Grace, wow. I'd never know you just had a baby two weeks ago."

Grace self-consciously smoothed her hands down her abdomen and smiled. "I have a bit of weight to go, but I'm able to hide it fairly well. Thanks, though."

Tammy smiled at her and then glanced over at Danny and noticed him watching her and smiling.

"Was he good for you, Dan?"

"Yeah, not bad, after I pulled him out of the bar, the ladies were going nuts for him. Then, getting him to go to sleep was tough; he kept wanting to watch porn. But, I talked some sense into him and got him to finally drink his bottle and go to sleep," Danny said. chuckling.

Grace walked to the recliner and reached down to pick up her baby. Before releasing him, Danny kissed the top of his head and smiled up at Grace. She smirked at him. "As soon as he can talk, you can't babysit anymore. I'm afraid of what he'll learn," she teased.

Danny laughed out loud, "Only what's necessary. You don't want him to be awkward."

Grace shook her head no, nuzzled her baby and walked into the newly finished master bedroom to place him in his car seat. Tammy and Danny both walked into the bedroom behind her and watched in amazement as Grace laid Noah in his seat and began strapping and buckling.

Danny said, "Where do you think he's going to go? He can't walk yet, holy cow, poor little guy is practically strapped in a straightjacket."

Grace smiled down at Noah and tucked his blanket around him. "Gotta keep him safe. There are terrible drivers out there."

Danny reached over and pulled Tammy into his side and wrapped his arm around her shoulders. He kissed the top of her head as he inhaled her scent. Tammy's arms snaked around his torso and squeezed as they both watched Grace package up Noah. Grace turned around and hugged Danny. "Thank you, Danny. I appreciate you watching him. I hope he wasn't any trouble."

Danny squeezed Grace and said, "He was perfect. We just relaxed in the recliner the whole time."

Grace stepped over and hugged Tammy. "Nice seeing you again, Tammy."

"Nice seeing you, Grace. Truly."

Grace stepped back. "Paul and I would like to have Thanksgiving at our house. Janice will be there, so you won't get to hold Noah probably. She tends to hog him," she said laughing.

Danny looked down at Tammy, "You available, babe?"

Tammy smiled up at him. "Yeah." Looking at Grace, Tammy said, "We'd love to come. What can we bring?"

"Let me talk to Paul and call you later, okay?"

Tammy stood in the house and watched out the window as Danny helped Grace load up Noah and all his paraphernalia. The diaper bag alone seemed four times larger than Noah was. She smiled as she saw Danny walking back into the house. She turned to face him as he stepped through the door. He briskly walked straight to Tammy and wrapped her in a warm, tight, welcoming hug.

"Now, let me welcome you home properly."

He kissed her firmly, delving his tongue into her mouth and claiming her. His hands roamed down her body and rested on her ass, pulling her forward into his quickly thickening erection. She wound her arms around his neck and hung on for dear life.

Breaking the kiss, Danny rested his forehead on hers and said, "Let's talk about this home thing."

Tammy smiled shyly and nodded. Danny grabbed her hand and pulled her into his recliner, sitting on his lap. He pushed back, bringing the foot rest up, and wrapped her in his arms.

"This feels good. Just like this. That first night you stayed here, it felt perfect holding you. I slept so well that night. Peaceful. It was the first time in a long time."

Tammy leaned back to look into his eyes. "Really?"

Danny nodded, his mouth a straight line.

"It does feel good here, like this."

"So, what do you think about moving in with me?"

"It's sudden. Are you sure?"

"It's not sudden. We've been together for a few weeks now and mostly, you're here anyway. Besides, Tammy, it feels right when you're here. It seems like the natural thing to do."

"Is it because of the nightmares?"

"No. Is that what you think? That I was scared because I had a nightmare?"

"No. I didn't say that. I asked about them. I just want to make sure, Danny. We haven't had a lot of time to process all that's happened and while we talked about that damn video, we didn't really talk."

"We didn't? What did we do then?"

"I mean, we didn't share our feelings."

Danny abruptly pushed the footrest down, throwing the recliner upright quickly. Tammy braced herself with her arms. She could sense his irritation at her and worried he was mad. As soon as she had righted herself, she hopped off his lap and stood facing him.

Danny stood too and started walking into the kitchen. He went to the refrigerator and pulled out the iced tea pitcher and carried it to the counter. Pulling a glass out of the cupboard, he looked over his shoulder at Tammy to see if she wanted one. She shook her head no and waited while he poured his tea. She watched him swallowing several times and knew he was trying to calm himself down.

Tammy fidgeted with the bottom of her sweater, rolling it between her fingers and stretching it alternately. She was afraid to move. She didn't mean to make him mad, but it looked like she had. He drank about half of his glass of tea and refilled it. Turning he put the pitcher back into the refrigerator and walked again to his glass. He turned and watched Tammy stretching the crap out of her sweater and softly swore, "Shit."

Walking toward her, he watched as the worry on her face grew, her lips trembled and her eyes were glassy. Danny stopped her hand from stretching the bottom of her sweater any further, and pulled her to the sofa. He sat, pulling her down next to him. Blowing out a long breath, he said, "Okay, tell me what we didn't share."

Tammy swallowed. "You didn't tell me how you felt about the video. I know you're bothered by it, and you've said you've talked to your counselor about it, but if we're going to take this big step and move in with each other...before we can do that, we have to talk to each other. You still need to talk to your counselor, but you need to be able to talk to me too."

Danny searched her eyes for mocking or falsehood, but he didn't see it. He watched the strain on her face, the tightness of her normally plump lips and the wrinkle in the middle of her forehead deepen as she waited for him to respond. Taking a deep breath, he nodded, "Okay."

He rubbed the back of his neck with his hand and then slowly rotated his head to ease some of the tension. Straightening his back, he looked into her eyes.

"I hate it. I hate everything about it. I hate that, while neither of us were virgins when we met, to know that other people know what you look like in that most private time...I hate it."

Danny rubbed his hands down his thighs and watched her bottom lip quiver.

"But, I don't blame you for it, Tammy. I hate that it's out there, that I'm helpless to do anything about it, I hate that it hurts you, that you're embarrassed by it. I hate that that fucker is out there, gloating and laughing, I hate all of that. It enrages me, because I can't change it for you."

The surprise registered on Tammy's face. She watched him trying to self soothe by rubbing his hands down his thighs and across the back of his neck. He kept swallowing, his breathing rapid and sharp.

Swallowing the sob crawling up her throat, she said, "You don't blame me?"

"Fuck no...Why would you..." Taking another breath he locked eyes with her and gently brought his shaking fingers up to her cheek to wipe away the lone tear trekking down. "I love you, Tammy. I love you so much and mostly, I feel powerless to help you. That's been my battle from losing my leg forward, this sense of powerlessness and then, I felt it all over again when you told me about the video. But, mostly, I love you."

CHAPTER 29

TAMMY JUMPED UP out of her chair and ran around the table as Danny pushed his chair away. He turned toward her as she jumped onto his lap and slammed her mouth against his. She wrapped her arms around his neck and kissed him wildly, tears wetting their cheeks. She felt him grab a handful of hair at her nape and hold her tight to his mouth. She could feel the shaking in his hand and the heat rising from his body. She continued to ravish his mouth with her own until she felt him tug gently at her hair to pull away. He looked into her eyes and softly said, "I love you."

Tammy held his handsome face between her hands, wiping the moisture from her tears with her thumbs. "I love you, too."

"Thank fuck."

She giggled as relief washed over her. Relief and happiness. He loved her. "We'll have to work on your language though."

"That right?" His husky voice rasped as his eyes caressed her face.

"As Noah grows a bit older, you're not going to be able to say fuck, shit, damn, son of a bitch, bastard or any other crazy ass words you say." Tammy giggled.

"Ha! Neither are you."

"I don't swear that much."

"Darlin' you just said ass. You don't realize it, but the f-bombs fly out of your mouth once in a while too." A smirk revealed itself on Danny's face.

Tammy wrinkled her nose. "Okay. We'll both have to work on our language."

Danny kissed her soundly, a quick peck, then another. "So?"

"So what?"

Danny looked into her eyes and saw humor. "Are you moving in?"

Tammy pursed her lips and raised a finger to her cheek as she acted like she was thinking. Danny pinched her sides causing her to yelp then squirm. "Yeah, I'm moving in. I have to give notice though. Sixty days."

"Sixty days?" his voice rose.

"It doesn't mean I have to stay there the whole time, I just won't officially be out of my lease until then." She leaned forward and kissed him again. Loving how his full lips felt against hers.

"What will your parents think about it?"

"Well, I'm sure they'd prefer I didn't cohabitate with anyone before marriage, but they like you, so I'm sure it'll eventually be fine. There might be a few lectures until they feel it's futile and I'm moving in anyway. Oh, and my dad is traveling during Thanksgiving, so they're having Thanksgiving dinner at their place on the Saturday after. You don't have to work, do you?"

"I'll talk to Dog, I'm sure it'll be fine." Danny leaned back to look once again into her face. "When is Mr. Moneybags going back home?"

Huffing out a breath, she said, "He took Sally back to Seattle in his 'private jet' this morning." Private jet in air quotes, along with an eye roll. "She stopped in briefly to say goodbye and drop off her keys and security card and such. She was nice and actually kind of smug, like she stole Zeke away from me or something. It gives me a little time to do some research though, so I'm glad they're gone."

"I'm glad he's gone too. I hate the thought of him eye-fucking you all the time."

"Language."

"Noah isn't here." Grabbing her waist, he picked her up off his lap and set her on the floor. Standing himself, he put his arm around her shoulders and walked her toward the living room. Flopping into his recliner, he pulled Tammy down onto his lap. He reached over to pull his laptop off the table and set it on Tammy's lap. With his arms around her, he said, "Before Grace got here this morning with Noah, I did a little snooping myself. I found on the City's website the list of builders vying for the coveted job of developing the downtown area."

Tapping a few keys he pulled up the list of builders. "Here's what I found."

Tammy read through the list of builders. "Hamilton Enterprises isn't on there. I thought for sure that's what was behind all of this. Dammit."

"Language." Danny chuckled at Tammy's huff. "I thought I might spend a bit of time researching these builders. They could be using an alias or a dummy company. I don't know why they'd do that, but you never know."

"Great idea. It could very well be that they are trying to pull something."

"Yep. So, Lex will be flying in on Wednesday. Coop will be in Thursday afternoon and Dirks Thursday around dinner time. They're staying here with us, there's plenty of room upstairs now that we're down here."

"Danny, I can stay at my place while they're here. I don't want to intrude on your time with them."

"Nope. I've told them all about you and they can't wait to meet you. Besides, you're moving in, so, this is your place now too." He kissed the side of her head and breathed in the fresh scent of her hair.

Tammy turned as much as she could to face him. Staring into his beautiful brown eyes she whispered, "Wow, I'm a lucky girl."

Danny chuckled. "Not as lucky as I am."

* * *

Tammy sat at her desk at work, poring over financial and activities reports. It had been a frustrating week. She and Danny had been unable to link Hamilton Enterprises with any of the builders on the City's website. Lex was coming in any minute now and Tammy promised to come home early. Home. It felt absolutely...right. She sat back into her chair as a smile creased her face. Her phone chimed and without thought she reached forward and grabbed it off the top of her desk. Swiping her thumb over the face of her phone to unlock it, she gasped as she saw another alert that the video had received comments. Why was this happening again?

Scrolling to her favorites, she touched the picture of her mom and tapped again to connect the call. Listening to the second ring Tammy glanced at her computer screen to see that it was two forty-six p.m.

"Hi baby, how are you?"

"Mom." Tammy broke out in a sob hearing her mom's voice.

"Honey, what's wrong?"

"It's starting again. The video, it's starting again." Tammy looked out of her office door to make sure no one was around.

"Shit. How do you know?" Denise Davis held her breath and pinched the bridge of her nose.

Lowering her voice, Tammy said, "I'm getting alerts. Two in a week. It stopped for so long, now it's starting again. Can you call Attorney Gratz?" Tammy's hands shook at the thought.

"Yes. I'll call him right now. How are you doing?"

"I'm basically okay. I have Danny in my life now, I just hate that this is all coming up again." Tammy bit a fingernail.

"Have you told him about it?"

"Yes. We talked about it and it's good. But, if it takes off again like it did before, it's going to get rough. Plus..." Tammy choked back a sob. "I can't...go through that again." Her voice cracked and her pulse raced.

Denise looked out her kitchen window and watched the neighbor's cat jump on top of the wooden fence and gracefully strut the length of it. Turning her mouth down at the corners, she turned around and leaned against the counter. "I'll call Derrick right now and tell him about the video and see what he can do. You know he's going to ask me. Have you seen Scott at all? Have you spoken to him? Is there any reason he would post this himself?"

Tammy let out a long breath as she stood and began pacing the floor in her office. "No. I haven't seen him, spoken to him, or even seen anyone we both would know. I can't think of any reason why he'd risk violating the restraining order now."

Denise nodded. "Okay. I'll call you later, baby. Love you."

"Love you too, Mom." Tammy ended her call and stopped at the credenza lined with the pictures of the people she loved. Except Danny. She needed to get a picture of Danny for her credenza. As she allowed her thoughts to flow over to more pleasant topics, her phone started playing "I'm proud to be an American" by Lee Greenwood. She smiled as she swiped her finger across Danny's picture. "Hey you."

"Hey. I just picked up Lex and his dad, Mr....Charles. Anyway, I wanted to make sure you're still able to come home a bit early."

Looking at the clock on her computer, she nodded, though he couldn't see her. "Yeah. I'll be leaving here in about fifteen minutes. Should I stop at the store and pick up something for dinner?"

"No. Charles wants to take us out to dinner. Just come home. Love you."

Tammy's smile widened at hearing those words flow so casually off Danny's tongue.

"Love you, too." She ended her call and set her phone on her desk. Taking a deep breath, Tammy fought to get her head around cleaning off her desk for the day.

CHAPTER 30

"IT'S A PLEASURE to meet you, Mr. Page." Tammy extended her hand to Lex's father, a beautiful smile on her face. She was nervous to meet these people who meant so much to Danny. Their newly declared love seemed so fragile right now.

"Charles, please. It's a pleasure to meet you as well. Tammy." Charles shook Tammy's hand with a firm grip and a broad smile. He was in his early fifties, with graying hair which in his youth was a warm chestnut brown and clear blue eyes that sparkled. Very handsome. On top of the polish was a faint but noticeable Southern drawl which added to the whole package. Lex looked very much like his father, though, there seemed to be a haunted look in Lex's eyes. Tammy shook Lex's hand as Danny continued with the introductions.

Danny put his arm around Tammy and drew her into his warmth. He kissed her temple and gave her a squeeze. "I thought we could eat at the Top Hat, what do you think of that?"

"That's fabulous." Looking at their guests, Tammy said, "Do you like big juicy steaks and steak fries?"

Lex laughed, "What are steak fries?"

Tammy and Danny both chuckled. Tucking her hair behind her ear, she said, "Okay. Um, they're thick slices of potatoes deep fried like French fries."

"Oh, in that case, yes. That sounds delicious, darlin'." Tammy smirked, there was something about that slow Southern accent that could make a girl fall head over heels.

They enjoyed an evening of getting to know each other. Lex and Charles were very much the Southern gentlemen. Lex would float off once in a while, lost in his own thoughts, but just when Tammy started to worry, he would come back to them as though nothing had happened. Charles watched Lex closely and more than once Tammy caught his eye. He would nod once and softly smile, though it never reached his eyes.

"Dan. What have you been doing about your PTSD?" Lex asked. He fidgeted with his napkin. His eyes flicked to Tammy and then back to Danny.

Danny sat forward, leaning his arms on the table and looked directly into Lex's eyes. "I still see my counselor twice a month and, recently, I started going into Stateside Home for Veterans and talking to the guys there. It's amazing talking to those guys, Lex. I was hoping you'd come with me when I go on Sunday. All of you. The men will love meeting you and it's amazing talking to them. They have so many experiences to share and they're interested in hearing about ours." Danny's smile was broad and he pleaded with his eyes for Lex to agree to join him.

"That sounds like a fantastic idea, Buddy." Charles pleaded.

Lex looked at the hopeful look on both Danny and Charles' faces and remained silent for so long Tammy began to get nervous. Hands in her lap, she twisted her fingers together and held her breath. Her eyes froze on Lex as they waited.

Taking a deep breath Lex looked from his father's eyes to Danny's. He nodded without saying a word. As if on cue, everyone let out the breaths they held and the mood lightened.

* * *

Watching Danny pour their cups of coffee, Tammy sat at the table, admiring the muscles bunching in his back as his slow methodical movements were silent and effortless. He brought their coffees to the table and kissed her softly as he set her cup down in front of her.

"You smell good." She inhaled the fresh spicy scent of his shower gel as he kissed the top of her head and scented her hair.

"So do you. I love the smell of your hair. I bury my nose in it to get to sleep at night."

"You do not." She laughed.

"I do." He sat in the chair next to hers and watched her realize he was telling the truth. When her eyes grew round he smirked and nodded.

"I had no idea."

Danny smiled and lifted his cup to his lips.

"So, tonight we have a house full. I didn't know Charles was coming on this trip, but he's worried about Lex and asked me to help him. I'm hoping having the guys all together will help. But, I thought we could all sit around tonight and relax. You good with that?"

Tammy smiled as she searched his face for worry. His brown eyes were bright and clear and the little creases around them crinkled as his smile grew. She reached up and smoothed them with the pad of her finger before leaning in to softly peck his lips.

"Of course I'm good with that. My offer stands though; I can go home if you want time alone with them."

Tucking her hair behind her ear, Danny kissed the tip of her nose. "You are home and I don't want you anywhere else."

"Good morning."

Lex walked into the kitchen wearing a t-shirt and a pair of jeans. He was slim, not muscular like Danny, more like slim from not eating a proper diet. His hair was damp from the shower and he was clean shaven. He approached the table as Danny stood and pointed to the chair across from him and Tammy.

"Still take your coffee black?"

Lex smirked and nodded. Pulling the chair away from the table he sat gingerly, not like 'one of the guys,' more calculated and measured. Tammy felt intensely sorry for him, clearly he was suffering.

"Did you sleep good, Lex?" Keeping her voice soft and looking him in the eye, she noticed he fidgeted a bit.

"Ah, yeah, I did. It's quiet here."

Danny brought Lex's coffee to the table and sat in his chair, leaning back and draping his arm across the back of Tammy's chair.

"This is a great neighborhood. It's one of the things I fell in love with when I first saw this house. What's it like where you live in Kentucky?"

Sipping his coffee, Lex closed his eyes as the hot liquid slid down his throat. Opening his eyes, he looked at Danny and said. "It's quiet. You know, we live on a farm, so we don't have neighbors that close to us, but when the ranch hands start pulling in in the morning, it can get busy."

Tammy set her coffee on the table, her eyes large and round as she said, "Ranch hands? How big is your farm?"

Lex's lips formed a straight line; he fidgeted as his lazy haunted gaze shifted from Danny to hers. He cleared his throat, seemingly nervous and hunched his shoulders then stretched them back.

"We have a large horse ranch north of Lexington. My dad's into breeding some of the finest race horses around. He grew up there and so did I. The ranch has been in his family for generations."

Tammy's brows rose. "Wow. That's amazing."

Lex's soft smile formed slowly. "Yeah," was all he could say.

"Morning, all." Charles strode into the kitchen, dressed casually in khakis and a light blue button-up shirt. He focused his attention on Lex as he entered the kitchen and then not wanting to seem rude, he looked over to his hosts and nodded. "Coffee smells wonderful, do you mind if I help myself?"

"Not at all, but I'm happy to get it for you." Tammy smiled.

"No need, darlin', I'm a grown man. At home my wife isn't an early riser and I'm used to taking care of myself in the morning. She makes up for it the remainder of the day by cooking, cleaning, and preparing fabulous feasts for us though, so you'll never hear me complain. Right, Charlie?"

At hearing Lex's given name, Danny's head snapped back as he shot his gaze to Lex. The movement didn't go unnoticed as Lex smirked. "Not used to hearing my name, Schaefer?"

"Not at all. I forgot you had any other name than Lex."

"Why do you guys all call each other by your last names or nicknames anyway?" Tammy asked.

Both Danny and Lex shrugged. "Just do, sweetheart. I think it starts in Boot Camp. Drill Sergeant will call you something and it sticks. I'm Lex because there was another Charles in our unit. He was from Boise and that didn't stick, so the DS called me Lex from day one."

Growing quiet, the room suddenly felt awkward and uncomfortable. Tammy grabbed her phone off the top of the table and looked at the time. Standing she smoothed her soft gray dress and centered her wide coral belt. "I've got to run to work, there's plenty for me to get done before my bosses come in next week."

Danny stood as well, "I hope you aren't talking about Mr. Moneybags. I hate that guy and I haven't even met him yet."

Tammy smirked, "No, our parent company is coming in next week to see how things are going. If the offer is accepted with Hamilton Enterprises, I suppose inventories and a plethora of other duties will be handed down, so I want my desk cleaned up before all of that happens."

At the mention of Hamilton Enterprises Charles turned around but didn't say anything. He looked over at Lex whose mouth pinched together and his eyes squinted, just a bit.

"I'll see you all later then, have a great day." She leaned forward and kissed Danny's lips before turning and walking toward the garage. Once the door closed Danny sat back down and Charles took up a spot at the end of the table.

"Hamilton Enterprises as in Zeke Hamilton and company?" Charles slowly drawled.

Danny's face registered surprise. "Yes, as in."

Charles nodded as he took a sip of his coffee. "What's going on there?"

CHAPTER 31

TAMMY FLIPPED ON the lights in her office and strode across the room to her desk. Flipping her computer on at the same time, she bent and opened her bottom drawer and deposited her purse, then she pulled her chair away from the desk without even fully standing. She had practiced this routine for years now and it didn't require thought.

As she typed in her user name and password she watched as her computer woke up. Mentally cataloging her day, she knew she needed to find some time to investigate some of the builders on the City's list. There had to be something there she was missing. Clicking open her email account she scrolled through a few emails that could wait; she had one from Molly, which she would read right away and then one from Zeke. Stifling a groan, she opened the email from Molly and read with delight. She missed Molly; they'd both been so busy with their new men that they were losing touch with each other. Tammy tapped out a message back to Molly and took a deep breath as she opened her email from Zeke.

From: Zeke Hamilton
To: Tammy Davis
November 13, 2014 8:34 a.m.
Subject: Opportunity made just for you
Dear Ms. Davis,
I hope this email finds you quite well. Isaiah has Sally firmly under his wing and indoctrinating her in all she needs to know to help Hamilton Enterprises with its nursing homes. She has plenty of experience and proves to be a quick study, so she should be on her own before long.
This brings me to you. Isaiah and I have been talking about the passion

you showed toward Stateside and the cause of Veterans in general. After our dinner we came to agree that you would be the perfect fit for a position here in Seattle at Hamilton Enterprises where we would put your passion, business acumen, and strengths to good use. I extend this offer immediately and will telephone you later today after you have had some time to think about it to discuss it in further detail. I apologize for the email, I simply cannot get away until early next week to fly back and extend the offer in person.

> Zeke Hamilton
> CEO, Hamilton Enterprises

Tammy sat back in her chair. Seattle? Well, no way. She nervously tapped her fingers on the top of her desk. If she left here, there would be no one to ensure this home stayed intact. He was probably trying to get her out of here so there was one less hurdle. Forget it, not interested!

She didn't bother to respond, he said he would call later and he could simply wait. Irritated at his email, she jumped up out of her chair and decided to stroll through the building and visit with the men and women who called this place home.

* * *

"Tammy? Mr. Hamilton is on line one," the disembodied voice of Lana, Stateside's receptionist, cooed through the phone.

Tammy shook her head. Shit, even Lana was enamored by Zeke. Crazy women were all nuts.

Taking a deep breath and sitting up in her chair Tammy picked up her receiver and tapped the flashing button. "Hello."

"Ms. Davis, I hope this call finds you well."

Tammy rolled her eyes. "Yes, very well. How may I help you?" she purposely didn't offer the same platitude to him.

She heard the humor in his voice as he responded. "Since you received my email this morning, I believe you know how you can help me. I've called to discuss the position we're creating for you here at Hamilton Enterprises."

Pursing her lips, Tammy scowled before replying. He could simply fire her once he owned the place, so she really had nothing to lose in telling him her thoughts.

"I'm not interested Mr. Hamilton. I don't want to move to Seattle. I don't want to leave my family. I don't want to leave my boyfriend."

"Ah, yes, the boyfriend." Tammy's brows rose at the acid that rolled off his tongue with the word 'boyfriend'.

Continuing on, "I haven't even fully told you about the job here. What if it's your every dream come true?"

"I have the job I've always dreamed of. Here. At Stateside. There's nothing more I could want."

"You haven't even listened to my offer."

Quickly becoming irritated with his tone and his complete disregard for her wants and desires, she tersely told him, "I've already said, I have my perfect job, here. I live close to my family, who are very important to me and I have a boyfriend, whom I love very much. I'm happy here, in Wisconsin."

Sensing her closed mind on the subject, Zeke changed the conversation. "Very well, it sounds as if you're not interested in discussing it at this time. Then, allow me to forewarn you that I'll be returning to Wisconsin early next week and intend to discuss this with you again, in person."

Tammy chose to stay silent, lest she make a total mess of things. But, she wasn't interested in anything Zeke had to say and she had absolutely no desire to move to Seattle. She wasn't Sally.

"I really do have quite a lot of work to finish up before I leave today, Mr. Hamilton, so if there's nothing else, I really do need to get back to it."

She heard his smile through the phone as he said, "Right, then, I'll let you get back to work. I'll see you next week, Ms. Davis."

Tammy hung up, irritated again at his pompous tone. Really? Creating a job and thinking she'd simper off like Sally did. Did the man ever hear the damn word 'No'? Tammy shut down her computer and prepared to go home and meet Dirks and Coop. As her heels clipped along the highly polished tile floor of Stateside, she heard the dreaded notification on her phone again. Barely missing a step, she continued towards her car without looking. Her mom was right, she should get rid of the damn notifications altogether. She was just torturing herself watching for it all the time, but something perverse in her needed to know what was going on with it.

Sliding the key in the ignition she heard the notification tone again. Once more before she merged into traffic and again as she pulled into the driveway at Danny's. She blinked back the threatening tears, took a deep breath and told herself to be a brave girl and ignore it. She would call her mom later to see what Attorney Gratz had to say. Locking in her resolve, she nodded and opened her car door. Taking deep breaths as she walked across the garage to the kitchen door soothed her nerves, almost completely.

She opened the door to the kitchen and heard a strange voice say, "We can leave while you talk to her about it if you like, Schaefer. She should know."

Tammy's stomach rolled and flopped. What did he have to tell her? Did they see the video? He said he didn't want to. Panic slammed itself into Tammy's body full force, nausea swept through her stomach and she turned to run outside and in the fresh air when Danny called to her.

CHAPTER 32

"HEY, THERE YOU ARE. I'm glad you're home." Danny kissed her softly on the lips and stood back to look at her pale face. "Babe?"

Tammy shook her head to stave off questions. Placing her hand over her stomach to quell the nausea, she looked up at Danny's concerned face. His brows furrowed and his eyes bored into hers. When she looked down, he gently tucked his hand under her chin and tilted her face up to meet his gaze. "Babe, what's wrong?"

Licking her lips, she whispered, "The video's getting a lot of hits today. I heard what someone said when I walked in. You guys didn't watch it, did you?"

Danny's posture became rigid. The muscles in his chest bunching under the tension. "No, babe, I told you I didn't want to see it and I haven't. I would never do that to you. I have other news for you."

Never looking away from his beautiful dark eyes, Tammy's lips quivered into a smile as she let out the breath she'd been holding. She blinked rapidly to stave off the tears that threatened as Danny's arms wrapped around her and held her close to his body. There was nothing more soothing than being held by him. Laying her cheek against his chest and listening to his strong heartbeat brought home what was important and real in her life. The nerves in her body, strung tightly, began to loosen as she breathed in the scents she associated with Danny. Strong, solid, refreshing and comforting. She began shaking as the tension left her body. She heard him whisper into her hair, "Baby, I'm here and it's going to be alright. I promise."

Squeezing him tighter, she hung on for long moments until Lex's southern drawl was heard saying, "They're probably making out in there."

Danny chuckled and Tammy found herself chuckling with him. He stepped back and looked down at her, "You okay?"

Nodding she replied, "Yeah. Sorry. Tough day."

Shaking his head no, he helped her with her coat and grabbed her hand and walked her into the living room. "Dirks, Coop, meet Tammy."

Shaking each of their hands and giving her brightest smile, she greeted each of them. Danny sat in his recliner and pulled her down on his lap as the others were seated on the sofa and the other chair in the room.

Tammy looked at each of these friends who meant so much to Danny. Coop was a tall lanky man with the brightest red hair she'd ever seen. His deep brown eyes coupled with this hair was very striking. When he smiled at her the dimples in his cheeks created quite a picture.

Dirks was shorter, around five foot eight and a bit stocky. His close-cropped blonde hair gave him the appearance of being bald until the light shown on his hair. He had the most appealing blue eyes she'd ever seen, besides Gunnar and Molly's. Dirks' eyes were a deeper blue. He was the prankster if she remembered correctly. Danny had told her he was the one always rubber-cementing their equipment to tables and chairs or throwing popcorn kernels into their shoes and drawers.

She noticed that Lex looked a bit more at ease this evening and Charles seemed to relax as the men all talked and renewed their friendship.

Finally, Coop said, "Tell her, Schaefer."

Tammy turned to look at Danny. His full lips parted into a perfect smile. "Charles knows a bit about Zeke Hamilton and is going to help us dig into his fascination with Stateside."

Tammy's brows raised as she looked over at Charles, who'd leaned forward in his chair, his forearms resting on his knees. "Yes ma'am. I called home this morning and have some of my associates digging up some dirt for us as we speak."

Bewildered Tammy looked into his clear blue eyes as she noticed his lips tighten. "That's fantastic, but, why? How do you know about him?"

Lex snorted in disgust as Charles sipped his drink. "Hamilton Enterprises, Zeke in particular, came sweeping into Lexington several years back trying to buy up some of the horse ranches in our area. Some of the other ranchers had done some digging and found out he wanted to commercialize our area. We live in the most beautiful part of Lexington, North, and our land is pristine, our horses highly sought after race horses. When I look out my windows, any window in my home, I see beautiful green rolling hills, a lake on one side of our home, our horses grazing or training and nothing more. Nor do I ever want to see anything more. The thought of him coming in and cutting up our ranches, building malls and commercial businesses, sickened us. We banded together and vowed to never sell to him. Once he realized we were sticking together and not selling, no matter the price, he eventually left. But, I have a bad taste in my mouth for Mr. Hamilton, he's a sneaky bastard and I don't trust him in the least."

Tammy's lips turned down into a frown. "I'm afraid that's what he's going to do to Stateside. The men and women who live there can't afford to go to a traditional nursing facility. Our home was subsidized since the beginning by the government. With budget cuts, we've lost our funding and I don't know where those folks would go. Their only options are substandard housing where the care is inadequate. I just can't let that happen." Tammy's eyes grew bright with unshed tears as she fought to keep her emotions in check. She swallowed a few times before she spoke again. "Thank you for all of your help, Charles, I appreciate it so damn much."

Charles smiled at her and slightly nodded, "You're welcome, darlin'. We'd do anything for Dan and that extends to you. I should know more in a day or two."

Danny squeezed Tammy's waist and she turned her head to look at him. "It's going to be okay, babe. It's all going to be okay. We'll figure it all out."

Tammy nodded as she laid her head on Danny's shoulder. Maybe things would be alright after all. The perfect moment for the doorbell to ring.

CHAPTER 32

DIRKS STOOD AND STRETCHED a bit, "I'll get it."

Danny raised his voice, pushed the footrest down on the recliner and set Tammy on her feet, "No, Dirks, I've got this."

Dirks blew him off with a wave and quickly made it to the door as he was pulling out his wallet. Opening the door to the pizza delivery man, Dirks smiled broadly and promptly handed him a fifty dollar bill. He took the three pizza boxes from the man and nodded as he stepped back. As the man started to stammer about change, Dirks smirked at him and said, "Go have a drink after work, Bud, this job must suck." With his free hand he closed the door and walked the pizzas back to the living room and set them on the coffee table, careful not to knock over their beer bottles.

Still standing Tammy said, "Oh, I feel so bad, you guys, I'm happy to make something besides pizza. It seems so rude to order pizza and then have you pay on top of it. You're our guests."

Coop grabbed a big slice of pepperoni pizza and inhaled deeply. "You kiddin'?" Taking a big bite, he chewed a few times as Lex, Dirks and Danny all dove into the pizza themselves.

Coop finally swallowed and explained, "I've been looking forward to this for months. We used to sit around in Afghanistan and talk about getting home, ordering pizza and drinking beer together without being shot at. When Schaefer got his leg blown off, I didn't think it would happen." He shot his gaze over to Danny. "Buddy, honestly, you scared the ever-living-fuck out of me. Us."

Lex froze mid-bite while his eyes flicked over to Danny, who swallowed hard as Dirks chimed in, "Me too." Taking a big bite of his slice, Dirks moved it around his mouth a bit. Then, with a full mouth and without swallowing, he muttered, "Shitty way to get attention, man. You could've just gotten the flu or something." Then he smirked while still chewing his pizza.

Danny picked up his slice and sat back in his chair. "Well, with you constantly pranking us, I figured it was the only I was going to out-punk you." He chomped down on his slice and smirked at Dirks then his eyes sought Lex, who still hadn't taken a bite and was warily watching Danny. Danny nodded to him once and said, "Eat up or these two pigs'll eat it all." He patted Tammy on the ass. "You to, babe, seriously, these guys eat like horses."

Tammy looked over the group and relaxed as she saw Lex finally bite into his pizza. She asked Charles in particular, "Would you like a plate? Anyone?"

"No thanks, darlin'. When in Rome…" Charles leaned forward and grabbed a slice as the men all dug into the pizza like they hadn't eaten in weeks. Lex was beginning to relax and eat and Coop and Dirks were already on their second slice. Tammy wiped her moist palms on her thighs and walked into the kitchen to grab everyone another drink.

*   *   *

Lying awake for several hours while Danny slept peacefully beside her, the sound of her phone chiming over and over rang through her head as the evening had progressed, even though she'd left it tucked in her purse. Tammy once again looked at the clock and watched it change from one fifty-nine to two o'clock a.m. Danny was breathing deeply and hadn't moved much since falling asleep after they quietly made love. Of course, the several beers he had with his friends helped. No telling how he'd feel in the morning, but for now, he was good.

Softly rolling to the edge of the bed, slipping from under the covers and grabbing her robe from the end of the bed, Tammy wrapped herself up and padded to the door. As she softly opened and stepped through the doorway, she looked back and smiled at Danny's soft snore. Bare feet whispering across the living room carpet, she walked into the kitchen and flipped on the light above the stove illuminating a small portion of the kitchen in a soft yellow hue. She opened the refrigerator, pulled the pitcher of water from the top shelf and stepped over to the counter. As she reached above her head for a glass from the cupboard, she heard footsteps approaching. She turned to see Lex appear in the kitchen, his chestnut hair standing up in tufts around his head, his eyes sleepy, but oddly alert. Tammy held up her empty glass and Lex nodded. Reaching for another, she quickly poured two glasses of water.

She turned toward Lex and nodded to the kitchen table. Each of them pulled out a chair and settled in for a quiet conversation. Taking a sip of her water and waiting until Lex did the same, she smiled at him. "Not able to sleep, I see. I'd have thought the beer would've helped. Danny passed out right away."

Lex's smile didn't reach his eyes. "I don't sleep much these days." He nervously rotated his glass, watching the water ring at the bottom smear across the top of the oak table. Tammy stood and pulled a napkin from the holder on the counter. She smiled as she laid it down in front of Lex. He smirked as he picked up his glass and set it neatly on the napkin.

"Are you seeing a counselor?"

Lex nervously looked into her brown eyes, seeing only compassion. "Yes. I see him twice a week, every week. It doesn't help. Nothing helps. When I close my eyes, I see Danny laying on the ground, his leg laying yards away, blood spilling from his wounds and he opened his eyes, but he didn't seem to register who I was or where we were. I've never seen anything like that in my life. I thought I was going to lose him."

Tammy nodded, sipped her water and waited to ensure he was finished. When he continued to fidget and swirl the water in his glass, she spoke.

"Danny suffered for a long time afterwards as well. Learning your life is forever altered is difficult to get your mind around, especially when you're in physical pain as well. He came home and Kathryn broke up with him when she saw him. He's dealt with so much. But then, he met Jeremiah from Rolling Thunder and he and his army of men and women raised enough money to build the bedroom and bathroom for Danny. That's when I met him. Then, he got his job at Rolling Thunder, which he loves. And we love each other and are building a fabulous relationship. Life can get better after tragedy. It keeps going; you must as well."

Lex stared into Tammy's eyes as the seconds ticked away on the clock above the stove. "I don't know how. I need to get rid of the nightmares so I can sleep. Then, hopefully, I'll heal. I thought I lost my brother. He's the only one I've ever had. When I first met him, immediately we had a kinship that's lasted through war. I have to get rid of the nightmares."

Tammy sipped at her water again and took a deep breath. "I have Molly. She's not my sister by blood, but she's my sister in heart. We've known each other since early childhood. We went to school together, high school dances, prom, graduation, and some horrible things Molly lived through thanks to her stepfather. Nothing will ever tear us away from each other. I know how it feels to love someone not your blood and see horrors. I've helped Molly through the worst kind. I had nightmares after I found out what happened. I felt guilt. Remorse. Sorrow. Hatred. But, I focused on helping her heal. Our friendship grew stronger. By helping her heal, I healed."

Tammy didn't look away from Lex. She wanted to drive her point home. He nodded after long moments. She noticed his hand shaking as he wiped the sweat beading on the side of his glass. He dragged his hand through his hair and let out a loud, staggering breath. "What do I do?"

"Follow Danny. Ask him how he's doing. You'll see, he's healing and doing well. Go talk to the men at Stateside with him and learn about them and tell them about your experience. Stick close to your buddies. You have some great friends here with Dirks and Coop and of course Danny. See that they're healing and you can, too. Allow yourself to heal with them."

Lex nodded as they sat in silence for long moments. Tammy wasn't going to go to bed before Lex and leave him here alone. She'd stay up the rest of the night if need be, but she hoped it wouldn't come to that; already sleep was calling her name. Lex finished his glass of water and stood. "I'm going up to bed. Thank you for taking the time to sit and talk. I can see how Schaefer fell so hard for you."

He put his glass in the sink and as he walked past Tammy's chair, rested his hand briefly on the top of her head. Then he softly made his way out of the kitchen and up the stairs. Tammy let a sigh escape her throat as she set her glass in the sink and turned off the oven light. Slipping into the bedroom, she silently slid between the sheets and scooted over to Danny. As she laid her head on his shoulder, he lifted his arm for her to rest her head in the crook. She smiled as she heard him breathe deeply into her hair and relax his muscles as he once again found sleep.

CHAPTER 33

DANNY WOKE TO TAMMY'S soft breathing and smiled as his gaze drifted to the window and the sunlight peeking through the split in the curtains. Replaying the conversations of yesterday, he tried getting all of his thoughts in order. His buddies were here and it felt great. It was past time for this get-together and he owed Jeremiah a big thanks for that. Charles was digging for information about Mr. Moneybags, but Lex, he needed to help Lex. And Tammy. This video business was shaking her. The look on her face last night said so much. When he first walked into the kitchen to greet her, she was on the verge of cracking. If he ever got his hands on that Scott son-of-a-bitch, he'd go insane on him. How could a human being do that to another? Dishonorable. Danny had no patience for people like that.

He looked down at Tammy, still nestled in the crook of his arm and smiled. One of her legs was resting over his and when she breathed, he could feel her breast move against his chest. His cock began to swell. He gently laid his cheek on the top of her head and breathed deeply of her fragrance. Would he ever tire of the smell of her? The feel of her? He doubted it. He finally knew what love felt like and it was fantastic. They hadn't had much time to just simply be. Once his friends left, hopefully they'd have the time without all of this other work and video business creating turmoil in their lives.

He kissed the top of her head and gently slipped his arm from under her. Rolling to the edge of the bed and slipping on his prosthetic, shorts and a t-shirt, Danny walked into the bathroom. Washing his hands he slipped out of the bedroom and made his way to the kitchen. He wanted to make his guests a giant breakfast. He saw the two water glasses in the sink and wondered who'd been up during the night. Pulling out a griddle and his mixer, he set about making pancakes and eggs.

"What's on the agenda today, Schaefer?"

Danny turned to see Dirks walking into the kitchen, scratching the top of his head. He was wearing shorts and no shirt.

"Dude, go put a shirt on. I don't want my girl looking at that pale chest of yours."

Dirks smirked, "Yeah, she'd be running to me in a heartbeat."

"You wish."

Dirks turned and walked back upstairs. He was down in a minute donning a shirt and walked to the table where Danny had set a steaming cup of coffee for him.

"You cook now."

"Yeah. It started as part of my therapy, then it became a challenge. Now I find that I love it and I look forward to spoiling Tammy with great meals when she comes home at night. We've not had much time for that, but we will."

Dirks nodded. "Yeah, there's time."

"We'll go over to Rolling Thunder this morning. Dog wants to meet you guys and we've finished modifying my bike. I want to show you guys."

"That's really cool, Schaefer." Taking another sip of coffee he watched Danny cook. His motions smooth and efficient. "You good, Schaefer? I mean really good."

Danny turned around and looked into Dirks' baby blues. "Yeah, I'm good. Mostly, my nightmares have gone away. I only have them now and then. Usually when something bad happens. I get around good on my new leg and I have a smokin' hot girl." Turning to flip the pancakes on the griddle they were both silent. When he finished he turned back to Dirks. "What about you, Dirks? Are you good?"

"Yeah, I'm good. I see my counselor monthly, work out regularly and eat good. I haven't had a nightmare in about two months. That's a first for me."

"What are you two hens cackling about in here?" Coops' copper hair was slicked back from the shower. His t-shirt was Army issue, his shorts too. He sauntered over to the coffeepot and pulled a cup from the cupboard. Pouring his coffee, he took a deep breath. "Damn, Schaefer, that smells good. When did you start cooking?"

"A while ago."

Dirks looked at Coop. "Schaefer's taking us to Rolling Thunder today to see his bike."

"Sweet. I bet you're excited to get her back on the road. Too bad it's freezing outside."

"Yeah. It can wait. I'm used to it, living here. But, at least you can see it."

"Morning. It smells good in here." Tammy walked into the kitchen, ready for work. She was dressed for comfort today. She wore black dress pants, a red silky tank, red flats and a white flyaway. The flats made her look even smaller than she actually was. She walked over to Danny and had to stand on her toes to give him a peck on the lips. He looked down at her feet and smirked. She slapped his arm as she turned to pull out a coffee cup. She looked back at the guys and saw their cups half empty. Before filling her cup, she took the coffeepot to the table to refill their cups. She refilled Danny's cup and poured the last little bit into her cup. She set about making another pot of coffee while Danny finished up breakfast.

Danny began carrying food to the table and said, "We'll eat now and Lex can eat when he gets up."

"He'll probably sleep a bit more, he was up during the night," Tammy said as she set the butter on the table.

Danny stopped carrying food and looked at her. "How do you know?"

"I got up because I couldn't sleep and he came into the kitchen as I was getting a glass of water. We sat at the table and talked for a while."

"He okay?" Dirks asked as he sat back in his chair.

Tammy shrugged. "It's up to him to say something. I just think he needs your support."

Danny hugged her from behind. He kissed the side of her head. "Thanks for talking to him."

Tammy smiled. "Of course. Let's eat; I've got to get going."

CHAPTER 34

WALKING INTO ROLLING THUNDER, the guys were happy and talking crap with each other. Charles stayed behind to get some work done and allow the guys to have time alone. They walked straight to the back of the shop where Danny's bike was up on a lift, one of the students wiping it dry after washing it.

"Thanks for taking care of her, Drew." Danny clapped him on the back and looked at his bike.

Drew's face flamed a bright red as he nodded, saying nothing in return.

"Holy fuck, Schaefer, she's a beauty." Dirks walked around the lift looking at the shiny chrome, gold, and black bike. His low whistle sounded over the shop noises.

"Schaefer, is that a softail slim? No fucking way. You said you were into old bikes, but you never let on you had this in your garage. Lucky bitch." Coop knelt down to take look at the pipes. "You had the pipes gold-tipped? Shit, Schaefer."

Danny laughed at his friends and their awe. He scratched the top of his head and ran his hand around and down the nape to his neck. His smile was electric, his dark eyes shined.

Lex walked forward and ran his hand along the painted two-tone shiny black and flat black tank and across the shiny cool leather seat. No front fender, fat front and back tires, gold tips and accents everywhere. "Narly, Schaefer. Fucking narly."

Drew lowered the lift to the ground and Danny hopped up on the bike. "Wanna hear her?"

"Fuck yeah," was said in unison by all the guys.

Turning on the ignition switch, he checked the shifter to make sure it was in neutral and hit the starter. She roared to life with a loud crack and the low rumble only a Harley can give. The smile from each and every one of the guys was a sight to behold. He twisted the throttle a few times, making the pipes crack and growl. The guys shook their heads and smiled from ear to ear.

"She sounds perfect." Jeremiah walked up to the guys, hands in his pockets, a smile on his face.

Danny turned the ignition switch off and dismounted. "She does. I never dreamed I'd hear her again."

Danny shook Jeremiah's hand. "Thanks, Dog. Wow, you got her running top notch."

"Actually, Gunnar and Ryder worked on it last night and this morning. They knew you were bringing your friends around and they wanted you to be able to start it up."

Danny looked over the shop. "Where are they? I'd like to thank them and introduce them."

"They're upstairs. Joci needed them to move things around in the office and I snuck out." Jeremiah smirked.

Danny shook his head. "She gonna be mad?"

"Naw. I threw you under the bus, saying you were here and I needed to come down and help you with your bike." His smile broadened.

"She gonna be mad at me?"

Jeremiah shook his head.

Nodding, Danny made introductions. "Dog, these are my friends, Lex, Coop, and Dirks."

The guys each shook Jeremiah's hand, commented on the bike and made small talk.

"Why don't we go upstairs and I'll tell you what I have in mind for the Veteran's Ride."

* * *

"Hey, girl. I thought I'd pop in and see how you're doing. You haven't painted in a while." Gerry wheeled his chair into Tammy's office, concern on his face.

Tammy set down the report she was reading and sat back in her chair. She smiled, for the first time since she'd arrived at work today.

Her smile faded to a slight frown at the concerned look on Gerry's face. "Yeah, I want to make sure I do a good job in Sally's absence and I guess I've buried myself in here, pouring over reports and budgets."

"So, the rumor out there is you're leaving us, too. That true?"

Tammy's brows pinched together. "No. It isn't. Who's spreading that rumor?"

Gerry shrugged. "I don't know where it started but some of the nurses were overheard saying Mr. Bigshot who took Sally away was trying to steal you too."

"Oh. Okay. So someone overheard something and decided to spread around what they thought they heard?"

Gerry chuckled. "Something like that."

Tammy leaned her forearms on the desktop. Smiling broadly at Gerry's faded blue eyes and lopsided grin, she said, "I'll tell you what. If I decide to leave here, I'll tell you second. How about that?"

"Second?"

Tammy laughed. "Danny would be first, Gerry."

Gerry nodded. "Makes sense. So, is Danny still bringing his friends in on Sunday?"

"He sure is. He's been telling them all about you guys this week."

CHAPTER 35

"OKAY, FIRST OF ALL, there's something I didn't tell you about Tammy. She paints. I mean, she's friggin' good, too." Danny smirked as he stood in front of the door to the activities room.

He pushed open the door and led the way into the room, his friends behind him. He waved to the men who'd already gathered around, each drinking coffee or tea and gossiping away. Men were just as big of gossips as women, maybe even more so. But, what caught Danny's ear froze him.

"She said I'd be second to know if she leaves here. Danny there..." Gerry pointed to Danny, "would be first."

"What are you talking about, Gerry?"

"Tammy. She told me if Mr. Bigshot steals her away, I'd be the second to know and you'd be the first."

Danny swallowed. "Have you heard that he's trying to steal her away?" His heart began thumping away in his chest.

"Oh sure, the rumors are all over the place lately." Harry waved his wrinkled old hand wide as he said it.

Lex watched Danny's face grow hard, his Adam's apple bobbing up and down as he swallowed to calm himself. Giving Danny the time to recover from this shock, Lex stepped forward and shook the hands of the men sitting around the table. Coop and Dirks followed, making their introductions.

Turning around Dirks whistled, "Is this what you were talking about? Tammy paint this?"

Danny slowly turned and mentally shook himself out of his shock. "Yeah." Clearing the frog from his throat he tried again. "Yes. She painted that. It's not finished yet."

They all looked at the far right of the wall where the background was roughed in, but no scenes appeared.

Gerry wheeled forward. "She needs someone to help her with this war. We've each spent time in here with her while she paints, explaining what it looked like, what we went through, how we felt." He wheeled closer to the wall and pointed to the face of one of the men in the mural. "This is Hank's brother." Lifting his hand he pointed across the room at a tall lanky man, who was too thin for his size, sitting at the table.

"Yep. That's Johnny. He died at the beginning of Vietnam. I brought a picture of Johnny in here and Tammy painted his picture into the mural. Now, when I have something to say to Johnny, I come in here and talk to his picture. Every time I come in this room, I feel like he's here." Hank's look was far away, his thin lips formed a faint smile.

The guys stepped closer to the picture and looked at Johnny, staring back at them. Gerry continued, "This here is my Uncle Joe. He died at the end of World War II. I never knew him, but I have the pictures from my dad; I love that Tammy painted him there."

Wheeling forward a bit more, he swept his hand upward. "This is Phnom Pehn, where I was stationed. It was a beautiful place at one time, I hear it is again. When I was there, it was war-ravaged, but I told Tammy I remembered sitting in those swamps and being quiet and looking around for any movement and I remembered a day I saw those pink flowers peeking up over the swampland. It brought a tear to my eyes to see something pretty in such an ugly world. She painted these for me."

*　*　*

"Hey girl, how are you? I miss you." Tammy spoke into her phone. She was reclining in Danny's chair, taking a few moments to call Molly before the guys came back from Stateside.

"Oh, Tam, I miss you, too. How are you?"

Tammy closed her eyes, "I'm good." Sighing softly she opened her eyes and looked out the window across the fresh snow on the front yard.

"That isn't the sound of someone who's fine. I need to know what's going on."

Tammy proceeded to tell Molly about the video. Danny. Danny's friends, and everything that'd happened recently. Molly shared her life with Ryder and that they were moving in together.

"Oh, Molly, that's fantastic. We need to get together; maybe we can go pick out a Christmas Tree next Saturday. We'd like to get one put up right after Thanksgiving and that's next week already."

"Wait. We?" Molly smiled as she watched a movie play on the television, the sound turned down.

"Danny and I are moving in together. Actually, I'm moving in with him."

The two friends shared their lives as they were now. Talking to Molly had always soothed Tammy's nerves. No one was more levelheaded than Molly.

*   *   *

The guys rolled in around four-thirty. They were laughing and talking excitedly about the afternoon at Stateside. Charles sat back, a smile on his face as he watched his son talk animatedly for the first time since he'd come back from Afghanistan. Lex laughed and shared with everyone the conversations with the guys. Charles asked questions, they all raced to answer. All except Danny, he was more subdued. He smiled when he was supposed to, but it didn't reach his eyes.

Tammy asked him if he was okay and he just nodded and kissed the side of her head. She went to the kitchen and grabbed the dishes and silverware to set the dining room table. She'd brought some of her dishes from her place and used the cloth napkins she'd purchased at an estate sale a couple of years ago. She'd made a beautiful roast beef, baked potatoes, and candied carrots for dinner. Homemade buns were in the oven and for dessert she'd made an Oreo Lasagna. It was fun cooking in Danny's kitchen. It was the first time she had carte blanche to cook and make herself feel at home, wanting this dinner to be special since it was also the first time she'd cooked for Danny.

The men sauntered into the dining room and took their places around the table. "Schaefer, you're a lucky son-of-a-bitch. You have a house, that crazy ass bike, a smoking-hot mama, who paints and cooks. Shit, some guys have all the luck."

"That's right." Danny exclaimed. But, he didn't smile. Tammy watched his face as his eyes flicked over to hers and then down to his plate. The guys all dug in as the lively conversation continued. Apparently the visit to Stateside had been successful. At least for Dirks, Coop, and Lex. Tammy fought the butterflies that began to take flight in her tummy. Danny was disturbed about something.

"Oh, dad, you've got to see the mural Tammy painted at Stateside. It's fucking amazing." Lex's smile stretched across his face, his blue eyes sparkling with a life Tammy hadn't seen since he'd been there.

Charles set his fork down on his plate and used a napkin to wipe his lips. "I'd love to see it. Before we leave you can take me there."

"I'm going back tomorrow. Hank is going to show me some pictures from World War II. And then Gerry said he'd show me some of the pictures he has from Vietnam. Then..."

"Whoa, boy. You sure are excited about all of this." Charles leaned forward on his forearms and smiled at Lex's exuberance.

"Sorry." Lex's pale cheeks reddened as his eyes caught the looks of each person around the table.

"We're all excited. It was great talking to those guys today," Dirks chimed in with a mouth full of potatoes.

Tammy smiled; she'd seen it over and over at the home. Soldiers helping soldiers; it was one of her favorite things about working there. She glanced at Danny and saw him watching her. He gently shook his head and scooped up a succulent bite of roast beef.

CHAPTER 36

STEPPING OUT OF THE SHOWER. Tammy froze as she saw Danny leaning against the counter waiting for her. His eyes showed the heat of a man looking at the nude body of the woman he loved, but his actions were cool and distant. His arms were crossed over his massive chest, the bulge of muscle in his biceps pronounced by the stance. Her lips quivered into a soft smile as she held the towel tighter around her. Neither moved for long moments and Tammy's stomach knotted as her fingers tightened in the towel until he softly spoke, though the gruffness in his voice belied the casualness he was fighting for.

"So, has Mr. Moneybags been trying to steal you away?"

Tammy's brows rose as she allowed her brain a moment to grasp this comment. Taking a deep breath, she began drying her arms. "He offered me a position in Seattle. I told him 'no'. That's it."

"That right? When was this?"

Tammy watched his jaw clench and his lips thin. "Thursday morning, I received an email. He called Thursday afternoon. I told him I wasn't interested in leaving Stateside, my family or you."

Danny raised his arms and scraped them along either side of his head. He locked his fingers behind his head and looked directly into Tammy's eyes. "He gonna leave it at that?"

Tammy's lips thinned and her stomach lurched. "He's coming to town next week sometime. So, I believe he'll try to persuade me."

At Danny's jerk forward off the counter and toward the bedroom, Tammy raised her voice just a bit. "I'm not interested. Before he gets here, I need to figure out what he's up to." Following him into the bedroom, she quickly grabbed a t-shirt and shorts from the top drawer. Pulling on the knit pink shorts and throwing the white t-shirt over her head and pulling her long wet hair from under it, she sighed. "Maybe I need to go back to my place for a while. I think these guys are great, but while they're here I feel like I need to spend time with them and when I'm doing that, I'm not researching."

As a groan escaped Danny's throat, she quickly continued. "I don't want to be rude, but I'm a nervous wreck; that time is slipping by and I'm not doing a damn thing." She walked over to him and sat beside him on the bed. Cupping his face between her hands, she whispered, "The video's been getting a lot of action this past two to three days, Dan. My stomach is in knots. My job is falling apart, my crazy-ass world is caving in on me. I'm drowning here. I don't seem to be able to do anything about that frigging video, I don't know why it's been so active lately, and Zeke is going to steal Stateside away and tear it down or something."

As a tear trekked its way down her cheek she swallowed and said, "The only thing I can possibly change, possibly, is Stateside. I might be able to figure out what the Hamiltons want with it and do something to stop it."

Danny huffed out a breath as he gently laid his forehead against Tammy's. His voice hoarse, his heart beating wildly he whispered, "I don't want you to go."

Danny wrapped his arms around her and pulled her over him as he lay back on the bed. Her dark hair still wet from her shower dropped forward and onto his shoulder. Her dark eyes looked almost black in the darkening room, but she softly smiled at him and her perfect smile, well, there were no words. Danny's cock throbbed to life at lightning speed. He could feel her heat settled just over his length and that made him harden more. He lifted his hips as he pulled her down on him and rotated just enough to make her groan. He smiled up at her and she quickly claimed his mouth with an urgency growing quickly between them.

He swiftly rolled them over and scooted up on the bed. Balancing on his good leg and one arm, he leaned back just enough to unsnap his jeans. Tammy's hands quickly helped him shimmy them down past his firm ass, which she quickly cupped in her hands. Pulling him down on her, she raised her hips to add pressure.

With his free hand he slipped his fingers up the inside of her right shorts leg and pulled the stretchy material wide enough to slip his cock inside of her. Her eyes first registered surprise then closed and her mouth formed a perfect 'O' as he pulled out and slammed back in. She raised her knees and wrapped her legs around his waist as he rocked into her feverishly. His rhythm increased as he watched her breasts sway and circle under her t-shirt, which had become wet from her hair.

"Shit, babe, that's fucking hot," he ground out between thrusts, enjoying the wiggling with each hard pulse into her.

Tammy's eyes opened as she watched Danny's face bead with perspiration. The man could work her up in an instant. She whispered, "Do it. Cum in me, Dan. I want to see it."

He shook his head once. "You. First."

He rocked a few more times, watching Tammy's face contort with exquisite pleasure. Too much. He grunted once and spilled into her, groaning loudly as the pleasure washed over him. He dropped down on to her and cradled her head in his arms.

* * *

Tammy stood for long moments, as if memorizing each face, each scene, each piece of the lives she'd grown to love here. She silently slid her hands into the pockets of her soft gray dress slacks as she focused on the end of the mural where the painting had only begun. As soft footfalls sounded behind her, she looked down at the floor and sighed, waiting for whoever it was to announce their presence.

"It's beautiful work, Tammy. You clearly have a gift."

Surprised, Tammy spun around to see Charles standing behind her looking over the mural and Danny standing next to him, his dark eyes searching her face.

"Hello." Swallowing but not moving her eyes from Danny's she said, "I wasn't expecting you two to visit today."

Charles stepped forward. "Lex was so excited last night after coming here I needed to see it for myself. I woke early this morning and hoped to catch you before you left, but Dan said you needed to get here early this morning. I'd love to spend a few moments speaking to you and Dan if you can spare the time."

Tammy's eyes quickly darted between the two men as she nodded. "Of course. We can go to my office if you like."

Charles smiled, his eyes crinkling at the corners. "Yes, but first, can you explain your mural and offer me a tour of Stateside?"

Her forehead slightly furrowed, she hesitated. "Sure."

Charles chuckled as Danny walked forward and put his arm around Tammy's shoulders.

"I think you'll find this visit a good one, babe."

Tammy proceeded to explain the mural softly detailing the little nuances of each scene depicted. They toured Stateside as she explained the different areas and introduced Danny and Charles to the men and women who lived there. Charles asked questions about therapy, activities, the issues the building had, and the repairs that were needed. As they walked into her office, what they found was Zeke standing at the window over-looking the parking lot. Tammy froze as Zeke turned from the window and scanned her guests.

Danny's back grew rigid, his breathing stilted as he immediately realized who was standing in Tammy's office, as if he had the absolute right to be there. His usually full supple lips thinned and lightened in color. Then Zeke's gaze landed on Charles. Recognition registered almost immediately.

"Well, Mr. Page, fancy meeting you here."

Zeke slowly walked forward, offering his hand to Charles, which propriety dictated but which clearly was detestable to each man. Charles shook Zeke's hand as his blue eyes collided with the steel gray of Zeke's. Each man's posture immediately growing as rigid as the unpleasant atmosphere in the room. Charles quickly introduced Danny.

"Mr. Hamilton, may I introduce Daniel Schaefer."

Zeke's left brow raised as who Danny was dawned on him. Shaking Danny's hand, which was much larger than his own, Zeke quickly pulled away as he looked down at Tammy.

"I didn't realize you had guests this morning, Tammy. I came into town today for a couple of meetings and wanted to further discuss the position we have for you at Hamilton Enterprises. Perhaps later this afternoon would be better."

Quickly flicking his eyes to Danny's and smirking, he added, "Perhaps dinner would be better so as not to interfere with your work here, which must be ever-growing now that Sally is happily ensconced in Seattle."

Danny's lip curled as he started to retort, but Tammy quickly interrupted. "Dinner isn't better. I've told you I'm not interested in the job you have in Seattle and my mind won't change."

"Well, you may change your mind when you find out that we'll be submitting our formal proposal to purchase Stateside Friday morning. If we decide to go ahead and close it down, you'll be in need of a position. I can't think of a position that would suit you more or pay you better than anything I can offer you." He said the last with his eyes firmly fixed on Danny's.

CHAPTER 37

AFTER THE ENCOUNTER with Zeke, Tammy, Danny and Charles closed themselves up in her office, with the door locked. Not wanting to seem as though she was talking down to them, they moved the chairs in front of her desk over and Tammy pushed her chair around the desk, causing them to form a tight circle. Charles sat back in his chair as Danny leaned forward and grabbed Tammy's hand.

"After you left this morning Charles and I had a long conversation. He's been busy while he's been here. After our conversation earlier this week, he had some friends dig up any information they could find on Hamilton. While the guys and I were here yesterday, he did a bit more work. All the research you wanted to do is done, babe, just listen to what Charles has to say."

"Tammy?" The faceless voice chimed in over the intercom.

"Yes." Tammy looked at Danny and Charles, her lips forming a frown.

"Mr. Isaiah Hamilton is on line two for you."

Letting out an irritated huff, Tammy said, "Put him in my voicemail please and hold the rest of my calls."

Leaning forward and pressing her 'Do Not Disturb' button on her phone, Tammy sat back down. Crossing her legs she nodded to Charles and tried not to fidget as he spoke in his usual calm, leisurely manner.

"When the Hamiltons came to Lexington, myself and the other ranchers formed an alliance to, basically, run them out of town. We were successful and after they left, we formed a corporation. This corporation has since been used for many things. We've purchased local businesses in decline and run them. We've even ventured out of our town and state and purchased businesses and turned them around. We have a manager who oversees our business ventures and reports back to us on all business activities."

He paused and smiled as he watched Tammy's eyes begin to register where this may lead.

Leaning forward, resting his forearms on his knees, he continued. "Zeke Hamilton wants to raze this building and build a mall. As you suspected, he has no intention of keeping Stateside open. We found plans he submitted for approval to the mayor, who just happens to be college friends with Matthew Hamilton, Zeke's father. They plan to push this all through the next City Council meeting. Council members are being contacted on the side and suddenly, their bank accounts are growing. We assume, of course, that the Hamiltons are buying the Council members off."

Tammy sat forward. "But they don't own Stateside yet. Why would they be buying off Council members when they don't even know they own Stateside?"

Danny sat forward as well. "Because they're arrogant. They assume everything will go their way. They also don't want to tip anyone off just yet who may see what's happening and pull the rug out from under them. I'd bet that's why they aren't submitting their formal offer to purchase until Friday. The City Council meeting is next Thursday evening."

Tammy shook her head trying to keep up. "But, why Stateside? There are many buildings for sale just one block away from here. They could put the mall there."

Charles smiled. "Turns out the State plans to move the highway during the road construction, which is slated to start next year. That highway will go through those buildings. They aren't worth anything now. When the State comes through and purchases, they only pay assessed value and many times less than that. Those plans haven't been approved by the Governor yet, but I'd bet money is being exchanged or promises made to make that happen."

Charles pulled a map out of the briefcase he had sitting on the floor next to his chair. Spreading it out on Tammy's desk, they all stood to get a better look.

Pointing to Stateside on the map Charles followed the path of the proposed highway and where the other buildings were located.

"This is prime real estate for a mall with this location. Just off the highway and with the traffic counts it'll soon have, it'll be easy to fill and command prime rent."

Tammy stood silent as her eyes traced the lines Charles had just pointed out. She slowly looked up at Danny, her eyes shiny with unshed tears and softly said, "It's hopeless then. There's nothing I can do."

Danny tucked her hair behind her ear and traced the little lines at the corner of her eye with his thumb. "You need to have faith. Charles and his men have a plan."

CHAPTER 38

DRIVING HOME, DANNY was lost in thought. It was close to lunchtime and he knew the guys had gone to Rolling Thunder, but Danny wanted to speak to Charles alone. "Want to stop for lunch?"

Charles smiled, "That'd be very nice, Dan."

Racing to figure out where to stop, Danny pulled into The Wheel. "It should be easy to find a place to sit since it's only eleven-thirty."

Shifting his truck into 'park' Danny, unlocked his seatbelt and climbed out of his truck. Hitting the key fob to lock it once Charles' door was closed, they walked into The Wheel.

The hostess greeted them with a big smile. "Afternoon gentlemen. Just the two of you today?"

"Yes, ma'am," Charles offered.

The hostess turned and walked them to the first window seat in the dining room. "You're waitress will be here shortly to take your order. Her name is Talia."

Danny and Charles perused their menus. Folding his menu and pushing it back, Danny glanced out the window and saw Zeke strolling across the parking lot. Another man joined him not far from the window. The other man was shorter, blonde and had a bit of a gut. He seemed nervous and looked all around him to see if anyone was watching what they were doing.

"What do you make of that?" Danny asked Charles.

Turning to watch the scene unfold before them, they saw Zeke pull a thick letter-sized envelope out of his suit jacket. The two men continued talking, though now it looked a bit heated. Zeke's hands were jerky and staccato as he addressed the shorter man. Finally the other man pulled a small item out of his front pants pocket. He looked down at it in his hand and closed his fingers around the object. Zeke grew more irritated and turned to walk away. The shorter man put his hand on Zeke's arm as Zeke whipped around and glared at him.

Taking a step back the man held his hand out and opened his fingers, revealing the small object. Danny and Charles both sat straighter in their chairs trying to see what it was. Zeke reached forward to grab the object as he handed the thick envelope over with his other hand. The sun glinted off the object as Zeke picked it up. He shook it at the other man's face a couple of times, tapping the end of the man's nose before pulling it away.

"That's a thumb drive." Danny sat back in his chair, not wanting to look so suspicious. He slowly reached into his pocket and pulled out his phone. Snapping a few pictures, he got Zeke holding up the thumb drive and the other man opening the envelope and counting what looked like money.

"That lowlife son-of-a-bitch just bought something very valuable to him. The wad of cash in that envelope is easily ten thousand dollars or more. Probably more. That's how he operates." Charles turned back to Danny his lips drawn into a tight line. "Did you get good pictures?"

Sliding his thumb over his phone, Danny looked down at the pictures and nodded. "Yeah. You can see both of them clearly."

He handed his phone to Charles who scrolled through as he nodded. "Perfect. I don't know what we'll need them for, but it's good to have them."

Danny began tapping away on his phone. "I'm emailing them to myself, Tammy, and you. I don't want to risk losing these."

*　*　*

Tammy walked back into her office, her feet whispering on the carpet, her heart heavy. Her nerves were getting the best of her. Every time she turned around she expected Zeke to jump out at her. She hadn't heard from him all morning and she half expected him to show up after Danny and Charles left. Setting the stack of reports on her desk, she walked over and looked out the window of her office. Not a great view, just the parking lot, but it was a window. As she stood here now, she realized she needed to come to terms with the fact that this place would be gone soon.

Hearing her email chime, she walked over to her computer and entered her password to unlock the screen saver. Her lips lifted at the corners when she saw Danny's name. Opening the email, she saw 'Don't show Mr. Moneybags these pictures'. Clicking on the first one, she gasped. There stood Zeke talking to another man. She clicked the next picture and her heart began hammering in her chest. The heat crawled up her body, her neck, her cheeks, as her hands began shaking.

Grabbing her cell phone she slashed her thumb across the screen and scrolled to Danny's picture. Tapping to connect the call she closed her eyes as she listened to the ringing on the other end. She took a deep breath to calm herself and keep her voice from shaking.

"Hey, babe. Did you get the pictures I sent?" Danny's voice calmed her through the phone line.

"Ye..." Licking her lips, she tried again. "Yeah. Where did you get these?"

"Charles and I stopped at The Wheel for lunch. We sat by the window and I saw Mr. Moneybags stroll across the parking lot like he owned it. Then I watched as he stopped and started talking to that guy. Then we saw the exchange."

Tammy's voice rose. "What exchange?"

Danny's brows pinched. "Did you look at all the pictures?" He stood quickly and motioned to Charles that he was going outside. Looking down at his phone, he clicked speaker, and scrolled to his sent emails to make sure he sent them all.

"Oh, my God. Oh, my God. That fucker. That mother-fucker," Tammy wailed.

Danny's head snapped up. "Tammy, what...what's going on?"

Leaping to her feet, Tammy closed her office door and began to pace while holding her phone to her ear. "It's Scott. The other guy is Scott. Fucking-video-Scott."

Danny's face pinched. He looked at the pictures again, slowly scrolling through each one, looking closely at the blond man talking to Zeke. He quickly headed to his truck so no one would hear their conversation. Climbing in and closing the door, Danny's breathing came in spurts as he watched the exchange through pictures again. The realization of what was probably on that thumb drive turned his stomach. Tammy's video. That's why it had been getting a lot of attention lately. As her soft crying came through the phone, Danny's guts twisted.

"Babe, we'll figure all this out. First, you need to call your attorney and send him the pictures. When you went to court to get the video pulled and put a restraining order on Scott, did the Judge add in the restraining order that he wasn't allowed to sell or physically distribute it?"

Sniffing and wiping under her eyes, Tammy shook her head. When she didn't hear Danny respond, she realized he couldn't see her. She softly replied, "No." Pulling a tissue from the floral tissue box on the corner of her desk, Tammy swabbed her nose and tossed the tissue in the waste basket. "He wasn't allowed to upload to any internet sites, email, message, share links in any way to anyone. He isn't allowed to comment on it if he sees it out on the internet, he isn't allowed to forward, like it, or otherwise. But…" she sucked in a deep breath. "I don't think we ever dreamed he'd download it to a thumb drive and sell it. I'll have to check the language in the restraining order."

Softening his voice so he could soothe her, Danny said. "Okay, hon. Hang up and call your attorney. I'm going to go in and finish my lunch with Charles and I'll see you at home."

"Oh, my God. Danny, please don't tell Charles about the video. It's so humiliating."

Danny hesitated. "Babe, we need to tell him. He needs to know what we're up against here and he saw the exchange. He might have some connections that can help us with this. Tam, wait till you hear what he has in mind. I had no idea, and I mean, no idea how connected Lex's family is. Blows my mind."

Flopping into her desk chair Tammy closed her eyes and pinched the bridge of her nose. Choking back the sob threatening to escape, she softly said, "Please don't, Danny."

"Babe? My counselor would tell you that you have to talk about it and stop giving it the power to paralyze you."

"Yeah, I know," she said softly.

"I love you. It's going to be alright."

That did it. The flood gates opened and Tammy allowed herself a good cry. Through her sobs and tears she managed, "Love. You." before she hung up.

Danny tapped the back of his head against the headrest a few times while getting his emotions under control. He wasn't a bit hungry any more, but, for Charles, he would go and fake it.

CHAPTER 39

GETTING HERSELF UNDER CONTROL, Tammy pulled the little pocket mirror out of her desk drawer and scoffed as she looked at her smeared mascara, red eyes and nose and virtually no other makeup on her face. Wiping, adjusting and fixing what she could, she grabbed her lip gloss and swiped it on her lips. It would have to do. She was going to kill Zeke and Scott and make this shit stop. She had enough of being a victim. And she was sick and tired of waiting for that video to jump out and destroy her.

After she felt a bit better and thought she could talk to her mom without crying, she picked up her phone and tapped her mom's number.

"Hey, sweetheart how are you and Danny doing?"

"Mom." Feeling her voice crack, she cleared her throat, sat straighter in her chair and started again. "Hi, mom. We're good. Danny's friends are leaving tomorrow. I'm sorry we didn't get over to you and dad, but you'll meet them next time. I promise."

"Oh, don't worry, honey. We completely understand and your dad's traveling right now anyway, so, we'll meet them next time. But, I do expect you and Danny for Thanksgiving on Saturday."

"Yep. We'll be there."

Tammy relayed the story as she knew it and forwarded the pictures to her mom. She knew she should talk to Attorney Gratz herself, she was a grown up, but her mom had a way of handling the crotchety old bugger and Tammy didn't much like him or that snippy receptionist in his office. Ending the call with her mom, Tammy stood and started clearing her desk for the evening.

One light tap on her door and she heard the handle turn. She knew who it was before she even looked up. "What do you want?" she snapped.

Zeke's stupid eyebrow raised and a smirk slid across his face as he walked through the door, hands in the perfectly tailored pockets of his perfectly tailored suit. Dammit, he was a smug bastard.

"While I hoped for a better reception, I'll take that one. What has you knotted up?"

Tammy stopped moving papers for a split second before continuing. When she'd closed the last drawer and righted the step file on her desktop, she calmly slid her hands in her front slacks pocket and met his gaze.

"What makes you think I'm knotted up?"

"You've never spoken to me like that before. I don't know if I find it sexy or irritating."

Slightly shrugging her shoulders, "I don't really care how you find it."

Now his smirk turned into a smile. "What happened, the boyfriend let you down? He's a cripple, so he probably can't satisfy you, for long anyway."

Raising her voice, she almost yelled, "He. Is. Not. A. Cripple."

"Well, potāto, potato. Missing a leg, even though he can camouflage it."

Zeke sauntered further into the room, his eyes never leaving hers. Tammy remained firmly fixed behind her desk.

"I'm getting ready to leave for the evening. What did you want?"

Unbuttoning the button on his suit jacket, Zeke sat in one of the brown leather chairs in front of her desk. Tammy watched him get comfortable, crossing his right ankle over his left knee and casually draping his right wrist over his leg. Refusing to get comfortable herself, she remained standing, coolly staring him in the eye.

"I thought we could talk about the job offer a bit more. At least, you should hear what it is."

Shaking her head, Tammy kept her voice calm and even. "You must have a hearing problem, Mr. Hamilton, I believe I've told you three or more times now that I'm simply not interested. Quite frankly, you could give me your job and I wouldn't be interested."

Zeke silently assessed her face. His eyes traveled down her body, stopping at her breasts which thankfully were encased in a bright yellow sweater. His eyes continued to travel until he got to the desktop. Slowly sliding them up her body he looked her straight in the eye, his mouth forming what could only be called a sneer.

"I wouldn't be so quick to discount what my job might entail, Ms. Davis."

Tammy refused to answer him, she simply stood staring. When he realized she wasn't going to inquire, he stood, reached into his front pocket and pulled out the thumb drive he'd purchased from Scott.

"If you accept my job offer, I can make that nasty video of you go away forever."

Tammy's hands balled in her pockets. She continued to remain stone still staring at him. When she didn't act surprised he raised both brows and slightly nodded.

"You're not surprised I have this."

"Nope."

"How could you possibly know I have it?"

Remembering Danny's email telling her not to tell Zeke about the pictures, she pursed her lips tighter.

"Maybe you should be more careful in selecting the location for transacting a purchase."

Zeke's head snapped back just a bit and Tammy actually smirked to see the surprise on his face.

"Well, it doesn't matter. It's not illegal to help a friend out financially."

Tammy merely shrugged. Friend, right.

Zeke leaned forward placing both palms on her desk as he leaned in. She could smell his aftershave, surprised at the fact that the first time she met him and smelled him, she thought he was rather sexy. Now she thought he was a bastard and though he smelled of money, he was the lowest form of life.

"My offer is this, Ms. Davis." Leaning forward just a bit more, his voice took on the tone of a man negotiating a deal - - even, cool, emotionless. "You come and work for me in Seattle. We've created a position there for you where you'll be in charge of locating charities for us to work with. We assume you'll no doubt gravitate to Veteran's charities and causes, and we'll speak to that at a later date. We find we have to siphon off a few million dollars each year to charities for tax purposes. Plus, it keeps the public happy. You will of course, report directly to me. Then, I'll give you this video and make sure it's never seen again."

Tammy's throat became dry and she needed to lick her lips. He was offering her something she'd dreamed about since Scott released that video in the first place. He slowly deposited the thumb drive into his pocket, buttoned his jacket and moved away from the desk. He started to turn to leave, when he stopped. "I'll give you two hours to decide. I'll call you later."

Before Tammy could say anything he was gone. She stood transfixed on the door, her knees shaking as she thought about it. She could go to Seattle, get the video, wait for him to wipe it away from the internet and quit. She'd come back here to Danny and it would all be good for them.

CHAPTER 40

ENTERING THE KITCHEN from the garage, Tammy smelled something delicious. "Hey, Tammy, welcome home." Lex's smile was electric.

"Hi, Lex. Wow, you look happy." Tammy returned his smile with a brilliant one of her own.

"Hey, stop flirting with my girl." Danny walked into the kitchen wearing jeans and a long-sleeved t-shirt, the ridges and planes of his muscles shown easily through the soft gray material. Sexy.

He walked straight to Tammy and wrapped her in his arms. He nuzzled his nose into her hair and breathed in deeply. She felt his heart beating strongly against her cheek and she closed her eyes and allowed herself to relax. This. Is. Where. She. Wanted. To. Always. Be.

Danny felt a shiver run through Tammy's body and he squeezed. He knew she'd been having a rough time of it lately. His guilt that he'd been enjoying his friends visiting and failed to see all that she'd been going through made him feel like a dick. Sucky boyfriend he was. He needed to start thinking like a teammate and less like an individual, because, he wanted Tammy here with him.

Pulling back he looked into her eyes. "Wine?"

Her full lips spread into the most beautiful smile he'd ever seen. "Yes, please."

Danny kissed her nose and turned to pull the wine out of the refrigerator. Tammy watched him a moment and then realized Lex was…cooking. She cocked her head and Lex smirked.

"Schaefer taught me how to make pot roast."

"That's fabulous, Lex. Some lucky woman is going to snap you up in a heartbeat."

Lex's face flushed as he looked over at Danny, who was walking toward Tammy with a glass of wine. "See, Schaefer, your woman likes me."

"*Pfft*. Don't get all full of yourself because you learned to make pot roast."

They all burst out laughing.

"Well, hello, Tammy, welcome home." Charles' salt and pepper hair was slicked back and he was dressed in nice jeans and a blue three-button placket shirt. He smiled as he made his way across the kitchen to look into the pot Lex was scooping vegetables from. He clapped his hand on Lex's shoulder as he praised the food. "Looks as good as it smells, Chaz."

"Thanks, dad. I think I could do this on my own."

Charles smiled at Tammy and Danny. "When you both have a bit of time, I'd like to fill you in on what my partners have been pulling together."

As Tammy looked around the table, Danny's friends were smiling, happy and so supportive of each other, she made a split second decision.

"If everyone is finished, I think we should talk."

Danny looked into her eyes and saw determination. He reached over, wrapped her hand in his and squeezed for support.

Dirks pushed his plate back and patted his belly. "I'm finished. If I eat one more bite, I believe I'll explode, and it won't be pretty."

Chuckles were heard and Tammy gave Danny's hand a little squeeze before pulling away and folding her hands on the table. Taking a bolstering breath, she began. "Danny's been keeping a secret for me, because, I'm embarrassed and, well, actually mortified to tell you this." She tucked her hair behind her ears with a shaky hand and began again. "More than a year ago, I dated Scott. We'd been dating only about six weeks when…" She looked at Danny. At his slight nod and wink, her lips quivered into a soft smile. "Scott videoed us having sex without my permission. I didn't know he was recording. The next morning I woke to the video plastered all over the Internet. He sent it to his friends, co-workers, uploaded it to several social media sites and YouTube. I was devastated."

Tammy continued telling the gory details as the guys all sat and listened without interruption. She finished her story with, "The reason I'm telling you this is because..." She looked at Danny and then Charles. Swallowing to force the fear and tears down, she continued. "Because the man you saw Zeke Hamilton with today was Scott. Zeke came into my office this afternoon, showed me the thumb drive and told me it was the video. He said he'd make it go away forever if I go to Seattle with him and 'work' for him." Work in air quotes.

Slowly Charles said, "Well, that son-of-a-bitch never ceases to lower himself one notch lower than before."

Tammy looked at each of the guys one-by-one and nodding once she said. "I'm sorry guys. I hope you can forgive me."

Lex's brows pinched together as he looked at her. "Tammy, there's nothing to forgive. You're the victim in this and that bastard Scott should really fry for doing something like that. But worse, is Hamilton. Blackmail is absolutely bullshit."

Tammy's lips formed a straight line across her pretty face.

Dirks spoke up next. "Is this Hamilton bastard the man trying to purchase Stateside?"

"Yes. And it appears he's also interested in Tammy." Danny's voice held a dangerous growl.

Coop added quickly, "Thank you for telling us, Tammy, I'm sure that was hard. You didn't have to."

Tammy smiled. "I did though. Danny was right today when he told me that coming clean would stop the video from controlling me. I've been so stressed trying to keep it a secret since you guys got here. I had alerts set up on the Internet and it's been terribly active again. I think it was Zeke, trying to turn the knife to get me to follow him to Seattle."

"Well, now it's my turn," Charles said. "My partners have come together as I expected they would. Travis, our business manager, called me just before you got home. We've submitted an offer to Purchase Stateside to FMS and it was approved this afternoon. LexRanch, our corporation, is the new owner of Stateside."

Tammy sat up straight as she looked at Charles' clear blue eyes and the beautiful smile on his face. "For real?"

Laughing, he nodded, "For real."

Tammy gasped as she jumped up, ran around the table, and hugged Charles. "Oh, my God, thank you so much. Thank you. I've been so worried about where these men and women would go. There are few places for them with their income levels and most of the facilities they could go to have long waiting lists."

Tammy turned and hugged Danny. He pulled her down onto his lap and wrapped his arms around her waist. "I told you it would be okay."

Looking into Danny's eyes, Tammy teared up as the relief began washing over her. "You're right. I never doubted, though I simply didn't see how it would ever be."

She lightly pecked his lips as Coop said, "Now how do we get rid of Hamilton?"

Tammy's phone started playing "You're So Vain" by Carly Simon. She smiled as she stood and pulled it out of her pants pocket. "Zeke said he was giving me two hours to decide whether to take his job offer."

The men around the table started laughing as the ring tone and the caller came together in their heads. Danny quickly pulled his phone out of his pocket and laid it on the table next to Tammy's. He tapped his record icon and winked at Tammy.

She answered her call while at the same time touching the speaker icon. "This is Tammy."

"Ms. Davis, your two hours are up."

Wrinkling her face, Tammy reached over and held Danny's hand. "I didn't need two hours. At the risk of repeating myself, I'm not interested in your job or anything you have to offer."

A moment of silence while they all waited for him to respond. Tammy's heart began a rapid beat as she wondered what he was thinking.

"You do understand what this means, don't you?"

"Yes. It means I'll be staying in Green Bay with Danny and my family."

"It also means you'll be out of a job by the end of the month and the little issue of your video will not go away. You may find I don't have the power to keep it from attracting attention in the days to come."

Danny's jaw tightened and he curled his hands into fists. His lips drew together as he looked over at Lex and saw the same reaction on his friend. Glancing at Dirks and Coop, Danny saw them both shaking their heads no. Dirks motioned with his hands - - brush it away.

"It's a chance I'll have to take. I've been through it before. It's unpleasant, but, I can handle it."

Surprised at her own confidence Tammy actually smiled. Still standing next to Danny, she laid her palm on his strong shoulder and took strength. He looked up at her and she felt it, he loved her through all of this.

"You'll find it difficult to obtain new employment with this nasty piece of imagery chasing you, Ms. Davis. I'll leave you with this, if you change your mind, you know where to find me."

"Are you staying in Green Bay much longer? In case I change my mind."

He chuckled on the other side of the phone. "Well now, are you offering to pay me a visit at my hotel?"

"I might be. I'm wondering if I'd be able to change your mind. About the video, I mean."

Silence. Danny looked at Tammy with what could be described as horror on his face. She winked at him and gently ran her thumb over his furrowed brow.

CHAPTER 41

"THIS WAITING IS SO INTENSE," Tammy said as she paced the living room, rubbing the back of her neck. The men were sitting around on the various pieces of furniture. Dirks was tapping away on his phone while sitting in the tan upholstered chair across the room. Lex and Charles were on the sofa, each seemingly calm and attentive to each other. Coop was sitting on the floor, leaning into the sofa next to Lex's legs and Danny was sitting in his recliner, forearms on his knees, watching Tammy pace.

"Maybe we should play a game or put in a movie to pass the time. A watched pot never boils."

Danny glanced at Lex, "When did you get so philosophical?"

Lex chuckled. "I've heard my share of clichéd sayings since coming home, Schaefer. Watching your leg laying yards from your body haunted me to no end. Coming here to see you doing so well is not only long over-due, but has put everything into perspective." Brushing his hand through his chestnut hair, he smirked. "Did dad tell you he's also negotiating with FMS to purchase two veterans homes in Kentucky, not far from our ranch? I'm going to counsel men and women there like you're doing here."

Tammy and Danny both looked at Charles. Sliding her hands into her pockets, a slow smile spread across her face. "Really? That's fantastic."

"Just seeing the change in him since he came here and talking to Dan this week has me hopeful that Chaz will heal completely and help others in the process."

Danny nodded still leaning forward. "I actually think those guys counsel me, not the other way around. Either way, it helps and they seem genuinely happy to talk to me, so it works."

Tammy's phone rang and she quickly pulled it out of her pocket. "Hello, this is Tammy."

She quickly looked at Danny and nodded. She listened intently for a few minutes. "Thank you, Sergeant. What happens next?"

Finishing her call, she walked to Danny. He reached up and took her hand in his waiting for her to tell them what'd happened.

"They have the thumb drive. The police knocked on Zeke's hotel room door and when he opened it, they told him he was in the possession of property secured by a restraining order. I'm so glad my mom and Attorney Gratz spoke today. Apparently, Scott wasn't allowed to do anything with the video. Not downloading to another media device or anything else. It's off-limits." Looking into Danny's eyes, Tammy continued. "However, Zeke's lying about how he got the video. He told police that he didn't know what was on it and that Scott is a friend and asked him to hang on to it because it's valuable."

Lex jumped in. "Well, you have pictures of the exchange. You can prove he exchanged money for it."

"The pictures don't show what was exchanged, just that there was an exchange. Scott's going to need to fess up for it to hold water." Danny stood, clearly irritated with the turn of events.

"The police are on their way over to Scott's to see if they can get him to talk." Tammy ran her hand across Danny's back to soothe him.

Dirks wrinkled his face, his bright blue eyes slightly squinting. "Well, at least that prick Hamilton can't do anything with the video. Provided he didn't already download it to his computer."

Tammy's eyes grew wide and a gasp escaped her throat.

"Sorry, Tammy, but you need to be real about this."

"God, I didn't even think about that."

"Well, the way it looks now, the police know that Hamilton had the video. If it shows up on the Internet again, they'll be able to trace the IP address of the computer. There isn't a restraining order against him, but, it'll be fairly easy to get it. You can create reasonable doubt with the pictures and the money, so a judge may just decide to slap a restraining order on Hamilton, too," Coop ground out. His face took on the hard lines of a big brother protecting his sister. Tammy smiled at his concern. All of their concern.

Danny wrapped his arm around Tammy's shoulders and kissed the top of her head.

* * *

"What do you intend to do about it?" Ryder asked as they sat in the break room at lunch the following day.

"I'm going to go over and beat some truth into that shit bag, that's what I'm going to do." Danny threw his sandwich wrapper into the waste basket with force.

Ryder's eyebrows shot up as he watched the wrap smash into the garbage and Danny slam his fist on the table top. "You can't go alone, Schaefer. You'll do something that'll make this all worse."

"I'm not taking Tammy to go and see that prick. I don't want her within fifty miles of him. I'd prefer it if he moved across country."

Ryder chuckled.

Danny's eyes narrowed on Ryder causing Ryder to sit back and put his hands up in defense. "Whoa, easy now. You have to admit, it's kind of funny."

Danny's lips formed a reluctant smile as he shook his head.

"I'll go with you. Your friends all left this morning, right? You can't go alone. I'll go with you. Molly's working tonight, so I have the time. We can go right after work."

"You don't have to do that, Ryder."

"I know I don't. I want to. That's what friends are for."

Danny looked into Ryder's green eyes and saw a friend looking back at him.

"Okay. Sounds good."

CHAPTER 42

"THIS IS IT HERE. The yellow house."

Danny pulled into the driveway of a house at the edge of the downtown area of Green Bay. Not the worst neighborhood, not the best. The houses were interspersed with old Victorians that'd been lovingly restored and older nondescripts homes that needed some TLC. Scott's house was the latter.

Danny's truck looked too big for the narrow driveway and stood taller than the front door. They looked at each other before climbing out of the truck. Ryder broke the silence. "Let's do it."

Danny nodded and climbed out. Upon approaching the door, it jerked open and there he was, Scott in all his glory. He was wearing a ratty pair of shorts and a t-shirt that had cheesy yellow streaks across the front. He was glassy-eyed, his hair was mussed and looked in serious need of some shampoo and water. Scott's glassy eyes narrowed in on Danny for a long moment. He slid his gaze to Ryder and then back to Danny.

"I don't know you two. Whataya want?" His speech wasn't quite slurred but not clear either.

"We'd like to talk to you."

"I'm expecting company."

"Now you have it."

Scott chuckled, "True. But not you."

"Who are you expecting?"

Scott's eyes narrowed as he looked at Danny again. "Who are you?"

"Danny Schaefer."

Scott's eyes widened and his mouth flopped open just enough to show his mouth yellowed from...Cheetos?

"You're with Tammy now. I've got nothing to say to you."

"I have something to say to you. I don't know why you did what you did. I can't see any reason to hurt someone like you hurt her. She didn't do anything to hurt you. It was dirty. It was nasty and underhanded. But that's over. What I don't understand is why you'd do something to hurt her again. What the fuck is wrong with you?"

Scott finally showed some real emotion, his voice raised as his hands flew wide. "What the fuck is wrong with me? Look at this shithole. I can't afford to move anywhere else because I have fucking attorney's fees up the ass. I lost my job because of that whiney bitch. I'm broke, and I found someone who was willing to pay for something that I can't do a fucking thing with for fear of going to jail."

Danny's fists balled at his sides. Ryder watched him trying to get a grip on his anger, worried this was a very bad idea.

"Did he contact you?"

"Yeah. He found me from Court records. Offered me twenty thousand dollars and said I would never be tied to it again."

"So, naturally, being the piece of shit you are, you couldn't wait to get your hands on the money."

Scott turned and walked inside. Danny and Ryder watched him go in and when he didn't make a move to close the door, Ryder shrugged and walked in first. He saw Scott sprawled in a chair in the corner of the room. He looked back at Danny and jerked his head toward the inside. Danny followed him in.

Scott looked at the two hulking men standing in his minuscule living room and swallowed. Grabbing his beer can off the side table he finished what was left of it and smacked it back down on the table, sending the empty Cheetos bag to the floor.

After a long silence, he added, "I didn't jump at the chance."

Danny's brows shot up. "That right? How's that?"

"He threatened me."

"Hamilton threatened you?"

Scott nodded his head, barely, but it was enough to be noticed.

"With what? What could he possibly threaten you with?"

Scott heaved out a heavy breath and leaned forward. "He said he has a whole team of computer geeks who could upload that video to the Internet and make it look like I did it. I'd go to jail for violation of the restraining order and there'd be a trial and he said nobody would be able to unscramble the metadata enough to know it wasn't me."

Danny's thoughts went back to the day in the parking lot. "Is that what you were arguing about with Hamilton?"

Scott looked up at Danny, surprise on his face. "How do you know that?"

"I saw you. I was sitting in The Wheel having lunch."

Scott groaned and dropped his dirty head into his dirtier hands. After a few seconds he yelled out, "FUCK."

Allowing him the time he needed to gather his thoughts, Danny and Ryder stood and waited him out. As Scott lifted his head, his eyes were glistening with unshed tears.

"Look. I'm sorry I ever did that to her. She didn't deserve it. I not only fucked up her life, I royally fucked up my own. Even my friends think I'm dirty now and most of them won't have anything to do with me."

He folded his hands together in front of him, sniffed a few times and finally watched as both Ryder and Danny's faces softened, just a bit.

"Whatareya gonna do? Kill me? Call the cops? What?"

Ryder actually chuckled. "We look like murderers to you?"

Scott looked Ryder and shook his head no. "You don't. He looks like he could kill me."

"Well, that's why I'm here, to make sure that doesn't happen. He doesn't need to sit in jail because of a piece of shit like you."

Taking a calming breath, Danny finally said, "Here's what we're going to do. We're going to call the police and have them come out and take your statement."

Scott's unshed tears actually started sliding down his cheeks, leaving a clean trail in their wake.

Danny pulled out his cell phone and tapped the numbers to dial the police department. He stepped outside with a nod to Ryder and spoke for a few moments before returning to the smelly house.

CHAPTER 43

STANDING ON THE SIDEWALK across the street from Stateside, Tammy clapped her hands as the last of the screws was inserted into the new sign.

"It's so beautiful," she cheered as Danny stood next to her, lovingly watching her delight.

She looked up at him and smiled her brightest smile. Unable to resist, he leaned down and kissed her lips. "You're chilly. Let's get you inside, we have a lot of unpacking to do before going to Paul and Grace's."

"Oh, my God, I'm so excited. I can't believe Noah's sitting up now. And so damn cute."

"Language."

Laughing she said, "Right. Sorry."

Walking into the new Stateside Home for Retired Veterans, Tammy's smile was bright. Employees and the residents and their families were bustling about as everyone was moving in today. Charles and his company, LexRanch, built them a beautiful new building on the edge of town, nestled on fifty acres. They were able to add things they wouldn't have been able to add in their old building. They had gardens and those who were able and willing would be able to work in the gardens where they intended to grow vegetables for their meals. They had a veterinary clinic at the front of the building which doubled as therapy for the veterans but also as an income source for Stateside as they would be able to care for pets, either in the 'extended stay' area or just as a daycare. Grooming stations were set up as well and the small pet store attached should act as a fabulous income source. LexRanch ensured they had beautiful medical facilities on site and the kitchen and dining rooms were spacious and highly appointed.

Danny and Tammy walked hand-in-hand into the activities room which was comfortable and relaxing. The furniture and colors of soft tans, deep brown-oranges and soft greens were inviting. The light oak wooden tables glistened with a high polish and the soft floral arrangements beautifully decorating various tables and shelves added the feel of home. The large entertainment center graced one wall in dark mahogany. But Danny's favorite wall was across from the entertainment center.

Charles had personally spared no expense to make sure Tammy's mural wall was carefully cut out of the former Stateside building and brought to this new building. Upon installation, Tammy set out to finish her mural. Lex, Dirks, and Coop came back to visit and talked her through their experiences in Afghanistan, Danny right there with them. The residents sat and listened and asked questions as she worked her brushes across the wall, adding a perfect picture of each of them in battle.

She looked up at his beautiful face now and softly smiled as she saw the pride so often on his face when he looked at the mural. He led her to the end where he and his friends were lovingly memorialized and he smoothed his hand over the soft cool texture. He slowly turned toward Tammy and held her face between his palms. Staring into each other's eyes, each were lost in the other. Slowly, Danny knelt on one knee as Tammy's hands flew to her face.

"I love you, Tammy. More than I'll ever be able to tell you. More than I'll ever be able to show you. Because of you, I'm whole. Because of your love, I'm strong. Because of you, I see a future with little brown-haired, brown-eyed babies. I want our house full of them. Tammy Davis, will you marry me?"

Tammy gasped as she wrapped her arms around Danny and fell on her knees to the floor in front of him. She buried her face in his neck as her tears wet his shirt. He wrapped his arms around her and pulled her in close and waited for her to compose herself. This year had been one of struggles, awareness, truths coming out of hiding, finding strengths where once weakness had been, learning to share, and gaining self-confidence. Danny turned his head slightly and breathed in the scent of her hair as he closed his eyes and committed it to memory once again.

Tammy pulled back and held his face between her hands. She looked into his chocolate eyes, bright with moisture and watched him swallow a large lump in his throat. She cocked her head to the side and her brows furrowed just a bit.

"You didn't answer me."

"Oh, my God, how could you think anything other than yes, absolutely yes?"

He squeezed her again as cheers erupted behind them. Tammy turned to see their friends and family standing there witnessing this momentous occasion in her life. Her brows shot up as she saw them. She turned and looked at Danny, who shrugged in return. He reached into the breast pocket of his deep purple dress shirt and pulled out a beautiful two carat oval diamond ring with two smaller pear-shaped diamonds framing the oval.

"Let's make it official, babe. Will you marry me?"

"YES!" she squealed. Danny slid the ring on her finger and the tears flowed down her cheeks like rain.

Danny stood and folded Tammy into a deep hug as she squeezed him with all her might. As they pulled away, Molly ran forward and wrapped Tammy in a hug as the two girls jumped up and down together while embracing. Ryder stepped forward, a smirk on his face and shook Danny's hand while loudly slapping him on the back with the other. Jeremiah and Joci came forward to congratulate them. Joci, about eight months pregnant, actually waddled. Danny's mom hugged Tammy and welcomed her to the family. Grace, Paul and Noah were there with ready hugs and sloppy kisses. JT and Gunnar were there as well as the rest of the crew from Rolling Thunder. Tammy's parents and her brother rounded out the family. Last but certainly not least were Charles, Lex, Dirks and Coop as well as many of the residents who'd grown to love both Tammy and Danny.

* * *

"That was fun. I'm glad Danny was able to surprise you, Tam. He was worried about it." Molly sipped her wine.

"I never suspected a thing." Tammy smiled as she looked across the room at The Barn, watching Danny, Jeremiah, JT, Gunnar, Frog and Chase from Rolling Thunder sitting around a table talking. The women had retired to the sofas in front of the fireplace about an hour ago. At eleven-thirty at night, it'd been a long day of moving and setting up.

"That's good, because he would've killed any of us who let anything slip out." Joci laughed as she absently rubbed her baby bump.

"How are things with you and Ryder, Mol?"

Molly's smile grew wide as she looked over and caught Ryder's gaze. He returned her smile with one of his own and winked. "He's still pissed that Lancaster isn't going to jail. But, I don't think we'll have to worry about him ever again. The thought of going back to prison and the fines he had to pay seemed to send him packing. Last I heard he moved to Florida. Good riddance."

Tammy shook her head. "I just don't understand our justice system sometimes. It seems criminals get away with far too much. Danny's pissed that Hamilton isn't going to prison for blackmail. But, basically, there wasn't enough proof. Scott set the record straight on his part of the whole mess, but Hamilton is like Teflon. At least he's out of the picture now."

Taking a drink of her wine, she leaned forward and set her glass on the table. Remembering something funny, she started laughing. "You should've seen the look on Zeke's face when he found out LexRanch got approval to build the mall on the former Stateside spot. It was priceless. I think he's more worried about LexRanch creating trouble for him in the future than he is about anything else."

Molly and Joci both smiled and nodded. Jeremiah walked over and kissed Joci on the top of her head. "Let's get you two home, baby. We're putting a crib together tomorrow."

Danny rolled his eyes as he settled in next to Tammy. "Good luck with that. I helped Paul put Noah's crib together and it took us all damn day."

"That's what I'm afraid of. Good thing I have three smart, strong boys to help me. Right boys?"

Ryder, JT, and Gunnar nodded, each looking a bit scared at the prospect. JT rolled his eyes as he gruffed out, "Man, I'm never going through that. You guys can have it."

Molly laughed. "You talk so big, but one day a woman is going to grab hold of you and you'll be purring like a kitty."

That got the group laughing. JT shook his head as he downed the remainder of his beer. He stood and walked to the bar to refresh his drink as Gunnar laughed at him. Molly looked down the sofa at him and said, "You too, Gunnar."

He held up his hands in a defensive gesture, not saying a word.

Joci scooted to the edge of the sofa as Jeremiah reached down to help her to her feet. "When's the wedding?"

Tammy smiled her brightest smile as she looked down at her ring, then up at Danny. He kissed her nose and looked at Joci. "As soon as I can get her to the altar. I know Ryder and Molly's wedding is coming up in about four months, but I want to be married right after them."

Tammy's brows rose. Joci laughed and shook her head. "Don't even say you can't get a wedding put together in that time. Jeremiah made me do it in less than six weeks. Two of those weeks I was in the hospital. If I can do it, you can do it."

Jeremiah smirked as he waved to the group, wrapped his arm around Joci and headed for the door.

Tammy looked up into Danny's face, cocked her head to the side and softly said, "How about September?"

"September is perfect. Now, let's go home and celebrate in private."

MEET THE AUTHOR

I'm a wife of thirty years, mother of four grown children and grandmother of three lovely grandchildren. When not writing a new story, I can be found riding my motorcycle and exploring this fabulous country of ours. My writing revolves around people anyone would love to spend time with. No self-absorbed billionaires for me.

Earning my Bachelor's Degree later in life fulfilled a dream for me. Then I found the courage to write and I haven't looked back. Currently I have four published books, Designing Samantha's Love, Dog Days of Summer, Rydin' the Storm Out, and most recently, Danny's War. I also serve as the VP of Communications for WisRWA and devote a large amount of my time helping other authors slog their way through this thing called publishing. I love to hear from fans, so look me up and touch base.

I come from a family of veterans. My grandfather, father, brother, two of my sons, and one daughter-in-law are all veterans. Needless to say, I'm proud to be an American and proud of the service my amazing family has given.

If you enjoyed this book, please leave a review.

If you want to receive news and information about upcoming releases and sales, sign up for my Readers Group here. http://eepurl.com/3X5yz

Check out my website: pjfiala.com

Follow me on Facebook: facebook.com/pjfiala1

Tweet me at: twitter.com/pfiala

See inspiration photos on Pinterest: pinterest.com/pattifiala

Goodreads: goodreads.com/author/show/7866768.P_J_Fiala

MORE GREAT READS FROM BOOKTROPE

Water, Stone, Heart by **Will North** (Contemporary Romance) Nicola and Andrew have each come to the tiny village of Boscastle to escape their troubled pasts. When they meet, they're bristly and sarcastic — and utterly attracted to each other. It takes a cataclysmic flash flood and a nine-year-old girl for Nicola and Andrew to see the truth about themselves and risk a second chance at love.

Unsettled by **Alisa Mullen** (Contemporary Romance) American Girl falls for an Irish boy in a summer filled with adventure, wonder, and the unexpected.

Unsettled Spirits by **Sophie Weeks** (Contemporary Romance) As Sarah grapples with questions of faith, love, and identity, she must learn to embrace not just the spirits of the present, but the haunting pain of the past. Can she accept her past in order to let love in?

Tripped Up Love by **Julie Farley** (Contemporary Romance) When Heather Meadows loses the only man she's ever loved, her perfect, ordinary life is turned upside down. Little does she know that her world is about to be turned upside down again when one wrong step puts her in the path of a new destiny.

Would you like to read more books like these?
Subscribe to runawaygoodness.com, get a free ebook for signing up, and never pay full price for an ebook again.

Discover more books and learn about our
new approach to publishing at **booktrope.com**.

Made in the USA
Middletown, DE
27 March 2016